About the Author

James Noble is quite a creative person, with interests in wildlife art, computer modelling and animation, writing of course, Napoleonic model soldiers, and model railways. He previously had a book published detailing the visits of Buffalo Bill's Wild West (show) to Yorkshire and Lincolnshire. It was titled 'Around the Coast with Buffalo Bill'. Having spent some years as a professional wildlife artist, he still paints and sells paintings locally.

Pawn Sacrifice

James Noble

Pawn Sacrifice

Olympia Publishers
London

www.olympiapublishers.com
OLYMPIA PAPERBACK EDITION

Copyright © James Noble 2024

The right of James Noble to be identified as author of
this work has been asserted in accordance with sections 77 and 78 of
the Copyright, Designs and Patents Act 1988.

All Rights Reserved

No reproduction, copy or transmission of this publication
may be made without written permission.
No paragraph of this publication may be reproduced,
copied or transmitted save with the written permission of the publisher,
or in accordance with the provisions
of the Copyright Act 1956 (as amended).

Any person who commits any unauthorised act in relation to
this publication may be liable to criminal
prosecution and civil claims for damage.

A CIP catalogue record for this title is
available from the British Library.

ISBN: 978-1-80439-884-5

This is a work of fiction.
Names, characters, places and incidents originate from the writer's
imagination. Any resemblance to actual persons, living or dead, is
purely coincidental.

First Published in 2024

Olympia Publishers
Tallis House
2 Tallis Street
London
EC4Y 0AB

Printed in Great Britain

Acknowledgements

Special thanks to Anne and Sarah, who put up with my insane imagination, and yet still encourage me.

Prologue – 3 June 1940, French Town of Dunkerque

"Light tanks, sir! Two of 'em!" The corporal advised excitedly, his eyes filling with tears that threatened to streak the grime from his face. "Just around the corner, and heading this way!"

The officer fell back against what was left of a wall, his legs straddling what remained of an old, shattered lamp post. He glanced across at the narrow stream of walking wounded being ferried from the house across the street, moving slowly with help from their comrades who exerted every effort to hurry them toward the beach.

"All right, corporal," the officer replied, breathlessly, "cover me from across the street if you can, I'll do my best to delay them."

"Very good, sir!" came the reply, as the man complied with the request and ran back to the shelter of a broken doorway, his final steps attracting a stream of bullets that raised the debris at his heels. The officer slid along the wall until he was close to the corner and risked one eye to see how far the tanks were. Twenty yards were all that separated him from the first vehicle and he pulled back immediately when a short, double burst of automatic fire roughened what was left of the edging bricks, causing dust and stone splinters to assault the left of his face.

They looked like Panzer 1's, and he was thankful that they carried small calibre, twin machine guns, which addressed the fact that he still had his face intact. Had they carried 50mm, he might not have been so lucky.

The sound of the Panzer advance came closer, too close. He knew that it was imperative to keep them from turning the corner, and looked around for something more useful than his service revolver. On the ground, to his right, lay the fragments of steel cylinder that had once been the lamp post, and as the German tank began to shake the ground around him, he found what he was looking for.

"Watch out, sir!" called the corporal across the street, but his voice was lost in the rumble of caterpillar tracks, just appearing around the corner.

Picking the right piece of steel, the officer waited until the forward drive wheel appeared, with its teeth gripping the track to heave the vehicle forward. He moved closer and with every sinew of strength pushed the metal pole between it and the following toothless support wheel.

Immediately the steel ground upon steel and the pole was chewed between the teeth of the drive wheel and the track, causing it to falter and fail. Although the track remained intact, it could not overcome the steel rod that flattened and held it immobile with its own drive teeth.

The opposite track continued to move, turning the Panzer to the right, and into the corner of the wall, where the remaining masonry ground the vehicle to a halt. The officer looked up as the turret began to turn, but it also found itself limited in movement, and it crashed with a shudder into the brick corner.

He glanced across the street, where the last of the wounded were moving away, toward the sea, and any help that remained.

The sound of metal on metal confirmed the opening upper hatch on the Panzer, and as a head appeared, it was hit by a well-placed shot from the corporal across the way, but another burst from the small arms of the Panzer caught the man through both legs and he slumped to the ground.

The far track ground the Panzer further into the fabric of the brick wall, then stopped, the driver beginning to reverse the vehicle and free it. The hatch slammed closed with the jolt but the British officer had already jumped up onto the level plating around the turret. He managed to gain a hold on the closed access hatch before it was sealed, and threw it back, just in time to deflect a small-arms burst from the following Panzer, bullets scarring the wall behind him.

As the victim of the corporal's bullet was dragged back down into the body of the tank, manipulated by others who were seeking to find the space to escape, the officer gripped his revolver and hanging down through the opening until he could find targets, fired quickly, until all were eliminated.

It had not been courage, or valour, or even rage that urged him on. They had written the rules and he had complied with them, without the fear of morality, or remorse, or even pity. They had entered the game, as he had, and should stand for the 'Birkenhead Drill', as he would, if it came to that. They had come for him, and by the same rules he would finish every mother's son of them, if it came to that. And it had come to that.

He heard the sound of the second tank, attempting to move around the side of the first, and from further behind, the sound of more, reinforcing their fellows. The officer hauled himself out of the hatch to see the other Panzer almost aligned with the one he now stood on, but the distance was deceptive, and the second Panzer surged into the tight space between its twin and the opposite wall, grinding metal as it stuck tight between them.

The gap was now sealed for any reinforcement armour coming behind. Slowly, the turret of the wedged Panzer began to turn toward him, but there was too little space for it to be a problem. He reached down again, into the open hatch where an armour piercing round for the main gun was lodged in a rack. Pulling the shell from its place, and himself from the interior of the German tank, he reached over, keeping most of his body covered by the open steel hatch. As the muzzle of the revolving gun came toward him, he reached out quickly and jammed the shell down into the barrel as far as it would go. Rifling of the barrel stopped the shell half way, but it was well seated, and he smiled to himself at the effect should the gunner fire without noticing the blockage.

More rounds spat about him as he jumped down and ran over to the injured corporal. He abandoned the man's rifle and pulled his arms around his neck, like a half piggy back, dragging him away from the lodged Panzers until out of sight of any machine gunner that might still find them as a target.

"Leave me, sir! Leave me!" The corporal croaked.

"Not likely," answered the officer. "If I was going to that, I'd be paddling in the briny by now. Anyway, I owe you one, so shut up."

German armour was advancing all around them, the sounds were obvious. But enemy infantry assaults had diminished in the last twenty-four hours. As the two men advanced, more British and French soldiers emerged from the side streets, ragged shadows of the pristine units they had once been. Eventually, they saw the channel, and smoking wrecks which had once been vessels of the Royal Navy. Smaller ships, lighters and ferries, and even sailing boats clipped the shallows, where streams of men waded out in the reddening waves in an attempt to find one near enough to board, and risk the occasional ME 209 that hoped to stop them.

"Good Lord!" Exclaimed the officer, craning his neck to see the Mole, broken and burning, with troops ignoring the dangers in their needs to be away from the hell that pursued them.

He knew that the corporal was losing blood and looked for help. Some distance away, nearer the shoreline, an ambulance still smoked from an earlier hit, the rear tyres still burning, but beneath a tarpaulin sheet extending over the engine, medics worked to see to the wounded. He hauled the man on his back over the beach, each step sapping his strength, until finally, he reached the vehicle, and he manhandled the corporal onto the sand.

"Would someone look to this man!" The officer called out, but all of the medics were occupied.

He stood up and shouted at the top of his voice, a hand on the empty sidearm at his hip.

"Would someone look at this man! NOW!"

A man in a red coat, which had once been white, turned to

him, his face drawn. For a moment, he just looked across, but then slowly came over and knelt on the sand, ripping open the corporal's battledress until the flesh was visible, then pressing a stethoscope to his skin. After a few moments, the medic looked at the officer, and put a hand on is arm.

"I'm sorry," he said, "there's nothing more that we can do for him. He's gone."

For a long, sad minute, the officer placed a hand on the corporal's arm as he sat by him on the sand. He stood when soldiers assisting the medics came over and took the man away to somewhere unknown.

"I can't remember his name," he said as the medic observed him briefly, then returned to his work.

A short distance away, the skeleton of a truck was buried up to its axles in the sand. The officer walked over and sat against the nearest front wheel, his arms resting on his bent knees, the tears staining his jacket. He was exhausted.

A soldier from the medical station walked the short distance across and thrust a mug of hot tea into his face. The officer looked up and smiled, taking the tea, hardly remembering how good it tasted. Looking down, the man frowned. He pulled back and squinted for a better look at the officer through the blood and the grime.

"Mr Lawrence, is it, sir.

Chapter One
Conduct Unbecoming

It was an old clock at the end of the corridor that claimed the half hour of seven thirty on a cold, wet September morning. The white face with Roman numerals was surrounded by polished oak, and beneath it, rain speckled the eight small panes of a window that needed attention to the faded white paint. The corridor itself appeared neglected, without any enhancement, the walls split by a wooden rail which divided the original paintwork of green and cream.

Heavy footsteps followed the final chime of the clock, and stopped at the last door on the left. The man in smart khaki adjusted the Sam Brown belt that he wore, and waited for the response to his knock, before entering. He took off his cap, and inclined his head closer to the oak door, listening for the words.

"Come in!"

He grasped the brass doorknob, his eyes level with the smart red and gold plate which informed of the identity of the person behind the door, 'Colonel Denning'.

The man opened the door and entered.

Across the room, behind a large desk that appeared to be a residence for files, sat a middle-aged man, his shoulder brass betraying that this was indeed the person announced by the red and gold plate. He was balding, with a few pen lines of hair across his scalp, but with no trace of grey, and as he looked up, two pools of the deepest blue searched over silver bifocal spectacles. His nose was sharp, but not overly so, and his lips pressed tightly together. His shoulder designation read 'Royal Engineers', but this had been just to avoid questions for some time, and bore little reference to his true employment activities.

"Morning Rutter." He snapped, with little attempt at a more amiable welcome. "Anything?"

Major William Rutter executed a salute without the usual coming to attention that was normally associated with it. In this department, those things kind of went by the board, in deference to more important activities. He handed over three folders, reaching across the smallest of the piles on the desk.

"Yes, sir," he replied. "You should take a look at these, I…"

Denning held up a hand for quiet as he looked through each file in turn, spending some time on each. He leaned onto the desk with one arm, and supported his chin with his fist. Finally, he selected one, and read it though again, spending more time in reading than before. Taking off the spectacles, he looked up at Rutter, handing back the opened folder that displayed something near to what he was searching for.

"Lawrence." Denning read the name aloud. "In France with the BEF, taken off at Dunkirk, good training background, rank of Captain, speaks German, perfect, also French, with passable Russian. Facial features close, but we can enhance that. Good IQ. Reasonable training reports. Height about right." His eyes lit up.

"I like him, Rutter, I like him."

Rutter twisted his lip as he looked at the selection.

"Ah! Yes, sir," he said, almost apologetically. "I rather hoped that you might find something in one of the other two…"

Denning looked up, seeing something in his subordinate's features that was left unsaid. He pressed his selection.

"The others have something, but this one fits the bill. Especially since he's a linguist, and a good one by what it says here." He insisted.

Rutter shrugged at the idea.

"Yes, sir. But there may be something of a problem in securing this man," he said, nervously. "You see he's about to be hanged."

Denning sat back heavily in his chair, and took off the silver spectacles. His face dropped into something between disappointment and surprise.

"Hanged. When?" he asked.

Rutter looked at his watch, then back at Denning.

"Oh, in around fifty minutes from now," he confirmed. "In Pentonville Prison. Now if I might…"

Denning was already on his feet and hurrying over to a door which led to an adjoining room. He pushed it open, surprising a young typist, who was engrossed in her work."

"Angela, get me Pentonville Prison, straight away!"

Angela's wide eyes darted from Denning to the telephone by her typewriter, and picked up the handset, while with the other hand, she opened a drawer and searched for the number to dial. Rutter walked nearer to the door, to where Denning waited.

"I don't think they take any calls before an execution, sir, unless it's from the Home Office, or the Palace."

"Then get me the Home Office!" he ordered.

"It might be a little early to catch anyone at the Home Office, sir, especially after the raid last night," Rutter added.

Denning glanced at him, then back to the typist, who had dialled, and waited for someone to answer. She looked up at her senior and raised her eyebrows to confirm what Rutter had predicted. Denning was becoming impatient. He looked at his watch.

"Leave it, damn it!" he told the girl. "Have my car come around right away. Urgent!"

He retrieved the folder on his desk while the other man looked on, then barked an order.

"Come on Rutter. How long have we got before they stretch him?" he asked, making with considerable haste toward the door.

Rutter followed in his footsteps, checking his watch.

"A little over forty minutes, sir," he answered. "I really don't think we can…"

Colonel Denning had grabbed his Army greatcoat from the hook on the inside of the door and was already thumping down the corridor, hardly pausing as he glanced up at the clock above the window which confirmed Rutter's estimate.

*

"What time is it?" asked the man who was dressed in grey wool.

His right hand cupped his chin and his eyes raised in anticipation of an answer from his opponent. The other man smiled and shook his head as he moved his white Bishop. The grey man smiled back.

"You know, Officer Willoughby, I could have taken that white Bishop three moves ago, had I wished this game to end sooner."

Willoughby's face took on a thoughtful demeanour.

"Could you?"

"You know I could," answered the grey man. "You could

have compromised my Queen at least three moves ago, and forced a check which I would have found pretty hard to escape, forfeiting either Queen or Rook. But by letting you have the Queen, which I knew that you would find hard to resist, you'd let yourself in for checkmate in two moves." He leaned forward to put both elbows on the table, clasping his hands together. "I appreciate your attempt to let me win, just one last time, but under the circumstances, the victory is a little shallow."

Distant footfalls echoed in the cold, stone corridor on the other side of the cell door. Suddenly, the grey man knew the time. Before he could stand, the cell door was thrust open and a short, portly man in a blue suit came quickly toward him, followed by someone younger. As the man in blue spun him around to secure his hands behind his back, Willoughby rose and hurriedly slid a large oak cabinet to one side, revealing a door, which he opened. Within seconds, a hessian bag was dropped over the grey man's head and he was walked through the door toward a heavy wooden trapdoor, and ushered into the middle of it, where a leather strap was produced to hold his legs together. He felt the weight of the noose being placed around his neck, just behind his left ear, and tightened. It had all happened in less than a minute.

There was a rattle of metal on wood and a frustration of voices somewhere behind him. Lawrence waited for the end. He stood waiting, wondering if time had slowed, if it was always like this. He could hear his own heart beating and wondered if this was the way that the Gods always played the final dance, extracting every entertainment until the last spark?

Rough hands grasped him, pulled him by the arms and he hopped like a demented kangaroo to keep pace with the speed that they moved him along. He was pressed against a wall as someone removed the leg restraints. For the first time he smelled the odour of the hessian bag over his head, as he tried unsuccessfully to see through the weave. He was confused, perplexed and bewildered at why he still felt alive, manhandled and jostled without explanation.

Was it over? Was he gone, finished, and no more? Was this how it happened, following those that had gone before? Was this transition into oblivion?

"What? What's...?"

*

The man in the blue suit, and his assistant were ushered back into the condemned cell, where a confounded Willoughby was collecting the chess pieces and returning them to their box. He tucked the board under his arm, nodded to the military uniform in the seat that he had so recently occupied. After closing the door which connected to the gallows and replacing the cupboard, he left, clanking the cell door closed behind him.

Major Rutter stood at ease behind his Colonel, his face without expression. Across the small table which had once hosted the uneven chess battle, the two civilians stood in obvious astonishment.

"Please sit, Mr Pierrepoint." Denning waved a hand to the other chair, while the assistant mirrored Rutter and found his place behind.

The hangman pulled the chair noisily until there was enough space for him to comply. He spoke with a strong West Yorkshire accent, which his years in London had failed to diminish.

"Are you going to tell me what the bloody hell is going on here?" he asked, with obvious annoyance. "You have denigrated my professional employment. My aim is always to service the client in twelve seconds or under, and in this case, you have sullied my work, not to mention any stress caused to the unfortunate."

Pierrepoint's anger was written across his face, his forehead furrowed and his mouth left half open, waiting for the explanation. Denning raised a hand.

"Mr Pierrepoint, I understand your professional compromise." Denning began. "The person who you were about to deal with is someone that we need to ask a question of, in the interest of the conduct of the war." He folded his arms and sat back in the chair. "Now, there are two possibilities, depending upon the answer that we receive from yourself. One possibility is that within the next half hour or so, you will be free to continue your work, and nothing will be asked about the delay."

Pierrepoint sat upright, an odd expression of confusion on his face. He turned to glance at his assistant, who appeared to be just as taken aback at the happenings of the last minutes.

"And the second?" Pierrepoint asked.

"Ah! The second." Colonel Denning's face brightened a little. "The second possibility is that you will hear no more of this. You and your assistant will leave and go about your business, as if you have done your duty. Neither of you will ever mention this again, either to your family, or each other. You will be paid the usual amount, and we have a little bonus for you if you agree to these limitations."

"A bonus?" Pierrepoint asked. "And what would that be, might I ask?"

Denning looked the hangman in the eye, and spoke in a matter-of-fact way.

"Mr Pierrepoint, the war is coming to a close, it's just a matter of time. We shall win, of course, but when, we have no idea. Our hope that it will be soon." There was a pause. "Now, when we do make an end to this damn dismal unpleasantness, someone will be brought to book. I might guess that quite a number will be brought to book..."

"You mentioned a bonus?" Pierrepoint asked.

"Yes." Answered Denning, thoughtfully. "Quite a number of those that I have just mentioned will no doubt be put on trial for the excesses of the war, whatever the limits of those excesses are deemed to be. Of course, the declination of those excesses will be for others to decide, but what I can tell you is that those exceeding them will receive the severest of sentences." He paused, thinking of how to confirm his words. "If you see what I mean."

The root of a smile crossed Pierrepoint's features.

"Now," continued the Colonel, "I have information, from the highest authority, that the place of decision in these matters is likely to be Nuremburg."

"The German Nuremburg?" Pierrepoint asked.

Denning confirmed it with a nod of his head.

"So, once these scallions have been sentenced," he paused again and smiled, "after a fair and comprehensive trial, of course, there needs to be someone of the highest professional reference to deal with their exit from this world in the manner that they deserve. And I am confident that I can see that yourself, and your assistant, are offered the first refusal of such a lucrative contract."

Pierrepoint's face was mixture of surprise and elation. He took a deep breath. Denning went on.

"But should the continuation of today's duties be necessary, I can offer you two hundred pounds in appreciation of the same discretion, and fifty for your assistant." He put a hand on his chest. "Providing you don't mind a cheque?"

Pierrepoint turned to look at his bewildered assistant. His accent seemed even stronger.

"I think that those terms are agreeable, Arthur, don't you?" he said. "Providing that the normal travel expenses are additional, should we be required to attend your Nuremburg arrangements."

Arthur nodded his agreement with wide eyes. Pierrepoint turned back to the Colonel, his chair slaking a little on the concrete floor.

"I must advise you, Mr Pierrepoint," Denning added, "should the second of the possibilities arise, some of the... he looked for the right description... 'disposables...' maybe female. I trust you have no objections in that direction?"

The hangman turned back to Arthur just briefly, a wry smile upon his countenance as he looked over at Denning once more.

"Come one, come all, that's what we say, General."

Denning sat back.

"Colonel, actually, Mr Pierrepoint, it's Colonel," he verified. "Now, can we offer you some tea while we investigate possibility number two? I don't think we will keep you waiting too long, either way."

"That would be very nice." Pierrepoint replied, gratefully.

"Rutter, would you organise some tea for Mr Pierrepoint, and Arthur, of course. And perhaps some biscuits, if there are any?" Denning ordered.

Rutter had remained silent during the conversation.

"Of course, sir," he replied, starting for the iron door of the cell.

"Then, if you will join me in the other place."

The Major turned back as he found the door.

"Yes, sir."

*

Colonel Denning leaned against the cold corridor wall, waiting for Rutter to find him. He read through the file again, then the prison and police reports, and finally the military police testimony and the court account. It was hard reading, but sympathy was far beyond his armoury at this stage of the war.

The slight echo of footsteps preceded Rutter until he turned a corner and joined the Colonel. Denning looked up, doubt sweeping across his face.

"Have you read this, Rutter?" he asked. "All of it?"

The Major shrugged, not recognising all of the paperwork covers, and set his hands behind his back.

"Some of it, sir," he answered. "Not all." Rutter shuffled as if he had failed an important exam. "Killed his wife, and her boyfriend, didn't he? In cold blood? In a compromising situation?"

Denning looked back down, into the court files.

*

He had been roughly pushed through a doorway, his legs weak from the stress of the last minutes, so much so that they almost failed to support him. Swaying, and still hooded in hessian and his hands tied behind him, he was ushered along the stone floor a short way, then thrust sideways into another cell. His voice seemed to belong to someone else, being high pitched and almost croaky, and his breathing was heavy and fast.

"Why am I...? Am I...? "What...? Who are you?"

Firm hands pressed him into a chair, then slammed the door shut, heavily. For a moment, he just sat, trying to understand, then wept profusely until he choked with the effort. He tried to breathe deeply, but found himself exhaling in a staccato of short coughs.

"Is anyone there?" he asked, finding the silence provocative and fearful.

By now, he was convinced that he had not moved into the afterlife, but if he had, he decided that the first was better. Sucking in all of the air that he could, he let it out in a long shout-scream. There was still silence. He moved his foot around and found the leg of a table, confirming what it was by moving it with a little pressure, and translating the noise of wood on a hard floor.

It was hard to decide how long he had been in the room, alone. The hessian hood seemed to magnify the time, and time seemed a very valuable asset at that moment. He began to breathe heavily again, almost unable to control the staccato breaths, but stiffened and forced the stress of the situation back where it came from, wherever that might be.

A door opened somewhere behind him; the distance blurred by the hessian hood. He half turned, still restricted by the hood.

"Is there someone there?"

He heard the heavy door close and followed the footsteps by what he could hear. Another chair grated on the hard floor. The lack of an answer to his question made him feel even more intimidated. Had they worse tortures to inflict upon him, worse than he had already been on the brink of? Could there be worse?

Colonel Denning placed the folders on the small table and looked up at Rutter, indicating with a nod to remove the hood, which he did. The man blinked a little with the infusion of more light coming through the small high window opposite the door.

Denning looked closely at the man in front of him. A little hard-faced, hair prematurely grey and unkempt with a day's growth of beard, for which he found hard to condemn, under the circumstances. Eyes which favoured blue or grey, depending on the light, and lips full but pressed tight together. Denning spoke loudly, checking the information text on the table.

"Lawrence, William George, thirty-three years of age, late of His Majesty's service. Previously married." Denning briefly looked up without expression, and across at Lawrence. "Two children, both boys, currently with your one and only brother. You are at the moment a convicted murderer." He looked up again. "A speaker of German, Russian and French. Translator. Lately transferred to the German prisoner interrogation section. Advanced at the beginning of the war with the expeditionary force, returned with the general retreat from Dunkirk. Would you say that was an overall description of yourself?"

Lawrence looked over to where Rutter was standing behind the Colonel, then back to the man seated.

"German and French perfect. Russian uh-huh." He confirmed shakily, discounting his perfection of the latter.

Denning gave him a long glance, as if the answer had offended.

"Why am I still alive?" Lawrence asked, ignoring the Colonel's need for further confirmation.

Denning straightened.

"You may not be for much longer, if you do not co-operate. Do you understand that?"

Lawrence swallowed hard.

"Well, if you put it like that…"

"I do put it like that." Denning rasped. "The hangman is still in the building, so if you wish not to make his acquaintance again, I recommend that you take a more equitable attitude to your situation. Do I make myself quite clear?"

There was little room for verbal manoeuvring, in the wake of a stressful morning. Lawrence was aware of that, but something in his character wanted to fight back against the trauma of it all. He knew that he was thankful to be alive, but why?

"All right," he agreed. "But why?"

Colonel Denning seemed to soften. He sat back with both hands stretched out to rest on the table. Rutter remained silent, his hands behind his back, and Lawrence noted the unclipped hood on his leather revolver case.

"I understand how confused you must be, and I do not wish to prolong this any more than needs be. What happens in the next five minutes depends upon you. The choice will be yours." Denning said. "You will have the option of two directions." He paused for a moment. "Choose one and you will be returned to your original path and suffer the consequences as swiftly as possible in the interest of being humane. Choose the second, and you will be charged with responsibilities of impossible risk."

"Hobson's choice, then?" Lawrence declared.

Denning shrugged.

"Depends how you look at it, doesn't it?"

Lawrence asked.

"And just what is this responsibility of risk?"

A shake of a balding head denied that information, at least for the moment.

"I can only divulge that if you take the second path. Needless to say, that to pluck a man from the gallows at such a moment takes the highest authority." He raised an eyebrow. "In fact, you are the first, and no doubt the last, to experience such a privilege. That should tell you something." Denning looked at his watch. "Now, time is of the essence, so you must make your decision."

"And if I choose the second option?"

Denning paused in thought for a moment.

"It's only right to inform you, that should you do so, you will never see your children again, nor any of your family. No trace of you will be found, anywhere. To the rest of the world, your sentence was carried out at the proper time. If you are successful in what we ask of you, you will be given the sum of five hundred thousand pounds, and a new life in whichever country of the Empire you wish, with a change of name, of course."

"Very generous," Lawrence agreed, raising an eyebrow, "should I be successful, of course." He took in a deep breath. "I suppose either way, I won't see my boys again."

"So, you agree to the second choice?"

"Well," said Lawrence, "as you can observe, my options are pretty limited at the moment." His luck was slowly beginning to realise the stress of his salvation. "Any chance of a cup of tea, or maybe something stronger?"

Chapter Two
The Scotch Game

The black Humber Imperial coasted along Fleet Street and turned right, down Salisbury Court. From the leg room behind the driver, Lawrence guessed it was a long wheelbase vehicle, favoured by the top brass, and from the configuration of the rear doors, and the sound of the engine, perhaps a Lagonda, or maybe a Humber. It was just a guess, as the hood had been replaced upon his head, and heavy, steel shackles still confined his hands onto his lap.

Denning sat on his left, with Rutter on his right. Lawrence guessed that such a configuration allowed the latter's revolver to remain as far away from him as possible, in a secure place, between the Major and the offside door. He guessed that Denning was unarmed as the available space in the rear seat pressed the three passengers quite close, and Lawrence's left hip could detect no sign of a sidearm, unless of course, the man was left-handed. Apart from the occasional directive given to the driver by Denning, there had been little conversation, and Lawrence went along with the silence, just glad to still be a part of it.

The vehicle slowed and halted after another turn. A sound of iron gates could be heard as they clanked together and some kind of mechanism sealed them.

"Just sit tight for a moment." Denning ordered, as the men on either side of Lawrence got out and closed the car doors heavily.

There was a brief, muffled conversation outside, on his right, but it was hard to hear clearly, or assign meaning to the words. Lawrence considered making a run for it, weighing up the chances despite the shackles, if he exited through the left-hand door, on the side where Denning had been sitting. Slowly he tested the extent of his movements, when a cigarette lighter clicked, and a London accented voice from the driver's seat advised him.

"Won't be long, sir. Just a minute or two."

Lawrence let out a long breath and the minute or two passed. The right hand, rear door opened, and he was hauled out by strong hands that supported him until his feet were firmly on the ground.

"This way." Someone said, his voice making a slight echo in what sounded like a limited space.

Lawrence kept silent as he was guided through a door, which cut off the echo outside, and led to a carpeted stairway, the pile of which denoted a reasonable quality, and not the well-worn flooring that led into an officer's mess, assaulted by spilt whisky and heavy boots. At least, that was how he remembered them, and it was wartime.

He was pushed into a chair, and the hood removed. For a moment, he blinked at the light which flooded through the bay window in front of him, even though the day was overcast and a light rain persisted, running in ragged rivers down the glass.

Between himself and the window was a large table, unimposing and ordinary, behind which sat Colonel Denning. Lawrence turned to find Rutter standing just to his right, just out of arms' reach, and his revolver case still unclipped.

Further over to the right, sitting near the wall in an ornate chair, was an elderly man with his hands clasped, his elbows resting on gilt arms. Lawrence rattled the shackles and looked over at the silhouette of Denning, detail returning as his eyes accustomed to the light. Denning ignored the silent request, with no physical response, except to turn on the large desk lamp. Then, he reached for the large black telephone.

"Send her in." Denning ordered to whoever was on the other end of the phone.

All was silent, until a minute later when the door opened and someone entered. Lawrence half turned to see a strikingly attractive woman of about twenty-five swish across the room and halt in front of him. She was wearing a white, short-sleeved blouse and dark skirt, the latter ending just below the knee, where nylon stockings took over, real ones and not just the simulated kind where gravy browning and a pencil line along the calf made something like a decent imitation during the last few years. Black, high-heel shoes completed the outfit.

Lawrence looked up at her, then at the others in the room, wondering what the hell was coming next.

"Sprechen Sie Deutsch?" the woman asked, in perfect German.

Lawrence paused before answering.

"Ja."

"Weist du 'die Lorelei?'" she asked, referring to a folk song.

"Ja." Lawrence answered. "I know it."

"Singe es dann," she requested.

Lawrence sighed and looked around once more, hoping to avoid it, but there was obviously no escape from his poor recitation. He took in a deep breath and started.

"Ich weis nicht, was soll es bedeuten,
Dass ich so Traurig bin,
Ein Marchen aus alten Zetien,'
Das kommt mir nicht aus dem Zinn…"

It went on until Lawrence had completed every verse, with the woman intensely watching and listening. When it was done, he bowed slightly to the room.

"Die Lorelei'," he confirmed, "by Heinrich Heine, sung beautifully by…"

"That will do! Carry on.!" Denning ordered.

The woman went into a quick question and answer routine, which Lawrence parried for another fifteen minutes. Then, she paused, raised her eyebrows and pursed her lips as she turned to face Denning.

"Absolutely perfect," she endorsed. "Not a sign of an accent, apart from the slightest inflection…" She looked back at Lawrence. "… Bavaria, I would guess at?"

He smiled, and reverted to English.

"Bavaria, Füssen actually, near the Austrian border. They make great violins, if you're interested."

The woman smiled back.

"Do you want me to check his French?"

Denning shook his head.

"I think that will be all, thank you."

She looked back at Lawrence for a moment, and smiled to herself as she left by the same door that she had entered by.
The man in the ornate chair rose and walked over to him, halting a short distance away with his hands behind his back. Lawrence looked up at him, noting the slight frown on his forehead, the kindly demeanour, and the way that the man was returning his gaze with an almost challenging stare. His longer than normal grey hair dropped over one eye, and he pushed it back into place, his hand then finding the gold rimmed spectacles in the inside pocket of his suit jacket. He moved around, more to Lawrence's front, and revealed a slight limp, then he folded his arms and let his head drop slightly to one side.

"Would you tell us why you shot your wife and her…" He paused to find a word that might be less dramatic. "…friend?"

Lawrence sighed deeply and sat back, letting the shackles fall back into his lap.

"Don't you read the Sunday papers?" he asked, a little sarcasm in his voice. "I'm sure there are much juicier cases, if you like that sort of thing."

He saw the expression on Denning's face change a little, and Lawrence refined his irritation. It was clear that his association with the hangman might depend on it. He sighed again.

"What is it that you want to know?"

The elderly man shrugged.

"Just how you came to the conclusion that it was the appropriate path to take."

Lawrence shrugged back, and looked into the floor. He raised his eyebrows and shook his head.

"It wasn't the first time I considered it, you know." He began. "It might have happened a couple of times in the last nine years. Maybe it should have…"

"Such a dramatic response to… adultery, isn't it?" He was asked.

Lawrence smiled shallowly. There seemed to be little emotion behind it.

"I aimed at him, not her, but he moved, if you see what I mean," he answered. "So, the bullet went through both of them, two birds with one stone, in a manner of speaking."

Denning cut into the conversation.

"The man was your commanding officer, I understand?" he asked.

Lawrence nodded.

"I wondered why I always fell for the night duties." He explained. "Then one night I abandoned my order and went home, making sure that I had my sidearm of course. And well, the rest is history." He smiled again. "They never charged me for dereliction of duty, just for the illegal discharge of a firearm, and the repercussions thereof. The expedience of the law, you understand?"

"And your children?" the old man asked. "You didn't consider them?"

"Of course, I did." Lawrence answered. "Better they were brought up by my brother, than in an unhappy marriage.

"You were unhappy in your marriage?"

"No." Lawrence confirmed. "But she obviously was."

The lock of grey hair assaulted the face again, and was thrust back as the man found a notepad in his pocket and a pencil from the same place. He opened the pad and began to write steadily, mouthing the words as he advanced along the lines.

"Did you intend to kill your superior officer when you left your duties?"

Lawrence took a deep breath and looked the other in the eye.

"Damn right, I did."

"And then you waited for the police?" he was asked. "Why?"

Lawrence raised his shoulders.

"I wouldn't want them… my kids I mean… to think I was a coward, unwilling to face the consequences, now, would I?"

The scribbler took three photographs from the back of the notepad and showed them to Lawrence. They were of a horse, a dog, and an eagle. He held them up, one by one.

"Which of these do you prefer?" he asked.

Lawrence glanced at the pictures.

"The dog," he replied. "Maybe the horse?"

"Not the eagle?" the old man asked. "Why not the eagle, the

freedom of the skies, the majestic hunter of the north. Why not the eagle?"

Lawrence thought for a moment.

"Because one with two heads is dropping ordnance on us all, in case you haven't noticed," he said, almost becoming irritated. "If you go to a good library, you're sure to find a picture of one at the entrance to the Reichstag

"You find the thought of the eagle with two heads bothersome?"

"I saw enough of them before Dunkirk, and after," he answered. "On battle flags, along with the other piece of crap, red and white with a black swastika. And I saw the carnage that runs alongside them, every time they're flown."

Lawrence clanked the shackles at Denning again, to no avail. It went on for another forty minutes, strange questions about his preferences, with the odd probes about his military involvements, his personal life, childhood, and other things. Several loose pages emerged from a side pocket and he was asked to complete strange notations of symbols, historical questions and the identification of random shapes. Then, the old man turned and nodded to Denning and returned to his chair. Denning rose and walked around the table, until he reached the centre of the room.

"All right, then," he said, "Major Rutter will take you to the mess, where you can get something to eat, then we'll get you out of those prison clothes and proceed to the next step." Still standing, he folded his arms. "I must warn you, if you try to escape or make any move which can be interpreted as such, Rutter has orders to shoot you without warning. Do you understand?"

"Yes." Lawrence understood the implication, but clicked the shackles again.

"All in good time," Denning said. "Now off to the mess."

Lawrence led the way back through the door. Rutter followed at arms-length and gave a pert nod to the others as he closed the door behind him. Colonel Denning waited for a few seconds, the turned to the man in the suit, who pushed back the streak of grey hair again.

"Well? What do you think?" he asked.

The other man rose from the ornate chair and thrust his hands in his pockets. He was thoughtful for a moment. An hour before, he had probed quite deeply into Lawrence's past, reading segments of the files over, several times.

"A product of his time, I imagine," he began. "I detected definite childhood issues, but I think that much of the underlying layer of violence could only come from his experience in the service." He was thoughtful again. "But this violence he can control, up to a point, and when the line is overstepped then the result is cold and calculated, with no remorse, or fear of the consequences."

"A psychopath?" Denning asked.

The other shook his head.

"Far from it," he replied. "The man is emotionally frozen. The violence is selective, almost restitutional, and calculated, as if used to right a wrong with little concern for the aftermath. He knew what the result of his actions would be, and was prepared to accept it. A killer with a sense of responsibility. Remarkable."

"His record shows considerable presence of mind during the retreat to Dunkirk." Denning added. "When most were just thinking about getting off the Mole, he was actually taking the fight to the Germans, almost as if it were a game…"

"Or a challenge?"

"Right," Denning agreed. "That would fit into your theory about his mind set."

The man in the suit sat down again.

"Whatever you do, never wrong this man." He went on. "The result might be terrifying. There are no traces of narcissism, no guilt over his actions, just an over-reactive need to make things right, as he sees them."

"He was chosen in haste, due in part to his background and linguistic skills." Denning admitted. "But perhaps we have bitten off more than we can chew. Is he safe, to be released, to be given authority, to complete an assignment?"

The old man smiled, and ran a hand over his hair.

"Major Denning," he answered, "I suspect that whatever your intentions are for this man, they will not be carried out down Oxford Street or Piccadilly. To those around him, he will seem perfectly normal, perhaps reflecting his upbringing, his education, his loyalties. And remember, even though his wife's infidelity had happened before, this was the first time that he took it unto himself to resolve the situation in such a manner. I suspect this was due to his concern for the children, how the matter conflicted, until the resolution in his mind took over his regard for himself, or anything else. And even when the decision was made, it was that cold, hard resolve that carried it out."

"Anything else?"

"A slight aversion to authority, nothing major, but on the other side of the coin, considerable respect for it under the right circumstances. Loyalty to whatever he decides deserves it."

"You think that we made the right choice?"

He looked up at Denning.

"I would like a little more time to look into his background, it may be very useful, very enlightening. If you give me your authority, I may be able to give you a more definitive answer to your question."

Denning looked stern and thoughtful.

"Very well, but our time is short," he said. "If you can make your observations in the time available, they may be useful…"

*

He had been given fresh clothes and eaten alone in the small mess room. The choices were limited, but it was the war, and many would have been glad of it. Rutter had remained in the room with him, but just stood by the door. Lawrence finished the coffee and looked up at his keeper.

"If you had told me early this morning that I would be drinking coffee like this, any time today…" He paused in thought. "…what is the time, by the way?"

Rutter grasped the handle of his service revolver and looked sharply at his watch, then looked back up again.

"Almost Fourteen hundred," he replied.

"Ah," Lawrence said, rattling the hand shackles. "Any idea when I can have these off?"

Rutter shook his head.

"Been a strange day." Lawrence admitted, more to irritate than stir up a conversation. "Strange indeed, when you expected not to see much of it. Any idea when someone will tell me what I have to do to stay in such a condition, one in which I am hoping to remain for a little longer?"

Rutter shook his head.

*

Forty-five minutes later, Lawrence was returned, still in shackles, to the room where he had previously been. The ornate chair was now on the opposite side to the table to where Denning was already waiting. He was shown into it. Denning looked intently at him for a moment.

"You realise that you no longer have your commission, and that you are now plain Mister Lawrence? Or should I say 'were'. You are now Mister Nobody. To all intents and purposes, you were hanged this morning as scheduled, and no longer exist. Soon, you will never be known again by your current name. Never. Do you understand?"

Lawrence nodded his assent, knowing that his options were limited, if that. Denning opened a file that lay in front of him. The text held his attention for a moment, until a slight rattle of Lawrence's hand restraints made him look across the table.

"In a few days, we will give you the opportunity to shorten the war by months, perhaps a year. As you can imagine, the lives saved would be in the thousands, perhaps hundreds of thousands, not to mention the incalculable retention of material assets and other considerations."

Lawrence remained silent, wondering what the hell he was getting himself into, as opposed to the hell he had expected earlier.

"Whatever the outcome," Denning went on, "you will never receive any gratitude or acknowledgement of your actions, or any marked grave or ceremony. To all intents and purposes, you are a dead man, a convicted murderer, and as such you will be remembered. Is that clear?"

"It appears that I have little choice," Lawrence answered. "When will I know of what's in store for me? Am I allowed to know that, at least?"

"All in good time," Denning said. "But you may be reassured that we will give you every assistance to succeed. And should you be successful, there will be a certain reward, as I have already outlined, but more of that later."

"I would like…"

Denning cut him off brusquely.

"I will see you again, the day after tomorrow, when full details will be given to you." He explained, with no humour in his expression. "Until then, remember that you are still under consideration for justice to be carried out. You will now be taken under guard for physical assessment and training." He paused but retained his humourless expression. "You will remain silent of what I have told you, under pain of death. Until the appropriate time, good day to you."

It was abrupt, and clinically clear. Rutter led him from the room, he guessed to the point where they had entered the building, down the carpeted stairway to a closed outside door.

"Sorry, old man," Rutter said, "I'm afraid the hood has to go on again."

Once he was all but blind once more, he heard the door open to the slight echo that he remembered. It was the same car that he was ushered into, Lawrence was certain of that, with just the driver, and Major Rutter beside him, on his right-hand side, still keeping the revolver in a safe position, just in case.

It seemed quite a short distance before the vehicle stopped. Lawrence could hear no traffic, and guessed that this was their destination, and not just a pause at lights or a junction. Footsteps came closer, and Rutter told the driver to wait. Once they had passed, and drifted into the distance, the major issued an OK, and Lawrence was helped out onto what felt like a paved surface, then hurried past mesh gates that he managed to touch and identify with shackled hands. Another door, then another, and then stairs which were completely unlike those he had descended just a short time before. They were hard, heavy and manufactured from wood, with no apparent concern to dampening the noise.

Another door opened, and he was guided through, and brought to a halt on bare floorboards. Through the hood, Lawrence could just make out the glow of artificial light in several places.

"All right, just stand while I take the hood away," Rutter told him, and once more he blinked into the light.

He was in what looked like a gymnasium, with faded lines

over the board floor. Several green-shaded lamps lit up the windowless space, and in the centre of one of the long walls, propped against the wall, was a wiry man in service uniform, his hands in the pockets of his gaitered khaki trousers. A short battledress jacket completed the uniform, topped with a beret pulled over one eye, and a dark blue pom-pom in the centre. The man looked up from the floor, and over to the two men who had entered without changing his attitude.

A key was thrust into Lawrence's hand, then Rutter stood back, his hand on the grip of his revolver.

"I'll let you do the honours, old boy," he said, almost cheerily.

Lawrence divested himself of the manacles and offered them back to the Major, rubbing his wrists where they had chafed.

"Just chuck them near the wall," Rutter told him. "We might just need them again."

The third man in the room straightened and walked over. He nodded curtly at the officer without saluting.

"This is Colour Sergeant Bull," Rutter told Lawrence. "He may just help you to save your skin, so listen to what he tells you. There is no escape from this room, so I will see you again in due course."

Rutter made a gesture of salute to the Colour Sergeant with a finger to the temple, then left quickly. The noise of heavy bolts on the other side of the door told Lawrence that Rutter's words had been accurate. Lawrence, still rubbing his wrists, turned back to the Colour Sergeant, who smiled back.

"Good afternoon, sir." He greeted with a Scottish accent, without offering a hand.

"Hello," Lawrence said. "You can drop the 'sir'. It's kind of a mute-point, but I no longer aspire to the title."

The other shrugged, taking off his beret and throwing it to the wall, then began to unbutton his jacket to reveal a white vest. His face was regular and brown with the sun, with a latent humour that shone through. A permanent rising at one side of his mouth added to the effect of friendliness.

"I know nothing of your history, sir, and probably never will. Neither do I know much of what is intended for you, or when."

"I have a similar failure to rub shoulders with what the future holds." Lawrence raised an eyebrow. "It seems to be the normal these days."

"Well, we have to get down to business as time is short, sir, and I have a fair bit to enlighten you with." Bull informed him.

Lawrence found it amusing that the Colour Sergeant seemed to insist upon his title as 'sir'. It didn't bother him. The other man looked him up and down for a few seconds.

"You have already an initial training in the military, as I understand?" he asked.

"I was with the expeditionary force into France," he told the Sergeant. "Engineers, but redefined later as a translator, that kind of thing."

The Sergeant nodded, apparently pleased.

"Then we can start a little way along the line," he said, inclining his head a little. "Now, the first thing we have to bear in mind, sir, is that an enemy is chock full of dirty tricks, and will have no compulsion in using them on you. So, what I hope to teach you, are a few tricks much dirtier than his that might keep you breathing long enough to do your job." His eyes widened. "Do you understand, sir?"

"I do," answered Lawrence.

Sergeant Bull nodded.

"Have you used a knife, sir? On a man, I mean?"

Lawrence shook his head.

"Then, that's where we'll begin, sir. If you come this way."

He was led to the centre of the room, where Bull revealed a knife, which appeared to have an ornate handle. He held it up for Lawrence to see.

"German Officers spike, sir." He began his description of the weapon. "Good blade, if a little heavy on the handle, and not one to have about you unless you wear the appropriate uniform. I assume that may be the case, sir?"

Lawrence threw up his arms.

"I have no idea, yet."

The sergeant cocked his head to one side.

"Not to worry, sir, we'll go through it anyway," he smiled. "Not exactly a delicate weapon, nor as concealable as, say, a stiletto, and certainly no good for throwing. But accurate throwing knives would take a little more time than we have at our disposal, so we'll just keep to the conventional." He weighed the knife in one hand. "Now if you can use something as heavy as this, and most of my customers have the need to be accustomed to such spikes, then anything lighter is an advantage."

"Right," Lawrence confirmed his attention.

"Now, sir. If you take this…" Bull said, handing over the knife. "…and take the stance you would make, if presented with an enemy of similar disposition."

Lawrence took the weapon and hunkered down like an overweight boxer, bracing his left leg forward, with the knife in his right hand, held back, ready to thrust.

"What we have to remember, sir, is that we are looking for split seconds of advantage," said the Sergeant. "Now you have made the classic defence for such an occasion, and he will expect you to do that. He will expect you to advance on his knife hand, in order to grasp and isolate it, while you try to leave yours free to strike. So, you must do the opposite to what he expects, and keep your opponent's body between yourself and his knife."

He thrust his hand forward to demonstrate.

"So, when he pushes his left leg forward as a guard, you must keep moving around to your right, his left. He will find it harder to change position to counter you, and will use his body to make the turn instead of his legs, meaning serious unbalance. His shoulder will thrust forward, thus remaining between yourself and his weapon. Then, sir, you can make your move, but not at the body, at the leg which will now be close to you. The higher the better, as there are big arteries in the upper leg, and your opponent's appetite to continue will be seriously diminished. If not, sir, his loss of blood will soon be to your advantage.

"And if he plays the same trick on me?" asked Lawrence.

"Well, sir, my advice would be to pull back and manoeuvre, look for another try."

"And if it doesn't play out?"

Bull grinned.

"Well, you could pull your pistol and shoot the bastard." He put his hands on his hips. "Any time you enter a space, even if you're familiar with it, the first thing you do is look around and identify anything that you can use as a weapon. Bottles, lamps, even a chair or similar. Knowing that might just save your life, especially if the other guy has a knife and you don't, or your weapon is not enough to overcome him. Electric cable is a winner if you can get behind them, and don't fall for the old trick they might pull of faking unconsciousness, keep pulling on that cable until their bloody head rolls off. Remember, sir. Better them than you."

"I'll remember that," agreed Lawrence.

"And while we're on the subject, sir, if you would take up the classic guard position, please…"

Lawrence did so, bringing forward his left leg and shoulder, as before, with his right foot back. The Sergeant moved to his left, demonstrating what he had just said about keeping an enemy body between him and the knife hand by careful strategy.

"Freeze right there, sir," he ordered.

Lawrence did so, and could see the predicament he was in, and how his left leg could be in a compromising position. Bull explained a different compromise in the constant Scottish accent.

"Now, sir, if you are facing an opponent who is armed, and you are not, and the space that you are in has not given up something to defend yourself with, you may have a moment of grace in which to change the advantage. It will only be a moment, though, because your enemy will see his own advantage immediately, and come at you. He will still be cautious, mind, and I would advise you make the same manoeuvre, keeping him turning to his left. Then, when your balance is just so…"

Bull's right leg had gained good purchase, and his left shot forward and upward, stopping just short of Lawrence's crutch.

"Lady or gentleman," the Colour Sergeant explained, "such a strike would bring tears to the eyes, and turn the tables. Inevitably, such pain inflicted, if you hit them hard enough, will promote the receiver to pitch forward, whereby you can use your fist, or possibly grasp the head with your left arm and break the neck. The choice would be yours, of course."

Bull grinned.

"Now does all of the make sense, sir?"

Lawrence indicated that it did.

"Another thing to bear in mind, sir, in any compromising situation where you are facing an opponent, and are unarmed. Watch the eyes, whether they have a knife, a gun, or Satan's blazing firebrand. Before a person strikes, his eyes will always give him away, its human nature, the body's automatic response. The eyes will widen, and the eyebrows raise. It's that split second that you must look for to survive."

The Sergeant flipped the knife and caught it.

"A knife is just an extension of the arm, sir, but it's a fast weapon. Forget the urge to go for an instant kill. Go for the big muscles, where the major arteries are, wear your opponent down, until you are better shaped to defend and attack than he is. That's my advice sir, and I'm still breathing." He thought for a moment. "And rely more on the point than the blade to finish it, unless you're in a position to slice his jugular, of course."

William Lawrence nodded his agreement, and to show how he was trying to remember it all. It was far from the basic training that he recalled.

"And rolled up papers or magazines pushed up the sleeve, or in any other vulnerable place that doesn't impede your mobility is useful, if you have the benefit of time." He smiled. "Now, sir, tea time, and my guts are grabbing my testicles. We only have salmon sandwiches, due to the time of day, so I hope that's OK for you…"

*

Colonel Denning exited the Humber and ordered the driver to collect him in an hour. He watched briefly as the car pulled away down St. James Street, and tucked his narrow briefcase under his arm, then turned to the entrance to Boodle's Club. The door opened and he walked through, where he was greeted by a tall man in a black suit, white shirt and plain, dark tie.

"If you would leave your revolver here, sir," said the suit, producing a silver tray on which to put it. "He's waiting for you downstairs, sir."

Denning complied and divested himself of the Enfield, placing it with little sound on the plate.

"This way, sir. The suit said, leading Denning to a side door. "Will you be dining, sir?"

"Er, I think not," answered Denning. "My car will be back in an hour.

"Very good, sir. Please follow me."

Denning was led down the stairs on the opposite side of the door, then along a short corridor, to a rosewood door with brass fittings which reflected the electric light. He was surprised at the apparent lack of security. The man in the dark suit knocked twice, and waited until there was a response.

"Enter!"

The door was opened for him, and Denning walked in, then halting and saluting at attention. Opposite the door, a corpulent figure looked up from his meal and sat back in the over-elaborate chair that matched what could be seen of the small table, covered as it was with a dark red cloth. Cigar smoke infiltrated the room, even though the meal was only half consumed, and a half-full glass of whisky lay close to where the origin of the smoke was placed over a crystal ash tray.

"Ah! Denning." The portly man said, waving him over. "Do sit down. Now what have you got to tell me. I do hope it is good news. My wife tells me that I am impossible to live with if I have not had a little good news in the day."

Denning sat opposite the diner.

"Well, sir, he began. "We have our man. All of the necessary requirements, and perhaps a little more. Linguist, military service since before the war, BEF, returned via Dunkirk. Bit of a savage, I'm afraid… you received my telegram?"

"Yes."

"His name is…" Denning began, looking into his file.

There was a huff of annoyance.

"I don't want to hear his bloody name!" Expressed the diner, impatiently. "Or his collar size or his sexual preferences."

A stubby hand gripped a whisky glass and angry lips opened to finish the contents. Denning swallowed hard and continued as if the words had never been said.

"He's being upgraded, physically, as we speak," Denning continued. "Of course, there are the more invasive procedures to be completed, but that shouldn't take long. We have confirmation from over the channel that things over there are going to plan…"

"And if things don't go to plan, and we still have this man on our hands? What do you suggest?" he grimaced. "We can't just throw him back to the hangman, for God's sake. Not now."

"There's always the tower, sir, at least until the end of the war, then we can shunt him off to Australia, or some other place…"

The cigar was retrieved and more blue smoke filled the room, allowing a short silence. The smoker settled his spectacles more comfortably on his nose.

"Then, you have the authority, Denning, but I want to hear no more of it." He said firmly, "God knows after the war, both the British and the German peoples will break every bone in my body if they get to know of it. A murderer sent to protect Hitler, and a British murderer at that. It's an escapade that even Uncle Joe would doubt possible, and the President would no doubt disallow my mother's citizenship, even though she has been dead these many years."

"Yes, sir," agreed Denning.

The portly man raised a hand.

"And it must remain silent, whatever happens. What would I say to the King? You understand, Denning?" he said, frowning over the blue smoke. "Silent at least until I am mouldering in the grave."

"Yes, sir.

"I mean it, Denning, don't you do a Neville Chamberlain on me, or I will take you down with me. Do you understand? Silence!"

Denning looked drawn, but maybe he needed sleep. More

blue smoke than was necessary accompanied several deep draughts of the cigar, and a white napkin was cast roughly on the table.

"Yes, sir," he answered firmly. "I understand."

*

The salmon sandwiches with white bread were well past their best, having remained untouched for some time, and their state ignored, but Lawrence was glad of the break, and also a time to think what he was getting into. However, comparing the consequences, he felt that the choice had been a good one, despite the abyss that he felt that he might be looking into.

He thought of that night, so long ago now, when he had thrust himself into the consequences of where he now was. Strangely, it rarely passed through his thoughts, and when they did, it was with little emotion, and always led along the path that led to his sons, and their welfare. There had been no contact with them since before that night, and he wondered how they were living with the violent outcome that their father had created, one which had changed all of their lives forever. If he felt any remorse at all, it was because of them, and he wished that he could explain, apologise, or just accept his guilt.

Colour Sergeant Bull sat on the floor, on the opposite side of the room, looking from time to time at his pupil, apparently relishing the salmon and the stiffening bread that surrounded it. They remained silent, until the last cup of weak tea, then Bull arose and shook his shoulders.

"Shall we continue, sir?" he asked, but it was really a

statement.

Lawrence met him in the centre of the room, but the sound of the main door unbolting claimed their attention. Major Rutter entered and took the Sergeant over to the wall, leaving Lawrence alone in the centre of the room. A hushed conversation lasted several minutes, then as Rutter left, Bull walked over to a side door and entered the room beyond. For the briefest of moments, Lawrence could see a workshop of sorts, barred windows with people employed in various tasks, most of which he could not make out. The only noise was from a woman close to the door who appeared to be working on an old sewing machine, or something like it.

He went over to the main door and tested its security, but it was bolted fast, and putting an ear to it, could detect no noise. When he turned around, Bull was back in the centre of the room, watching him.

"Well, sir, shall we move on?" He asked.

A brief nod from Lawrence affirmed his agreement. He joined the Sergeant.

"All right, sir," he said, presenting an Enfield revolver. "No doubt you have seen one of these?"

"Yes, it's an Enfield Number Two, Mark One. Service revolver. Thirty-eight calibre, spur-less hammer, double action. Calculated at twenty to thirty rounds per minute, depending upon the user, round nose bullet with a muzzle velocity of six hundred and twenty feet per second. Effective firing range only around fifteen yards, I'm afraid, with a maximum range of two hundred, at which distance you could be fired at all day and still be there at breakfast. Six round cylinders, with a rear notch and front post sights, but bloody good at cracking skulls if you can get close enough."

The Colour Sergeant looked at him with what looked like admiration in his demeanour.

"Very good, sir!" He exclaimed with approval. "However, we won't be needing that information." He swapped hands and held out a German Luger. "This is the little beauty that we will be investigating. Here…" Bull said, handing it over. "Take a look at it, feel the weight, get to know the feel of the spring."

Lawrence took it, and slowly levelled it at Bull, who added a slight smile to the proceedings.

"You know very well that it's not loaded, sir. Now, shall we get on?"

Lawrence grinned and raised the weapon. He had seen them before, but looked anyway.

"I won't bother you with most of the detail," Bull told him. "Suffice to say it has the capacity for one hundred and sixteen rounds per minute, semi-automatic, of course, with an effective range of fifty-five yards, eight round detachable magazine, short recoil. Bloody lovely little beauty, eh? Now which would you prefer?"

"Well, if you put it like that…"

"You could grip the barrel and hammer nails in for an hour, and still be dead on target," Bull advised. "This model is the PO8, hardly altered since 1901, standard infantry pistol. Officers carry the Walther P.38, similar range and muzzle velocity," he paused. "You are familiar with side arms, then?"

"Yes," Lawrence answered.

"And you've used one, against a man, have you, sir?"

Lawrence thought for a moment.

"Yes, I've used one on a man."

The Sergeant's face brightened.

"Then we can skip the emotional section, sir. Get on with the important stuff."

He put the Enfield on the floor, and he presented the Luger at Lawrence's chest.

"Now," he asked, "what would your experience tell you to do in this scenario?"

Without waiting for the answer, Bull handed over the pistol, and indicated for Lawrence to hold it on him in the same manner. They were about three feet apart.

"Now then, sir, if you are compromised with a pistol, your automatic response is to make a grab for the weapon. My advice would be to wait your chance, wait for that split second of grace that we keep talking about," Bull said. "Human reactions are a difficult thing to avoid, they are automatic, inherited behaviour from when we were chased by all manner of nasty things, bears and mammoths and the like. So, if you can control your reaction, and your opponent can't, then you have a chance to turn the tide, as it were, then disarm him and beat his bloody brains out, before you can say, Jack Robinson. Does that make sense now, sir?"

"Absolutely."

"So, if you are close enough, you need to distract him for that half second. Now you can be as creative as you like, cough, sneeze, or feign a bloody heart attack if you want to, but distract him. Then, do not try to pull the pistol from his hand. Aim to grasp the barrel and then push upwards, so that the business end is under his chin or thereabouts. Because of what we just talked about, his natural reaction will be to take a tighter grip of the weapon, and that will include the finger on the trigger, but as his wrist is pushed further back, the two actions will hopefully coincide and blow the beggar's head off." Bull made a short grunt of satisfaction at the thought. "Of course, in a limited space, you might be fired upon from an opponent who is out of reach. In that case, consider doing exactly the opposite of what he expects. If you run away from him, he has a considerable advantage of the angle in which he is trying to level upon you. The probabilities are that you will stand a better chance of survival if you attack. First, it will throw him off guard, as his concerns will be inflated as to what you will do to him if he fails to stop you. Dodge erratically, and if he hits you, keep going. And remember, if someone has a gun in your back, the feet and shins are in perfect line for your heel, but take care with that one, as he might jerk back and pull the bloody trigger. I would use that one only if you are positive that to not make an effort will end in your demise."

Bull stopped and thought for a moment.

"However, if he gets lucky and scores a direct hit in a vital place, you may have to readjust your intentions. But an attacker is stronger in morale than a defender, or so the psychologists tell us. Do you have unarmed self-defence training, sir?"

The question almost surprised Lawrence.

"Just the usual stuff," he answered. "Never actually got close enough to use it. Never tried to. There, again, France was a different place to where I'm going, I suspect."

Bull frowned and screwed up his lips.

"Just forget the chop at the back of the neck stuff, sir. If you come into close contact with an enemy, remember that he intends to do just the same to you as you do to him. Think of all of the places that you'd rather not be kicked, clouted or grabbed, and make sure that you do it first, and hardest. Leave fists for the last resort; the eyes are a good mark, and if you can get a thumb into one of his, he'll use both hands to get you off him, leaving your free hand to put a spike into his neck. Another interesting technique is to use the heel of your hand and bang it into his nose, driving the nasal bone up into the skull, very effective."

Bull demonstrated each action as he spoke, and Lawrence had little doubt that the man had used most of them personally.

"If you can," he went on, "a sharp blow to his kneecaps with a foot can be very effective, and if you have his arm in your grip, for heaven's sake break the damn thing as soon as you can. Don't be squeamish, sir, and remember he will do the same to you if you let him. And a blow to his testicles will also have the right effect, fist or boot, sir, whichever you find applicable.

Now, if it comes down to fists, try to avoid the usual blow to the head. Heads are pretty sturdy, believe it or not, and there are far better targets to aim for. The kidney and liver areas, and the pit of the stomach can produce good results, and if he heaves his breakfast over you, you know you're right on the mark. But don't forget the elbows, sir. A crack with the pointy bit in his face will certainly demoralise him, maybe even giving you time to decide how to end his grimy little life, once and for all. Any questions, so far, sir?

"No, it's all perfectly clear, thank you Sergeant, I was just surprised that there were any of the Wehrmacht left for the rest of us."

Bull gave a curt nod.

"The essence of all of this, sir, is to do unto him before he does it unto you. Do it faster, do it harder, and do it twice as often, and you might just walk away at the end of the day."

"I'll keep that in mind," confirmed Lawrence.

"All right, sir. It's been a long day…"

The other agreed.

"Longer than I expected Sergeant," Lawrence said, nodding his agreement.

"Aye, well, we have another day tomorrow, but there's a cot in the corner, so get some sleep, and there's a bucket over that side if you need it. I'll be back around zero five hundred, and we'll look at a few more things that might be useful."

Lawrence watched as Colour Sergeant Bull walked over to the main door and knocked twice, replacing his tunic as he waited for it to be unbolted. A few moments later, as he left, a wooden tray of food was slipped inside, and then it was closed heavily once more. Soup and bread were on the tray, more than he wanted, but he finished the soup while it was hot, and went over to the other door, pressing his ear to the surface and trying the brass knob.

He found the door locked and no sound could be heard from beyond. Lawrence wondered if everyone who came to this place were treated in such a manner, and guessed that he was really a special case, bearing in mind his circumstances, and could not fault them for it. He slid onto the low cost and placed an arm over his forehead, thinking through the day, and could not decide whether he was lucky to still be alive, or not. For so long he had been counting the days, playing chess with the jailers, his only decision whether to let them win on that day, or not. And now here he was, pressed into a strange purgatory, with little idea of the direction in which he was being guided.

It had not been that he feared death, more that he had come to terms with it and just wanted it over. Since 1939, death had touched him more than once, and passed him over for easier targets, with no explanation or reason. Often, he had let providence tempt him into situations where something else took over, as if he were watching the events from some safe place, in which he was sheltered from without. It had been like that in France, and elsewhere, but then melded into his world at home, finally placing him on the scaffold and then taunting him with more to come. As if he were some minor chess-piece, moved by a dark hand that had far better experience of the game.

Sleep was difficult. It was at last becoming real, the last hours filled with more than enough to distract his assessment of what was happening to him. Occasionally, he wondered if this was indeed the afterlife, and passing over was a continuation of some dramatic torture, a punishment for all that had gone before, and Heaven knows he deserved it. How many times had he acted coldly, with no thought for mercy? Return the situation to the status quo, and damn those in between, then straighten his tie, and become the Englishman again.

*

Sergeant Bull shook him awake, with a white mug of tea. Lawrence was glad to be away from those re-runs of everything that had offended his dreams. For one brief moment, he thought that he was back in the cell, waiting the footsteps behind the iron door with the small, barred window.

"Zero five hundred, sir," Bull told him.

Lawrence wiped the tears from his eyes, hiding them with his arm as if the movement helped him awake.

"Oh." He feigned more drowsiness than was the case. "Oh, thank you, Sergeant."

"Aye, sir," he smiled. "A wee while, then we have to get on. Do you need the latrine before we begin?"

Lawrence nodded and used the bucket, using the time to cast aside the bad dreams.
A short time after the last of the tea had gone, Lawrence joined Bull in the centre of the room once more. The Sergeant put his hands upon his hips.

"Now do you remember any of what we went through yesterday, or shall we go over anything again?" he asked.

Lawrence shook his head. Of course, much of what he was being taught had been covered in basic training, and he was not inexperienced in looking after himself, but Bull's aplomb for the detail of discounting an enemy was far more enlightening than he remembered. He wondered if it might be a distant illustration of what was to be expected of him.

"Just a couple of slight additions to the unarmed self-defence methods that we explored yesterday, sir," Bull began. "Never underestimate the teeth. If you can get near enough to close yours around an enemy nose..." He paused and looked over at his pupil. "You don't have dentures installed, I presume, sir?"

Lawrence shook his head.

"That makes it a little easier, but if you face an enemy so enhanced, dislodging them further down his throat will certainly be to his disadvantage, and he might choke on them if you're lucky and save you the energy." He raised an eyebrow. "But back to where we were, sir. If you are close enough to restrict his breathing by closing off his nasal passages, his attention will be elsewhere, and if you bite the damn thing right off, the flow of blood will have the same effect." Bull shook his head. "Try not to be too squeamish, sir, the taste of blood is not all that bad, unless the bastard has a head cold, when I would advise spitting the snot away." He smiled. "But when you walk away in one piece, you'll forget all about the inconvenience."

Lawrence grimaced. It was far from basic training.

"And the ears too, sir," added Bull. "Not much of a strategic advantage overall, but better to take the benefit of relieving him of one of them, if the situation arises. He'll be mad as hell at the pain of it, and a bit distracted. Good for you, bad for him. That's the way I look at it, anyway."

Lawrence was beginning to like it. Whereas at first, it seemed just a bag of dirty tricks, far and above what the ordinary soldier was taught, this was an art, a means of survival in the worst of places, a level of detail far beyond what was expected by an enemy, far beyond what he had already inflicted upon those that he had been set upon.

For several more hours, Colour Sergeant Bull went through

meticulous demonstration of the advanced techniques that Lawrence might find useful in the days to come. Finally, they paused when more tea arrived. The pupil was thoughtful.

"Do you think the Germans have such ways of dealing with an enemy, Sergeant? From what I saw of them, they have a certain determination, a certain discipline…"

Bull fell back until the wall supported him. He took a long draught of the tea.

"What you saw was a different perspective, sir, a different environment altogether." He advised. "On a battlefield it's called strategy, a world of planning and dynamics, and big words like that." He flattened a palm to enhance his theory. "What I'm showing you is darkness a couple of feet away, and how to be ready for it, how to deal with it. And how to make sure it doesn't come at you again." He paused for a moment. "Now, your German, sir, is a herd animal, in a matter of speaking, well trained and certainly no coward for the most part, but fighting as a part of a whole, as dependant by those around him as he is on them."

Bull pointed a finger at Lawrence.

"Now you, sir," he said. "You are the whole, if you follow my examples, you are dependant only on yourself. And there are many like you across the channel, waiting for that moment when that split second of grace will give you the edge, keep you alive for long enough to put an enemy's lights out, until the day that we can switch ours back on again."

Lawrence smiled.

"And won't that be a day, Sergeant? Won't that be a day?"

Bull nodded, and went on with his thoughts on the enemy.

"Many Germans have quite a penchant for torture, and they're bloody good at it too, especially the officer corps. Far better than we are, with our Geneva Convention crap, so don't let yourself get into a situation like that."

He looked over at Lawrence.

"Entitled, you see, sir. I think that's what it is. They seem to think that it's fair game for somebody that comes against 'em, anybody that challenges their ideals, their outlook on the status quo, maybe an inability to split right from wrong, if you see what I mean."

Lawrence looked at the Sergeant, listening to the words, weighing the definition.

"Don't get into it yourself, sir, no matter how much you need to, the torture lark, Takes too long, and it's noisy, and hardly conducive to a good night's sleep." Bull took in one of his deep breaths. "Any questions, so far, sir?"

Lawrence shook his head.

"Very good, then, sir," he said with a look of satisfaction. "Now, we have a few things which may assist you in your objectives."

Bull walked across to the other door on one long side of the room. He knocked once, waited a moment, then went through and closed the door behind him. A short time later, he re-emerged with what looked like a German officer's tunic, and several other objects. Walking back to Lawrence, he held it out.

"Try this on for size, sir," he said. "I am not informed of the nature of your enterprise, but the officer has advised us that being appropriately dressed will be to your advantage."

Lawrence slipped his arm through one sleeve, and pulled the jacket on, fastening the buttons from the top. He shuffled to let it settle around his shoulders. Bull raised his brows as a question, enquiring as to whether the jacket fitted.

"A little tight around the collar," he confirmed, "but all right if you find the fashion to your taste."

"Quite, sir," said the Sergeant. "But one thing you can't knock the bosh for, sir, is the cut of their tailors," he paused. "We'll see to the collar presently, but first I'll just show you something that might be to your advantage."

He took Lawrence by the shoulders and jiggled the uniform, as if again checking the fit. His hands slid down the sleeves and pulled down the cuffs. Then, his right index finger and thumb took the nearest brass button to the cuff, and pulled gently. Lawrence looked down to see the button detach, pulled away from the cuff but still connected by some kind of cord.

"See this?" Bull asked. "It's connected around the collar to the same button on the opposite side, with a little slack to allow smooth movement. The buttons are connected by a flexible steel cord, narrow enough to be flexible, but strong enough to be almost unbreakable, at least by the human hand." He smiled. "If you find yourself compromised, and you can get yourself into a good position, pull out the button and slip the cord around the neck of your adversary. No matter if you're left or right-handed, sir, works as well either way." The Sergeant looked at the cable. "Beautiful workmanship, wouldn't you say, sir? A little trick up your sleeve, so to speak."

"And useful, I would imagine," Lawrence grinned. "If you need such an advantage.

Bull nodded his agreement.

"Now then." He went on, presenting a German Luger. "Just like the weapon we investigated earlier, and to all intents and purposes, exactly the same, but this one is a little special." Bull snapped open the butt of the pistol and ejected the magazine. "Usually, these sidearms have a magazine containing eight rounds. But we've re-engineered this one, reducing the calibre slightly, and with a bit of juggling with the original design, and re-rifling the barrel, we have added one more round. Of course, the stopping power is a little reduced, but it should be quite a surprise for anyone believing that you have exhausted your magazine."

Lawrence took the pistol and felt the weight. The Sergeant

clarified the other's thoughts.

"Just a few grams different in the weight. That's all, sir. But I doubt anybody will be pulling out the scales to check it."

"I'll let you know," Lawrence smiled.

"And finally," Bull announced, holding a long scabbard with a blade housed within it, the grip standing proud at the open end. "German bayonette, general issue, with a little jiggery pokery by ourselves."

He removed the scabbard and put it under his arm, then twisted the grip. Immediately, another, shorter blade that had been housed in the grip flipped out and clicked into place.

"No need for explanation there, sir," the Sergeant said. "Multiple options, depending upon your situation, at your own discretion, of course."

Lawrence took the weapon and rolled it over, examining the release.

"Thank you very much, I'll keep that in mind."

*

While Lawrence was engaged with his tuition, Truscott, the man with the unkempt hair was with Colonel Denning once more. He had slept little in the interim, using the authority that he had been given to probe into the past.

"Well, Truscott?" asked Denning. "I hope you're not bringing troublesome news?"

The lock of hair was pushed back again, and the face crumpled a little.

"It depends which way you look at it, I suppose." Came the answer, as he thumbed through hastily engendered notes on foolscap sheets.

"I was interested in his schooldays, his early years." He began. "The human mind usually falls into one of several patterns, the more so with aberrations, away from the normal, I mean. Of course, my time was limited on how deep I could dig... You did say that time was of the essence?"

"Yes," Denning replied. "It is, but we can't send a criminal psychopath into something we can't control..."

He remembered that he was already committed with his superiors.

"Well, we may have to," he admitted. "But at least we can try to understand what to expect of him. If we can trust what we see on the surface, and risk the outcome. It's too late to change the selection now."

"Just so," answered the other. "As I told you previously, it is not the surface that you need to be concerned about. Individuals such as this man usually have signs in childhood that betray what to expect of the adult, mistreatment of animals, bullying of those beneath them, general traits of dishonesty, that sort of thing. But not him, his violence is the reverse of that, the punishing of these things as he finds them. At school, he was reprimanded and punished for violence against such miscreants. His, is a disorder rarely seen, and hardly documented…"

"Are you trying to defend him?" asked Denning.

"Absolutely not." said Truscott. "I told you before, a killer with a powerful sense of responsibility, and who can deny that?"

"But the disorder…?" Denning asked.

The man opposite in the ornate chair was thoughtful for a moment.

"Colonel Denning, from what I see in the records, most of it overlooked by the military, for obvious reasons, this man was all but abandoned by his parents, for reasons unknown, and spent most of his time with grandparents, living in France and Spain, sometime after the first war. Hence his linguistic skills, but don't let geography fool you. Had he lived in Liverpool all of his life, the outcome would probably been the same. The geography only enhanced what was there already." He paused. "You are aware that he is a chess player of some skill?"

Denning shook his head.

"I've only known of the man for a day."

Truscott nodded his understanding.

"He was not interested in distinction, or reputation, although he might have reached those goals, had he tried. His concern was for the game, the follow through to a successful conclusion, which satisfied the disorder that claimed him."

"And all of this, from his past, his childhood, is responsible for his actions?"

"Colonel Denning," Truscott went on, "we have identified that this man exudes outer normality from all aspects, with an underlying justice that is its own personality, almost admirable in most circumstances." He paused again. "But have no doubt, he is a loner. He walks in darkness, with no guide but the shadows of his own mind. If those shadows reveal a perceived injustice, then who can guess at the outcome?"

"So, you think he is the right candidate?"

Truscott twisted his features in thought for a moment. He looked back at Denning, as if wondering whether to expand or not upon his concerns.

"Have you ever heard the term, 'sigma male'?"

Denning shook his head, and Truscott continued with his train of thought.

"In general psychology, Colonel," he began. "Mankind, specifically the male sex, can be formulated into a pyramid, which is roughly segmented top to bottom, with the larger, general population at the bottom. These normal, everyday individuals that make up the larger part of the inhabitants of the planet survive their existence quite happily. Other segments which occur as you progress to the apex will improve in intelligence, capability, creativity, aptitude, and so on." He paused for a moment. "What we understand as the sigma male is none of these, living completely apart from the pyramid, and without the same physical and mental constraints. They live by their own rules, undefined by anything that others try to impose upon them, or perhaps even by moral compass. Such men can evolve into anything, on any scale, from an uncompromising judge to the perfect safe breaker. They neither forgive, nor forget, and only their own minds dictate the paths that they must take."

"And you believe that this man is a… sigma male type?" Denning asked.

"Colonel, all I can tell you is that if you release this man upon an enemy, then God help them."

Chapter Three
The English Opening

It was just after mid-day. Colour Sergeant Bull had insisted on going over some of the previous day's instruction, but for Lawrence, there was little need, most of it inserted into the slices of memory that he wished to retain. As the main door bolts announced Major Rutter's return, Lawrence felt the need to thank his teacher, and held out a hand. Bull grasped it and smiled.

"It's been an experience, Colour Sergeant." The pupil said. "I would like to…"

A sharp sensation on the left side of his neck made him pause and glance downward, trying to move as little as possible. From the corner of Lawrence's right eye, he could see the shiny blade that caused the break in his sentence. Bull was grinning.

"Always on the watch, sir," he warned. "Always on the watch. Enemy or friend, no harm in keeping your defences primed. Sleep with one eye open, and your boots on. And at all times, know where objects in a space are, and how you might use them if the time comes." Bull gripped his hand tighter. "I doubt we'll meet again, sir, but I hope you fare well, and that when this damn war's over, you still have every part of your anatomy intact."

"I'll remember that, Colour Sergeant, and thank you."

*

Major Rutter was accompanied by two khaki clothed soldiers, at a short distance behind, one of which carried his new jacket and equipment, besides a shouldered rifle. The other soldier was more aggressively posed, with the Lee Enfield at the present. Rutter also, still rested a hand on his unclipped revolver.

Lawrence was led to an upper level, booted feet clattering on the boards. An open door led to a small mess room, where Lawrence received the best food that he had had since his hanging. He sat alone, silent, until he had finished the meal, with his guardians at a safe distance. Then, he sat back, and looked at Major Rutter.

"Now what?" he asked.

Rutter waved the two soldiers around the room, so that a triangle was made around Lawrence.

"Sorry old chap," he advised, "got to put the bracelets on again. Just for a short while."

He neared the table where Lawrence sat and put the manacles on the table, then stepped back.

"If you wouldn't mind…"

Lawrence looked at the handcuffs for a moment, then shrugged and clipped them around his wrists. He held them up.

"All right?"

A hood was replaced over Lawrence's head, and he was led down to the street level, where the Humber waited. Soon, they were back to the previous location, the carpeted stairs betraying his destination. Lawrence was guided through, seated back on the ornate chair, and the escort dismissed to a place beyond the door. Rutter took off the hood, and Lawrence was hardly surprised to see Denning on the opposite side of the table.

Without speaking, Lawrence eased his wrists against the steel of the handcuffs, slid back the serrated, hinged clips from where he had pressed them against the chain parts, instead of into the fastening aperture, and dumped them onto the desk with a clatter. He glanced over at Rutter, whose embarrassment was obvious. Denning also looked at his subordinate, but with different concern.

"Can we do without these from now on?" Lawrence asked.

The Colonel looked coldly at him, with a raised brow of concern.

"It appears that there is little point in declining," answered Denning, a hint of a smile beginning to change his expression. "Now. If we may continue, preferably without the theatrics."

Lawrence took a quick glance at Rutter, who had reclaimed his composure.

Some time ago," Denning started, "a plan was sanctioned to

assassinate Hitler, by a sniper at the Berghof, at the dictator's mountain retreat. It was named Operation Foxley," he paused. "Foxley was abandoned for various reasons, impracticality, difficulties finding the right operative... and other considerations."

Lawrence shook his head.

"You're trying to tell me that you've changed your minds?"

"No, not exactly." Denied Denning, pausing again before continuing. "Shortly after Operation Foxley was stood down, on July 20, an attempt to kill Hitler at his Wolf's Lair by members of his own inner circle in Poland, failed. The perpetrators, most of those implicated, and some completely innocent officers, were summarily executed. Now, Hitler's whereabouts are hard to pin down, because of the use of doubles and other deceptive methods, for obvious reasons. But thanks to our acquiring a German decoding device, and other confirmation sources, and I will spare you the details, we now have an accurate idea of his movements over the next week or so."

He frowned.

"Now, as for the failed assassination attempt in Poland, we are also aware that the Gestapo were unsuccessful in tracking down every involved member of the plot, and some will be in a position to make another attempt. In fact, we have cast iron information that in the days to come, such an attempt will be made. We know the day, the place, and the method, but sadly, not the identities of the plotters. And that is where you come in..."

Denning leaned forward and cupped his chin with his right hand, his elbow braced on the table top.

"What we want you to do is to defend him, to deny an attempt upon his life, which will take place several days from now."

"What!"

Lawrence laughed aloud. Denning remained deadly serious.

"What may seem an unbelievable request, I assure you is quite serious," he explained. "If Hitler continues making the strategic blunders of the past year, then the war may be over by some time next year. If more able bodies take over from him, and continue the fight, then thousands will perish and who knows when sanity may return to the world again."

"Is the gallows option still available?" Lawrence asked.

Denning ignored it. Lawrence fell back in the chair, trying to assimilate what had just been told to him. It seemed unbelievable, the British sending someone to stop the assassination of the world's most hated individual. Since his execution, what little they told him had spiked his imagination, and he guessed that it was just some perfunctory task that nobody else wanted to do, but this was completely different.

"And just how am I supposed to do that?" he asked the

obvious question.

There was a distinct hiatus, with everyone in the room harbouring a different thought. Denning broke it.

"Sometime in the next three days, you will be parachuted by the RAF, at night, into eastern Germany. Your drop will be covered by a conventional bombing raid to give you the optimum chances of reaching your destination. Your parachute will be black, and you must dispose of it as soon as you reach the ground, as well as the safety chute which you will carry upon a chest harness."

"Considerate," Mouthed Lawrence, acknowledging the danger that the main chute may not open.

Denning went on.

"You will be wearing a German officer's uniform, so it is imperative that you are not connected with the method of descent from the aircraft in any way," He warned. "A short time ago, we acquired the body of a dead officer, and it is this man's identity that you will be assuming. There is a certain resemblance to yourself, and hence the reason that your neck was not stretched at the appropriate time. Tomorrow, we will enhance your similarity to the deceased officer to increase your chances of survival. His papers and identification we received intact, which again will help you to navigate to the destination. There, you will do everything in your power to ensure that the attempt to kill Hitler is frustrated.

The attempt on his life will take place as he boards his

special train, probably by sniper, so your task is to locate and dispose of the threat. More details will be given to you later."

Lawrence spread his palms.

"That," expressed Denning, "is where your competency and aptitude comes in. You have seen action since 1940, and your ability to engage with a situation is well afforded." He seemed to hold back the words for a moment. "Both in the moral sense, and otherwise."

Lawrence was silent for a moment, wondering if there was any more preaching to come. There was not, but a question needed to be answered.

"And what's stopping me just landing in Germany, and disappearing, or just giving myself up? The war won't last forever."

Denning fortified himself to answer.

"As for the latter, later," he advised. "The chances are that you will be shot as a spy, wearing as you will be, a German uniform. Shot at best, but perhaps tortured beyond your endurance," he smiled. "As for the former, should you succeed in your objective, and the Fuhrer reaches Berlin safely, then you will receive the reward already mentioned. Additionally, your sons, upon reaching the age of twenty-one, will receive the sum of one million pounds each, which I dare say you would agree is a princely sum with which to set them up in whichever direction their lives take them." He paused for a second. "You will never see your boys again in this lifetime, but you can be assured of their future."

"So, my objective will be complete when Hitler reaches Berlin?" asked Lawrence.

Denning closed his eyes and inclined his head.

"Once he is on the train, the man is the responsibility of others."

"And if I fail? If he dies before then. If I can't find the assassin?" Lawrence asked.

"Then your children will still receive twenty thousand pounds. Quite generous, considering, don't you think?" Came the answer. "And we can only assume that under those circumstances, that you have been compromised." He let the words sink in for a moment. "So, you can see, how imperative it is that you succeed for all concerned, and not only for yourself and your children. The success of this endeavour would mean the saving of so many lives."

Lawrence felt his shoulders sag a little as he weighed up the chances of accomplishing what was being asked of him.

"And what happens after? If I survive, I mean, how do I extricate myself from all of this? Ring for a taxi?" he asked.

"All in good time." Denning told him. "Everything will be explained at your final briefing. But before that, we must ensure that you fit the profile of the German officer that you are to become. Now, we shall dismiss the hand restraints, but I'm afraid we must insist on the hood. It is only a short distance, and I dare say that you will now appreciate the importance of security."

He looked up at Major Rutter, and raised an eye.

"If you will see to that, Major."

Rutter moved closer and produced the hessian hood, glancing down at Lawrence before starting to put it back over his head. Lawrence looked up and made eye contact.

"Oh, go ahead," he remarked. "Getting rather used to it by now."

"Sorry, old chap," Rutter answered.

*

Despite his appreciation of still retaining a neck of a reasonable length, Lawrence was becoming quite bored with the constant moving from one place to another. Of course, he could understand the need for security, there was a war on after all, but he was starting to just want to get it over with, one way or the other.

There had been little time to really think it through, as if he were floating from one confusing dream to another, unable to wake up into reality. He thought back again, to that night when he abandoned his orders and went home to find what he had expected for some time. Where might he be now, had he not done so? Certainly not here.

After June 6, he had been stationed at Canterbury, waiting for orders to go to France as an interpreter, but all that had changed on that fatal night when he could not allow justice go unchallenged, his justice, his time and his place. He knew that it was not a conventional way to resolve such a matter, but something inside would not allow others to do it for him. Why he was that way, had never crossed his mind.

The strange thing was that he felt no remorse, even though he wanted to. That was something that evaded his moral code, somehow. Why had fate made him Judge Jury and Executioner? Even now, he just accepted it all for what it was, what he was, a piece on the board, of the least value, moved by some unseen hand without the slightest consideration.

Lawrence knew that he was different. He had always known it. Why, he had no idea, only that some force that guided his actions left no margin for doubt, when the time came.

*

The journey was a little longer than he expected, although the transport was the same. At least his hands were now unshackled, and having given his agreement not to resist, remained quiet until the destination was reached. Escape was never really an option since the future of his sons became an issue, but even before that, he had wronged the establishment and accepted the result. His only dispute was the method in which he was manoeuvred from pillar to post, as if gripping some huge steel ball on a gigantic pinball machine.

There had been so little time to mentally investigate what was in store for him, and the narrative that was unfolding slowly, one small piece at a time. So extraordinary was the picture that was being pieced together, that it hardly seemed true, and that at any moment it would be discarded to the dungeons of history, never again to see the light of day. And then, what of him?

The Humber stopped slowly, coasting to a halt. Rutter spoke first, and guided him by one arm. Lawrence tried to see through the mesh of the hessian hood, but could define nothing.

"Come on, old chap," he stated. "This way. Mind the step, just as you get out."

Lawrence turned in the seat, and raked a foot around to find the obstacle that the Major had referred to. It felt like a high kerb, with stone paving beyond. Soon, he was conducted into another building, with hard flooring and the noises of distant activity beyond his interpretation. A door opened and he was guided through. There was a strange smell, one he felt he should know.

"You may take off the hood," Denning's voice told him.

Lawrence did so, and found himself in a small medical anti-room, with a closed door opposite the one that they had entered by. A flat-bed trolley was positioned by one wall. He looked quizzically at Denning, who leaned against the wall near the door, and guessed that Major Rutter remained outside.

"Won't be long," Denning advised. "Just a small detail we need to get right. We can't let you go in without having the best chance of success." He made an odd smile. "And of course, your survival."

Lawrence found himself already falling under the spell of Colour Sergeant Bull, assessing the room for possible assets to his situation. Trolley, cabinet on the wall and a light chair in one corner. Best choice, he decided was the glass in the cabinet, once broken it could cut as well as a knife.

They both turned as the door opened and a tall man walked into the room. He wore a white coat, surgical cap and dark rimmed glasses, with an intense look in his eyes.

"This is the man, I take it?" he asked of Denning.

Denning nodded as the man in the white coat eyed him intensely, as if he were some prize bull at a cattle market. He leaned to one side to look closely at Lawrence's left cheek. Lawrence returned the gaze, with as much intensity as he could muster, but the effort was lost.

"Have you ever had septicaemia, any blood issues?" the white coat asked. "Skin ailments of any kind?"

Lawrence shook his head.

"Look, I had medical examinations in the…" He paused the sentence for a moment. "…Where I was, until recently." He smiled. "They said I was fit to drop."

The man in the white coat ignored him. He turned stiffly toward Denning, then back without speaking. He walked over to the small locker on the wall and Lawrence could see the man's reflection in the glass, until he opened it and drew out a small kidney dish. Coming back, he indicated the trolley.

"Have you eaten in the last four hours?" The white coat asked.

"No. But its damn time I did, my stomachs dancing a jig on my backbone."

There was just a slight nod of the head in reply, and almost a look of satisfaction at the answer.

"Just jump up on there will you?" the man asked.

Lawrence sighed and did so. He sat upright with his hands on the edge,

"Now, I'm just going to give you a small injection." He was told as the man took a syringe and filled it from a small phial."

Lawrence looked across at Denning.

"You afraid I'll catch something across there?"

Denning watched the injection being performed and just answered with a few small inclinations of his head. Then, when the needle was removed, and Lawrence rubbed his forearm, he took a step forward and put his hands into his army trousers.

"The man whose place you are to take," he began, "was quite an unfortunate."

"Well, let's hope it's not catching." Lawrence cut in, rubbing his eyes with the back of his hand. "And I have more luck than he did."

The white coated man began to return the instruments to the locker. Closing the door gently, he turned and looked over at his patient. Lawrence shook his head and blinked rapidly.

"Luckily for us," Denning continued, "the poor man was found by the resistance." He held the explanation for a moment as he watched Lawrence. "I won't go into the details, but you need to know that he died from a grenade, the outcome of which scarred the left side of his face quite badly. Now, all of this happened in the last week or so, and although we are fairly certain that his passing was not witnessed directly, we cannot be certain that the incident went totally un-noticed. What we do know is that his body was left unburied until found by persons loyal to the allies, which adds to our hypothesis that no-one actually knows that he is dead." He paused once more. "I'm sure that you will be pleased to know that he received a respectful send off by those that found him, but as I'm sure you will understand, there were no flowers." Denning made that odd half smile again, "The war, you know."

Lawrence's eyes had almost fully closed. He fought to keep them open, but it was useless, and he was already beginning to let himself fall back onto the trolley. Denning moved closer as the white coat guided Lawrence to a prone position.

"You understand that under normal circumstances," he said, "we would have needed a signature to complete your preparation. But, well, as you don't theoretically exist, we decided to dispense with the formalities."

He nodded to the surgeon, who opened the second door and began to push the trolley through. Lawrence was almost unconscious, but not quite. He found his movement limited, his reactions failing.

"When I... when..."

"I assure you that it will be quite painless." Denning reassured him. "And you will be on your feet in no time at all." He put a hand on Lawrence's arm. "I assure you that you will thank me, later."

*

The door to the small anti-room opened and the surgeon came out into the corridor, removing his mask and surgical gloves. He glanced up at Denning and held the eye contact. It had been just over an hour.

"Well, all done," said the surgeon. "Not exactly the prettiest piece of cutting I ever did, but I think it's damn close to what you asked for."

"Can it be reversed?" asked Rutter. "I mean, if it ever comes to that?"

The surgeon took a breath.

"Oh, I suppose to some extent, but there will always be a

vestige of scar tissue. I doubt that beard growth will cover much of it, unless he wants to look like Father Christmas," he laughed shallowly. "But I dare say he'll have to wait a year or two for that."

"How long before he comes around?" Denning asked.

"Half an hour or so, maybe less. It was only a light anaesthetic, but I would give him the rest of the day to recover all of his faculties."

Denning shook his head.

"Time that we don't have. But we'll do our best."

*

Lawrence opened his eyes slowly, trying to blink away the moisture that had crackled into solid form. He started to raise a hand to wipe it away, but found himself once more shackled to the hospital bed that he found himself on. There were white blinds all around him, looped on metal rings that supported them from a frame that was fixed to the ceiling. He hurt, more pain than just a simple ache, and he became aware of bandages, or some kind of binding around his head. Even closing his eyes made it worse.

"Hello!" he grunted. "Is someone there?"

A few moments later, the surgeon appeared, with a nurse. She was far from pretty, and eyed him as if he should be enjoying the attention.

"Do try not to talk too much." Warned the surgeon. "We can give you medication for the pain. It will be quite sore for a while, but it will ease down in a short time."

"Why am I bound?" Lawrence asked. "I want to get up."

His tone was anything but civil. Why should it be? He thought that all of that was behind him. The curtain was pulled back, and Denning walked through. Lawrence looked intensely at him. Perhaps they were fighting the same war, but these people had been anything but civil, or even friendly, unless he allowed the fact that they had saved him from the noose to enter the argument.

"What have you done to me?" he asked.

The surgeon gently pulled away an antiseptic cloth from Lawrence's left cheek. Denning examined it closely, bending over to view it better, so close that Lawrence could have pushed himself high enough and bitten off his nose, if he had been so inclined to implement the good sergeant's teaching.

Denning pulled back.

"Good!" he expressed. "Bloody good!"

Denning stood upright. He looked at the surgeon and the nurse.

"Would you mind leaving us for a moment?"

As they left, the surgeon closed the blinds. Lawrence had already assessed that the room was small, with him the only patient. He tried to control the anger that was rising inside him.

"Listen," Denning began. "The man whose place you are to take was quite severely injured by the blast of a grenade. I told you that. While there is a good likeness between yourself and him, there may be those who knew him, and whose path you may cross. We have given you the best camouflage that we can, by the best surgeon in the field. The wounds on your face are replicated to resemble his, at least as they were when he died."

"Wounds?" asked Lawrence. "You mean, you've cut me up?"

"Cut and cauterised." Denning answered. "Nothing too expansive, but expertly performed, and almost artistic, considering the time availability. Quite a job."

"Let me see! Let me see!" Demanded Lawrence, his eyes widening. "And get me out of these damn things!" He rattled the handcuffs.

"Now calm down." Denning said. "This may just save your life."

He swished through the curtaining and left. Lawrence fell back on the bed and wondered what nightmares were still to come his way. He thought of the boys, his boys, and knew that whatever was to come, this was for them. A few minutes later,

Denning returned with a large shaving mirror.

"Now," Denning said. "Take a look, but remember what I told you."

He presented the reflection and Lawrence looked at his own face, or what was left of it. On his left cheek, extending from the jaw line to the temple, was a large, inverted 'K'. He stared at it for some time.

"Christ!"

"The surgeon said that it could be partially improved at some later date, and we would deal with that when the time comes, of course." That shallow smile again. "Another reason to hope that you are successful, I dare say?"

Lawrence looked away from the mirror, and directly into Denning's face.

"And if I'm not, you think improving my good looks will be so important?"

"Well, let's hope so," Denning replied, almost seeming to be sympathetic. "But it is a remarkable piece of work. Now, let's see about getting you something to eat."

*

Painkillers helped the discomfort of surgery. He hoped that it was all worth it, and that what they had put him through over the last days did not turn out to be just more of the same with little reward. When he thought about what they had told him of what was expected, there was no denying that he had his doubts about his own abilities. And yet, if by some twist of fortune, he might succeed, and the war might be shortened, there was no denying that the incentive was worth the risk. It seemed an impossible balance, weighing the continuation of life with what might happen to him. And should he fail, for he had seen what the enemy might do to those who oppose them, he could only imagine the depths of pain afforded to one wearing the wrong uniform.

Suddenly, the hangman seemed to be an option worth considering.

It was getting dark outside. Somewhere in the distance, an air raid siren announced company. Lawrence felt that they were finding him more trustworthy, despite his more recent condition, travelling as he was through the darkened streets of the capital once more, this time without hood or handcuffs.

Rutter sat beside him in the back seat, with only the driver for company as the black Humber saloon moved slowly along streets still glossy with rain. He gurned his jaw a little, to ease the discomfort of the cauterising. It was more soreness than pain now, and he was thankful for it, and a large dressing covered all of the surgical area.

"Where are we going?" If it's not going to prolong the war to tell me?" Lawrence asked.

Rutter turned to face him as what little light there was penetrated to the rear seat and rolled across his face.

"A secure place," the officer replied. "Get you something to eat," he grinned. "The old man said it was the least we could do."

A few minutes later, Rutter looked across at Lawrence again.

"Look," he said, if you give me your word not to do anything stupid, and you can keep your mouth shut, maybe I can make this a little more…" He looked for the right word. "Edifying?"

Lawrence returned a look of surprise. He shrugged.

"All right," he answered, wondering if this was another ruse of the establishment.

Rutter leaned toward the driver.

"Left here, Albert," he ordered, "turn onto the Embankment."

"Very good, sir," said the driver.

Once on the Embankment, with the Thames on their right, the Humber made its way along, until Rutter ordered a stop.

"All right, let's go," the officer said to Lawrence, and then. "Albert, pick us up in forty-five minutes."

"Are you sure, sir?" Albert asked, turning to look into the back seat.

Rutter nodded, and put a finger to his lips.

"Not a word," he whispered.

The Humber pulled away, leaving a confused Lawrence pulling up the collar of his raincoat. The rain had stopped but it was cool for early Autumn. Rutter stood for a moment and watched the car as it moved away.

"Come on." He made a gesture with his right hand and led in the direction that the Humber had taken.

A short distance ahead was a rickety old catering van, its lights off but with subdued illumination from the business end and steam or smoke emitted from within. Someone was being served by a tattooed hand and they waited until the patron had gone before approaching the high counter. Somewhere out of sight, fat bubbled and spat.

"Pennorth's worth, and a tuppeny fish, twice," Rutter ordered.

He glanced at the astonished Lawrence.

"Lord, the price of things these days." He exclaimed. "Salt? Vinegar?"

Lawrence grinned until the scar hurt, and shook his head.

"And the condemned man ate a hearty supper…" he laughed.

The meal was presented in its usual condition, in Rutter's case, a week-old edition of 'The Telegraph'. He paid, and somewhere across the river, well into the distance, the boom of bombs repeated as a faint flash of explosions lit up the sky. Rutter led the way across the road, to where the pavement overlooked the Thames. He opened up the paper.

"Fingers before forks, I'm afraid, old chap."

Lawrence smiled, and followed suit, closing his eyes as the aroma filled his nostrils. How satisfyingly wonderful the memory of fat and vinegar and potato yielded.

"Been a while." He confided. "Even my last meal was nothing like this."

Rutter ate, but looked pensive.

"Aren't you afraid that I'll make a run for it?" Lawrence asked. "I could you know, and probably make a go of it with all of the stuff that The Colour Sergeant taught me."

The Major spoke while still eating. He made a gesture of apology.

"Not now, I think, don't ask me why," he answered. "Maybe because of your children. In all of this, I've seen no shirking of responsibility toward them. Of course, I don't condone the method you used to right the wrongs you perceived, but I can understand."

Rutter saw the faintest tears in the other's eyes.

"Those boys are everything to me," he explained. "Without them, I'd have faced the noose willingly. I did wrong and I would have paid the price for it. At least this way, I can do something for their future, even if I never see them again, and they hate me for what I did." He looked into Rutter's eyes. "They did love their mother, you know, and they'll never know the truth of it."

"I'm sorry," said Rutter.

Lawrence changed direction of thought and made a strange smile.

"Well, here we are though, feeling the breeze along the Thames with a belly full of fish and chips, and a tuppeny fish at that, and a free holiday across the channel to boot. What more could a hanged man ask?"

Another staccato stick of flashes far beyond The Houses of Parliament lit up the sky for a moment. Both men looked across and held the gaze beyond the barrage balloons.

"Not so many over the city since D-Day," Rutter said. "I think they're concentrating on the airfields now, the bomber 'dromes especially." He looked around at Lawrence. "You still have anyone over there?"

Lawrence shook his head.

"My grandmother in Germany died before the war, thank

God, but I still have another in France, last I heard."

"Quite a cosmopolitan bunch, then, your family?"

"I suppose you could say that," Lawrence agreed. "My father was French, mother German. My parents left France as soon as Hitler came on the scene in 1933, changed their name to Lawrence by deed poll, just in case he won. I guess they could read the writing on the wall even then." He paused. "They died in the first bombing raids during the Blitz. They had just gained British nationality two days before."

"I'm sorry." Rutter sympathised.

"Oh, I didn't know them too well. It was kind of a, well, an abrasive relationship, but they stuck together, probably due to the arrival of my brother. I spent a lot of my time before the war with my grandparents, then in boarding school, then the military." He looked out over the river. "But we were on nodding terms."

Lawrence put memories aside. He disliked talking about himself.

"You have children, Major?" he asked.

"Two boys, like yourself," he answered. "My wife was also killed in the first raids on the south coast. Silly, really. She was visiting her mother and stayed an extra day. Had it not been for that decision, she would still be here, with us."

They remained silent for a while, just watching the ripples

reflect what lights came from Westminster. Lawrence broke the quiet.

"So, what now?" he asked. "What's next, and when do I go into the abyss?"

Major Rutter shook his head.

"A good night's sleep, then tomorrow back with the old man. He will give you the last and most important briefing, updated, so you should then know everything that you need to know, probably far more than I do. It's kind of pulling everything together."

"Is it always like this?" Lawrence asked. "Fast and furious, with hardly time to breathe?" he smiled, wryly. "Actually, I suppose the fact that I can still breathe in any format available is a blessing."

Rutter shook his head.

"It's always need to know. My job is to find the appropriate character, investigate their backgrounds, skills, and recommend them upward. That's what I do, but the detail stuff is down to Denning. I don't know all established field operatives, only he knows that. I only know the ones that I am involved with, and others like me are the same. Our paths rarely cross. You know what the poster says, 'Loose Tongues Costs Lives', and although I know the general outlines of assignments, my overall knowledge is limited."

Some-time later, the black Humber drew up beside them. Lawrence glanced at the reflections in the polished skin of the vehicle, then back at Rutter.

"Thank you, Major, for such a delightful meal in such interesting surroundings. I hope that one day I might return the moment."

Rutter saluted, formally. Lawrence shrugged.

"You can't salute a ghost, Major."

*

Wherever Lawrence slept that night was masked by the darkness of the Autumn night. The rain began again, this time far heavier than before, and it reminded him of times during the last few years, when German bullets ricocheted all around him. Fortune had defended him, and claimed others far more admirable than himself. The rain increased, hammering upon the roof of the Humber, and spattering on the bonnet.

A fast exit from the black saloon into the shelter of a large house completed the short journey, and Lawrence was shown to a second-floor suite, complete with bathroom and twin beds. The curtains were sealed across the windows, to the point where tools would be needed to open them to the city beyond, but it mattered little, as there was nothing that he particularly wished to see in the extended dark.

"I'll collect you at seven-thirty," Rutter advised him. "Be ready if you can, as Denning's a stickler for punctuality." He paused as if deciding upon his words, then discarded the thought for something more mundane. "Sleep well, old chap."

The door closed and Lawrence heard the decisive noise of the lock being slipped. He wondered if, after all, Rutter did not totally trust his integrity. Remembering his recent advice, he looked around the room, lit dimly by two wall lamps near the beds. Small desk, light cane chair, a couple of obscure paintings, rugs, no electric cables that he could see, or any other item that might be converted to a weapon. He checked the bathroom. More of the same, with only a small shaving mirror bolted to the wall, which revealed polished steel instead of glass to give a reflection. Below the mirror was a sealed antiseptic dressing for the wound that had been imposed upon him. There were no wall cabinets, or shaving gear, just soap, so it looked like someone else had taken Bull's advice, but how the occupant might defend such a space if the German Army appeared was quite a puzzle.

Lawrence washed, taking his time with the hot water that had been only tepid in the days before his hanging appointment. He thought with a little fondness of Officer Willoughby, and the chess games that he thought he was losing willingly to the condemned man. Lawrence had let him make the moves that were so obvious, and went along with it, dancing with glee when he took the game after an hour of play, when he could have finished it within minutes. Willoughby's task had been a hard one, and Lawrence had no heart to make it any more difficult than it needed to be, so he played the game that Willoughby wanted, and let the man sleep easier.

He took off the raincoat, jumper and trousers that they had swapped earlier for his prison grey, and chucked them on the bed nearest the door. He decided to take the one nearest the window, turned off the wall lights and climbed in, under the sheets. Some way off, a car horn contested some minor displeasure, and such insignificant intolerance seemed so ridiculous now, especially to one such as he that had faced oblivion and made his way through it.

Lawrence realised that this was the first time that he had been truly alone over the last few days, but then, the fact was that he had always been alone, even when all around him was a chaos of human activity. Something in the confines of his skull had engineered the need for settling his own decisions, mark his own path, and keep his own personal confidence. Almost from childhood, he had known it, lived with it, even honed it to fit the person that he was. Emotions had always seemed fleeting, there for the moment, and then shelved when another situation demanded his attention, and taken down again only when the circumstances allowed. It was his way of coping with the world, the complexities of it, when those around him seemed to drift through without effort.

Sleep avoided him for some time. Thoughts of what was expected of him filled his mind, and he wondered where it would take him. He guessed that it would be a period of high activity, following the directions that he would learn more about tomorrow. Impersonating a German officer would not be easy, despite his perfection in the language. He'd had a fair idea of the culture within the Wehrmacht, and other parts of the German armed forces; heaven knew that he had served as interpreter in many an interrogation of prisoners. That had been his role for some time, but becoming one was a different kettle of fish.

He remembered the stoic backbone of many a bagged German, officers and other ranks, and seldom saw a deference to their captors. He hoped that he could maintain that kind of performance, at least until he had done his best to fulfil his duties.

Lawrence wondered how the boys were, and if they already hated him. How would they tell them of what he had done, so coldly, uncalculatingly and without even the passion of jealousy. He smiled to himself, and hoped that the same cold mental state that seldom failed him would walk with him once more.

*

A sharp rap on the door rescued him from more bad dreams. He knew that they had been bad, and lasted a long time, but could remember little of the detail that had been forced upon his sleep. The door opened, and a smiling woman in military uniform entered, carrying a tray which held tea and a substantial breakfast. She smiled briefly as Lawrence sat up in bed, her blonde, curls catching what little light filtered from the window.

"Good morning!" said the woman, gently placing the tray on the small desk.

Her voice rolled over him like dark treacle.

"Good morning," Lawrence answered. "Breakfast for the condemned man?"

She smiled back without comment, her eyes flickering toward the scar on his face that he had left uncovered.

"Is there anything else I can get you?" she asked.

"An Austin with a full tank of petrol and twenty-four hours

start." He joked, knowing it was stupid, but he said it anyway.

The woman smiled once more, and ignored it as if it was never said.

"Someone will be with you shortly." She parried. "I wouldn't let it get cold, eggs are pretty scarce in London, these days, and the powdered stuff is hardly worth eating, is it?"

She left and closed the door. Lawrence listened but heard no familiar turning of the lock. He rose and moved over to where his breakfast had been left and ate quickly, then washed, shaved and dressed, finally finishing off what was left of the tea. He changed the dressing to the wound on his face that he had found in the bathroom, then he sat on the edge of the bed, and waited to see what was next.

After the past couple of days, the morning had seemed to have slowed. He enjoyed the isolation for as long as it lasted, letting his mind ebb and flow without any particular direction, knowing that to focus might not be a good thing. Fifteen minutes later, there was a brief knock and the door opened to reveal the now familiar face of Major Rutter.

"Hello, old man. Sleep well?"

For some reason, the improvement of Lawrence's living quarters gave him a feeling of melancholy, perhaps because he was all too soon to lose it, and for what?

"Yes," he answered, standing. "Pretty good. Now what?"

Rutter straightened.

"Time to see the boss," he told Lawrence. "I think today you'll get all of the information you'll need. Where, when, how, that kind of thing."

Lawrence smiled.

"I think I feel the noose tightening." He admitted. "A distinct feeling in my throat when I try to swallow."

"Probably the eggs, if they gave you the powdered stuff."

Rutter parried.

Lawrence let it go and walked toward the door. He paused and turned around to glance back. It was just as he found it, apart from the unmade bed and the remains of his breakfast.

"Right, let's see what they have in store for me."

*

Back in the back seat of the Humber, Rutter produced the hood once more, but left Lawrence's hands free.

"Sorry, but security is essential. Under torture, our whole intelligence structure could be blown," he explained.

The hood turned in his direction.

"That's reassuring."

The journey became the longest that Lawrence had endured in the vehicle, lasting, he guessed, almost an hour. From the light that filtered through the hood, he deduced that they were heading south, and from the reduction of traffic sounds, it appeared that they were leaving the city. Now and then came the distinct sensation of tyres on gravel as the car slowed a little and cornered sharply. A lack of reflected sound convinced Lawrence that the journey had now entered the countryside, confirmed by the increase in speed.

Rutter spoke little, until he confirmed that they were almost at their destination. The car turned hard and stopped. Footsteps, and an opening of a side window announced some kind of security check. There was a shuffle of paper.

"Very good, sir." Came a harsh voice. "You know the way?"

Rutter confirmed that he did, thanked the man, and the car sped up once more, crunching along a road of hard chippings. For another few minutes, they continued in the same steady manner, then the Humber braked and almost skidded to a sudden halt on the uneven surface.

Lawrence was helped out of the car, and walked to a flight of seven hard stone steps, which he navigated with ease, then through a doorway of some kind, until he once more could detect the echo of a large interior.

"All right," Rutter told him. "You can take it off now."

Lawrence reached up and pulled off the hood. His eyes were

met by a large opulent hallway, complete with lush carpets and well-polished antique furniture. On the walls were military paintings from many periods, housed in magnificently worked frames. Lawrence walked over to one of the larger ones and looked up into the smoke and manoeuvring armies, being blasted by French guns. He turned to Rutter.

"Blenheim?" he asked.

Rutter shook his head.

"Malplaquet," he answered. "Same Duke, different battle."

Lawrence looked back up and followed the tight squares of horsemen with his eyes.

"A little different now, eh?" he observed.

Rutter shrugged and leaned his head to one side.

"Oh, I don't know. The same intolerance to decency, each with their own reason to stick two feet of steel into someone they don't know, and never will. To put a bullet into another for nothing more than the passion of the moment, to…"

Rutter paused, realising what he had just said. He glanced from the painting, over to Lawrence who was still searching the battle.

"I'm sorry, old man, I didn't mean…"

Lawrence appeared to be lost in the action of the painting. His answer was simple, as if he had hardly heard it, or cared.

"That's all right." He turned slowly to look at his companion. "Old man."

An oak door opened and an orderly appeared.

"This way, sir," he informed. "The Colonel is in the library."

Lawrence waited for Major Rutter's indication to follow. He had already used the time to indulge in Colour Sergeant Bull's disciplines, just for his own peace of mind, and to prepare himself. He followed Rutter past a large staircase, to where the orderly led them along a short corridor, and through a half open door that led to the library.

Daylight flooded through huge bay windows. Denning stood by a grand fireplace in the centre of one long wall, the only place not covered by occupied bookshelves. He looked up. Lawrence detected a slight change in his manner.

"Come and sit down," he said.

The door closed behind them and Lawrence followed Rutter further into the room. A large, low table supported an elaborate chess board, the pieces manufactured to represent some distant medieval armies. Lawrence stopped and stared down at the half-worked game. He folded his arms.

"You play, of course?" Denning half asked.

"You know I do," answered Lawrence. "Along with virtually everything else."

Without waiting for an answer, Lawrence jerked a thumb down toward the game, then back up at Denning.

"If you are playing black, then your opponent is playing you along. He has tried 'fools-mate' as an opening, and having failed to lure you to respond, has used the opportunity to secure the flanks, putting you into a defensive frame of mind. In three moves he will convert the situation to command the centre of the board, and there is little, I'm afraid, that you can do to stop him."

Denning smiled.

"I was playing white," he confirmed, and my opponent was… well… let's say his mind was on other matters." Denning released the smile. "We shall not be continuing the game."

Lawrence slowly circled the chess table, until he had isolated himself from the others. Taking a deep breath, he lifted his right hand to reveal Rutter's service revolver that he had eased from its holster in the Humber. Rutter's immediate reaction was to check the holster, but found it empty. Denning moved his hand slowly along the lintel of the fireplace, to something that Lawrence guessed would turn the tables and bring help. The revolver levelled at him.

"I wouldn't," he suggested.

Denning's hand pulled back. His face was stern. Lawrence

grinned, enjoying the flush of power for once.

"You know, sometimes the reputation of a convicted murderer comes in handy. If I were not of that character, you might risk it."

"Don't be a bloody fool, man!" Rutter advised.

Lawrence laughed aloud.

"Either way, I don't have much to lose, do I?"

Denning folded his arms.

"Now what?" he asked of Lawrence.

"I want an end to this damn nonsense," he told Denning. "No more hoods, no more being treated like something the cat brought in. I agreed to go along with this for the good of my boys, and I will. I've gone through every bloody check and balance that you've thrown at me. You've pushed me one way and another, even cut me up without consent. But whatever time I have left I want to be treated decently." He paused for a moment to think. "And you've told me what you'd do for my boys but I've seen nothing in black and white to confirm it. I just have your say so, and I have to be honest, what I've seen of you so far, Colonel, does not give me a warm trickle down my spine."

Denning thought for a moment.

"I cannot give you anything in writing. I simply cannot." He answered the charges. "But you have my word that the offer given will be honoured by the British Government. I can do no more than that." He pursed his lips. "If those terms are not agreeable, then this matter is closed."

Rutter looked surprised at Denning.

"Sir, we have gone too far for this to…"

Denning held up a hand, and Rutter halted mid-sentence. Lawrence was thoughtful for a few seconds. He glanced over at Major Rutter.

"Do I have your word?" he asked, emphasising the possessive.

Rutter looked nervous. He swallowed hard and looked across at Denning, then at Lawrence. Moments passed.

"Yes," he answered. "You do."

Lawrence took the revolver by the barrel and handed it over to Rutter by an outstretched arm. His eyes returned to Denning.

"Then let's get on with it."

An uneasy silence lasted for a few seconds, before Denning motioned Lawrence to an easy chair. Rutter found a seat by the chess game, and gave it a quick glance that betrayed his ignorance of the contest.

Denning moved a file from the armchair seat which he

chose, and balanced it on the arm rest. He sat back and clasped his hands together.

"A short time ago," he began, outlining history once more, "there was the plot to kill Hitler at his Wolf's Lair in Poland, as you may be aware. In the aftermath, seven thousand people were arrested, many executed, and many more might still be. The retribution not only focussed upon the assassins in the plot, but additionally any who might be considered as opposition sympathisers to the Nazis. Very convenient."

Denning paused while he lit a cigarette. He took the silver lighter that he had taken from his jacket pocket and put it on top of the file. He inhaled once, then continued through the blue smoke.

"Despite the number of individuals caught, shot or hanged, there were still those who escaped any connection with the attempted assassination, several of which still harbour the intention to do away with the Fuhrer, and are still at large. Our intelligence confirms that some of these officers are within Hitler's inner circle, and are now in no doubt as to the outcome of the war, and their doubtful places at the end of it." He put the cigarette to his mouth once more. "If Hitler is disposed of, and these officers are successful in taking over the German government, they may sue for peace, but not unconditionally, which the PM is adamant that they should do. It is also the view of the American President. Without the immediate unconditional surrender of Germany, the war could go on indefinitely, and cost innumerable lives."

"Would we not see these German Officers as kind of... allies?" Lawrence asked.

Denning shook his head.

"Germany is far from beaten, militarily," he explained. "You saw what happened with the Arnhem operation, and the Russians are taking considerable losses on the eastern front. In the west, intelligence already hints at some kind of counter attack in the winter months. If Hitler dies and competent officers gain control of the government of Germany, who knows how long we must fight on, perhaps years. The madman continues to make poor decisions and strategic mistakes that can only result in total collapse within months, providing he is kept alive, and the PM is resolute that he is."

Lawrence could see the logic of what he was being told.

"And I am to see to that, from what you have told me?"

Denning nodded. Rutter shuffled in his seat.

"How?" Lawrence asked.

The Colonel put out the cigarette without finishing it, stubbing it into a decorative glass ashtray on the small occasional table, by his chair. He took the folder and opened it.

"We are fortunate to have an agent close to Hitler's communication staff," he explained. "Encrypted messages from this source have been deciphered by an asset in Britain, quite close to where we are now. As we said before, the information gained confirms that there is to be an attempt on Hitler's life by sniper as he boards his personal train to Berlin, three days from now."

"And how am I to…"

Denning cut in.

"As we said, you will be dropped by parachute from a conventional aircraft, under cover as part of a bombing raid, as close to a small station town in eastern Germany as we can safely do so. Upon reaching the ground, you must find your way to the station, and locate the sniper. Rutter will give you guidance on the best way to do this, so you should have adequate time to complete your task."

"The station is close to the tracks, and there is heavy forest all around," Rutter interjected. "So, a rifleman will need to get pretty close to the target. Not only that, there will be German security to consider, so the options for a shooter will be limited."

"That's a relief," quipped Lawrence.

"Hitler has several doubles, and one of these has taken over the Fuhrer's general appearances since the July plot, some weeks ago." Denning continued. "The explosion shook him up quite a bit, so he has remained in convalescence until now. Once in Berlin, he will be flown to the Berghof, and any chance for the remaining plotters will be gone. He has a twenty-two-men SS guard on board the train, so once he is safely aboard, your job is done." Denning leaned forward a little. "Now for the detail."

He turned his head.

"Rutter, do you want to inform Mr Lawrence of his alter-ego?"

Rutter shuffled again, and took the folder that Denning offered. He opened it, and then looked up.

"Oberleutnant Kurt Maas was transferred from the war in the east, to the Netherlands, where he was injured by a grenade which affected the left side of his face. He was allowed medical leave of fourteen days, for which he was given a rail pass to Berlin, in order to also visit his mother who was, perhaps still is, terminally ill. Along the way, Maas was wounded again during a British air raid, after which he was killed, and relieved of his papers and personal items by Dutch partisans."

Rutter checked the file again.

"The items were passed to American OSS agents active in the area, and in a little game that we play with our allies, they found their way to us. About this time, our intelligence in the field advised us of the Hitler situation, and the possibility of another plot to kill him before boarding his personal train. The PM was most enthusiastic that we use this information in the best way possible.

Naturally, if we were to capitalise on Hitler's poor strategic capabilities, we needed someone on the ground who would stand a good chance of ensuring the Fuhrer's survival, someone who could speak perfect German, someone who bore a good resemblance, and pass as the unfortunate Maas, someone who had at least some military training, and so on, and so forth.

We had a few candidates for this role, but you were by far the best choice, not least because the others were half way around the world in other theatres of the war, and would take some time to locate."

Rutter raised one eyebrow. Denning lit another cigarette.

"Of course, even you presented considerable problems to be overcome."

The Colonel blew a blue cloud into the air. Rutter continued, and Lawrence's eyes were fixed upon him.

"The surgery was unfortunate, but we could not risk anyone putting Maas's name to an unscarred face. In the next few hours, you must memorise every detail we have of this German officer, according to his papers and personal items." Rutter grimaced. "How is the face, by the way?"

Lawrence raised a shoulder.

"Oh, great, so long as I don't laugh."

The Major continued.

"You will see that we have pretty comprehensive information of Maas's unit, its commanders, and its movements, and all of this information is valuable if you are challenged. The uniform that you will be wearing is accurate to the last stitch, the fabrics sourced from the correct locations, with a little addition to the tunic which might help, as no doubt you will be aware. Maas's papers should be perfect, so long as you remember the history of the man. Besides being somewhat similar in features, you are of a similar height. He had no natural marks on his body, and your hair colouring is quite close, eye colouring also. Any physical facial features will hopefully be discounted by the wound and the dressing. Try not to remove the dressing unless you are alone."

He glanced down at the folder once more to check if he had forgotten anything.

"Any questions, so far?" Rutter asked.

Lawrence shook his head.

"A million, but by the time I know what they are, I guess I'll be in Germany."

Denning put out his second cigarette.

"We realise the extent of what we are expecting of you." He said, almost sympathetically. "And that much of the detail of this operation can only be actioned once you are on the ground in enemy territory, but I hope that you will see that we are doing our utmost to give you every chance of success, and your survival. However, we must limit any information in the field to your particular operation. Should you be taken, and tortured, the whole of our network in Germany could be compromised."

"Well, let's look on the bright side, shall we? Fresh air, nice scenery…" added Lawrence, realising that levity was out of context, especially in his situation.

"Now!" Denning said, ignoring the remark. "Let's give you some idea of the area of operation."

He rose and led the other two over to a large oak table, upon which photographs had been spread.

"Hitler will be flown from a small chateau where he has been convalescing, to the station town where he will rendezvous with 'Brandenburg'…"

"Brandenburg?" Lawrence asked.

"His personal train," Rutter explained. "Used to be code-named 'Amerika', but I suppose he felt it inappropriate when the Yanks came into the war. It's a hell of a piece of engineering, with all of the luxury of a top-class hotel…"

"A moving hotel with flak wagons and an SS bodyguard." Denning added.

He continued.

"Normally, the train would travel all of the way to Hitler's headquarters in the east, but as the Russians advance, it would be a sitting duck for any of their fighters lurking around. Much safer to connect with the train over the border, and that has given us the time to react to the information of another assassination attempt, as Brandenburg was undergoing overhaul to one of the engines in Berlin…"

"One of the engines?" asked Lawrence.

"Yes," Denning confirmed. "It has two, double-headed, and another train precedes it all of the time, just in case there is an attempt to derail it."

"He thinks of everything, doesn't he?"

"I suppose that's why they decided on the simplest way to do away with him." Rutter interjected. "One man with a rifle is easier to discount, and if he succeeds, everything will just disappear into the chaos of those squabbling to take over."

Denning shuffled the photographs, and stopped on a clear picture of a typical German station halt.

"Bei Schallendorf," he pointed at it, with a finger browned by cigarettes. "The only place where Brandenburg can safely relocate the engines to the front of the train. It has a reversing loop, installed when the Germans invaded Poland. The time it will take for the train to reform, and move Hitler from the small airfield will be the best chance for a sniper to take him out."

Denning moved the finger over the photograph.

"It's a small place, quite isolated, with any forest cleared well away from the tracks and the station, so a sniper will have limited places from which to secure the shot, and the station buildings cover almost all of the long-range possibilities, which is why we think you have a chance of finding him."

Rutter cut in.

"Your main problem will be getting into the station area. Security around the place will extend well beyond the tracks. After you set foot in Germany, you should have a couple of hours of darkness, but if you are challenged, I'm afraid you'll have to bluff your way through."

"And if I can't?" asked Lawrence.

"Then you'll be shot." Denning answered with a turn of his lip. "But you'll reveal little information before you are, as you know little worth revealing. They'll just assume that you are a British agent, chancing his arm to kill the Fuhrer, or some other nefarious undertaking."

"And if I spill the beans?"

Denning laughed.

"Which story do you think they'll believe?"

It hardly encouraged Lawrence. No matter how few his chances of success were, they were definitely diminished in the last half hour. As the flush of avoiding the hangman had begun to give him confidence in his future, that conviction was now beginning to find holes, leaking his self-assurance by the minute.

"You should have plenty of time to search the area, look for any preparations that a sniper would need to make." Suggested Denning. "Anything unusual, any odd configuration of cover that a shooter would need to make, and also give him the chance to avoid capture. But the marksman will be good, remember, bearing in mind the security cordon around Hitler."

"And he may not be alone, so keep an eye on any small gatherings, and how they react. If they constantly look for the train, if they act nervously, if there are vehicles prepared to move quickly. In short, anything that gets your attention," Rutter added. "Then, whatever you need to do to disrupt their plans, you must do, with extreme prejudice. If you can do that, and remain undetected, then so much the better."

"If I can't?"

"Then you are on your own!" Denning said. "So, as well as everything else, I would advise that you plan a route of escape, and keep it in mind. The forest may be your best chance, providing you can reach it. Any pursuit will necessarily be on foot, like yourself, and give you the best chance of avoiding them. Under these circumstances, we can do little to help you, so I would advise that Poland might be your best direction of flight. If you can make it to the Russian lines, you may stand a chance of survival," he smiled. "But do ditch the German uniform first."

"And if I manage to see Hitler onto the train, all shiny bright and in one piece, and undetected, without any unwanted holes?" What then?"

Denning straightened.

"When you see with your own eyes that the man is actually on board, your job is done. It will take around twenty minutes for the security checks to be carried out on the train, before it moves off. Go directly to the small waiting room, and take away the dressing from the scar on your face. This is important."

He looked for his cigarettes.

"You will find a seat where you can be seen clearly. Someone will approach you, and ask which train you are waiting for," Denning explained. "Your answer will be, 'Berlin', eventually', but I am not sure of the time schedule'. Now repeat that."

Lawrence did so, perfectly in German, while Denning found the cigarettes and pulled one out of the pack.

"You will be given directions as to your safe exit from the area. And how and where you are to be withdrawn. Follow these instructions to the letter, and we may meet again under pleasanter circumstances."

"How am I to…" Lawrence began, spreading his hands.

"If you going to ask how you will be extracted, don't," Rutter told him. "The only people who know that are the partisans. Once contacted, follow their instructions. The fewer who know, the better, and the more chances you'll have of survival. We will only have information of your whereabouts once you are clear."

"Now," said Colonel Denning. "You will remain in this place until tomorrow night. You will be given the complete biography of Oberleutnant Kurt Maas, such as we know. Memorise it, for it will undoubtedly aid your survival."

"Have you jumped before, by parachute?" Major Rutter asked.

Lawrence winced.

"Only once, in training," he told the other. "Static line only, and not by choice you understand. Why anyone would volunteer to do such a stupid thing on request is quite beyond me. Present situation excluded I suppose."

"You'll be given adequate instruction before you go." Denning interjected through cigarette smoke. "But for God' sake don't break a leg, and stick the canopy where no damn Gerry will find it too soon, you understand?"

William Lawrence straightened and looked at the Senior Officer.

"I will do my best, Heaven knows it's in my own interest, isn't it?"

*

The room on the second floor in which Lawrence found himself abandoned was quite different to anything that he had expected to experience over the last few hours. After the door was closed, and locked once more, he walked over to the big bay windows and looked down into the twilight. The rain had stopped, and he could see many people leaving the building from the main entrance below, and others joining the throng from a row of Nissan huts across the lawn. They seemed quite young and mingled freely, as if all were acquainted, heading for whatever was beyond the big iron gates at the end of the short drive, where several army personnel kept a strong security point.

Lawrence flipped the switch on the tall standard lamp and flopped into the waiting armchair, where he continued his investigation of the mysterious Oberleutnant Maas. The papers were double spaced and clearly typed by experienced hands, with no spelling errors. He looked at a photograph, which had been taken from the man's body, long before his indiscretion with the grenade. It showed the officer with his mother, close in some well-kept garden, bearing an iron cross around his neck, without oak leaves or other adornment that enhanced the decoration. Lawrence stared intently at the man, surprised at the similarity to himself, and wondered what grief the old woman might know when the time came for things to be revealed, at some stage in the future.

Maas had been transferred from the eastern front shortly before the allied assaults at Arnhem, joining German Army Group B under General Model, presumably due to the lack of good officers after the D-Day invasion of Europe. Why he had been selected was not known, but Lawrence guessed that he was an officer of quality. Maas had fought west of Arnhem as part of Kampfgruppe Von Tettau, a mixed bag of seven battalions under

General Hans von Tettau, attached to the Waffen-SS. It was here that Maas had received the head wound from the grenade, an incident that eventually led to his demise under different circumstances.

There were huge holes in what was known of Maas, principally his wider family life. There were no other photographs to reveal his married status, and Lawrence guessed that fact alone suggested that he was a single man. Any normal soldier would always carry a picture of wife and family to bolster his courage in harsh conditions, but then Lawrence reminded himself that he himself had never done so.

Capturing the essence of a German officer was obviously the important issue. No matter how much individual information one assembled mentally, if the charisma of such a character failed, then the whole pack of cards fell with a clatter. Lawrence tried to recall all of the times in which he had been present to translate during interrogations of such men, making every effort to recall each little inflection, the tiniest twitch of the mouth, each detail of distain in the eye. He stood, came to attention, and clicked his heels sharply, inclining his head imperceptibly to one side, as he had seen so many perform, more to discolour respect than to show it.

In Lawrence's experience, German officers seemed to fall into two general categories. The older, Prussian kind, and the younger generation of leaders, who, due to the swift wartime promotion benefits, found themselves on a similar level to the former, but without the wisdom of proficiency. Of course, this was just a general observation, and there were some talented amateurs, as in any army, but many substituted a haughty twisted lip for expertise.

Lawrence looked again at Maas's photograph, and guessed

from his expression, age, and the fact that he was a professional soldier, that he was far from a Prussian straight-back, but had more to him than just a run of the mill officer.

The more times that Lawrence read through the file on Maas, the more that he came to respect the man. Something in his mind began to outline the character, bring him to life in his mind, and allow him to make a mental shape that he could step into. There was even a kind of sympathy that developed gradually for the officer, installed into the eastern front, then moved to fight against the allied brigades around Arnhem, only to suffer horrendous wounds, which led inevitably to his death at the hands of partisans. Hardly a fitting end. Lawrence put the thoughts from his mind, knowing that he might have to do the same for others of the officer's ilk, as he had done so before.

But these things hid away at the back of his mind for the moment, waiting to unleash themselves, almost involuntarily, when the time came and they could direct his actions.

Chapter Four
King's Pawn Advance

He was taken from the building while it was still light. Waiting with Major Rutter just outside the main door, Lawrence took in a deep breath and half smiled at the smell of freshly cut grass.

The door opened behind them and Denning appeared, several files tucked under his right arm. He joined the other two men as a black car appeared around the corner of the building, but his expression hardly changed as he spoke. Looking first at Lawrence, he said...

"Well, Lawrence. This is it. By dark you will be on your way. I trust that you will be successful in this enterprise. I wish you good fortune. Rutter has the files should you wish to refresh your memory until the last moment."

He nodded curtly and handed the files to Major Rutter. Lawrence returned the gesture without speaking and allowed himself to be ushered into the back seat. Rutter was about to follow when Denning took his arm and held him back, guiding him from earshot. Rutter looked at his superior with a look of surprise.

"Once he is in the aircraft, and off the ground," Denning told him, "Burn them, and confirm to me that you have done so."

*

Fear of the unknown was not something that Lawrence was new to lately. But to flip between one fear and another, possibly worse, tended to focus the imagination. As the car moved steadily along the narrow country roads, he balanced his fortunes. Perhaps it was fortunate to have avoided the justice of the hangman, but there again, his Majesty's executioner did not endeavour to pull out a man's fingernails or beat him to a pulp before stretching his neck. He wondered if his choice had been a good one, for at least that one would be all over, and now he would either know everything that there was to know, or not one God-damn thing.

Prior to leaving, Lawrence had been given his German uniform, and he had spent a little time getting used to the cut of the jacket. It felt like a good fit, and surprisingly the boots were more comfortable than they looked. He felt for the button that was attached to the wire and made sure that each side was housed correctly and was unseen. Looking into a mirror, he had tried on the fatigue cap, then snapped his heels and saluted, hoping it would be good enough to impress anyone who challenged him.

Even in the back seat of the Humber, the uniform felt comfortable, and it gave him a little encouragement. Not exactly Savile Row, but he decided that if it had been good enough for Maas, it would be good enough for him, so long as the final outcome was different.

"Ten minutes, we'll be there," Rutter said. "Anything you want to ask before you go?"

Lawrence shied but stopped when the discomfort of the scar

kicked in.

"You mean, have I changed my mind?" he suggested.

Rutter shook his head.

"I meant, more like anything that might help, when you're on the ground."

Pursed lips presented the doubts.

"So, apart from if I don't break my neck jumping from a perfectly sound aeroplane, I manage to find the way to the railway without being shot by a trigger happy 'kraut', I convince them that I'm a dead German officer, I find some top notch assassin who would just as soon put a bullet in me as the Fuhrer, and I manage to find my way back to some friendly Russians or Poles and convince them that I am not a German spy, despite the fact that I might still be wearing a uniform that they hate, I feel pretty confident about the whole damn thing. Right?"

Rutter swallowed and raised his brows. The car slowed and stopped at the airfield entrance. Which airfield was a guess, as the signage had been removed, just like it had at many others. Two armed sentries checked the credentials of the driver, and then Rutter through an open window. The soldier then ducked to check the other occupant of the back seat, and Rutter spoke in a low voice, showing more documentation, to which the man nodded his confirmation that all was well.

By now it was quite dark, and the automobile's lamp slits illuminated only parts of buildings that it approached. The tyres splashed through puddles from the recent rain and crackled over gravelled roadways until it halted by what appeared to be a large pair of hangar doors.

"All right, old chap," said Rutter. "Here we are."

Lawrence was led from the car to an unlit side entrance, down a small corridor and through a way into the main hangar. Low lighting illuminated a medium sized aeroplane, painted dark grey and carrying subdued British RAF rondels. Apart from the familiar war planes, Lawrence had little knowledge of more specialist aircraft, but he guessed correctly that this was some kind of night fighter, or reconnaissance plane. Several mechanics were busy preparing the aircraft, and virtually ignored the newcomers.

Along one side of the hangar, a long table stretched the full depth of the building, and in the centre lay a variety of equipment and clothing. Rutter led the way along the table and stopped opposite a folded flying suit. He reached up and switched on a small wall light.

Lawrence looked down and saw what he guessed was the modified Luger, sporting an extra round. There too was the altered bayonette which Colour Sergeant Bull had shown him, capable of spitting out an extra blade. There was also a small, black leather pouch with ammunition for the Luger, hardly discernible from the usual bullets.

"Better tool up," Rutter told him, throwing a glance at the weapons."

Lawrence reached over and took a quick look at the

bayonette, before slipping it onto his belt, then picked up the pistol. Before he could insert it into the holster at his side, Rutter took his arm to stop him.

"Just one more little trinket," he said, reaching into his pocket and drawing out what appeared to be a small black cylinder. "Not exactly regular issue, but I picked this up a while back. Knew it might come in handy, and I had it modified to fit the luger."

Lawrence looked at it.

"Suppressor for the Luger," he explained. "One twist into the end of the barrel and you can drop Gerry all day without worrying about the noise. Bloody good piece of kit, if you need it."

Lawrence tried the suppressor and found it a perfect fit, and easy to insert.

"Thank You," he added. "I was worrying about waking the neighbours."

Rutter looked at his watch.

"An hour and ten minutes. Get into the flight suit, and we'll go through the details one more time."

A short time later, they were going over the vital aspects of Lawrence's mission. Once again, he repeated the contact phrase should he be successful in reaching that point, methods of finding the shooter and many other small aspects that might just give him an edge to succeed. Then, from the side door by which they entered, three RAF personnel appeared, also clad in similar apparel and ready to fly.

Rutter greeted one of the men, who Lawrence guessed was the pilot. The other two walked over and grinned at him. Seeing the German collar over his unzipped suit, one of the airmen snapped a raised arm 'Zieg Heil' salute.

"Normally, we drop fellows wearing those jackets through the hatch without a parachute, but in your case, we'll make an exception." The man said.

"Very good of you," Lawrence tried to sound confidant. "Long time in the air, is it?"

The flying officer grinned, obviously aware that this was not a regular thing for the other.

"Don't worry old thing," he smiled, "once the ack-ack kicks in, tracer, fighters, dodging the eighty-eights, it'll pass in no time. Eaten today, have you? Nothing too greasy, I hope. Nothing worse than slipping around in this morning's breakfast for six hours."

The flying officer that Rutter had been speaking to walked across and cut into the conversation, and Lawrence was glad of it. He heaved a parachute pack over. The man seemed removed from the kind of repartee that his colleagues were prone to enjoying.

"Ever used one of these before?" he asked.

"Er… some time ago," Lawrence answered, "training only, never in anger."

He was helped on with the bulky pack, which made walking difficult due to the position of the equipment, and shown once more how to detach the chute once he had reached the ground, via a large flat clip on his chest. Last minute instructions followed on refreshing his knowledge of a parachute.

"You'll be on a static line," explained the officer. "We'll connect you up once you're aboard, so, all you need to worry about is jumping from the aircraft at the right time. Piece of cake. Any worries?"

Lawrence nodded.

"Plenty."

Rutter had finished a brief conversation with one of the other crew members and came over.

"You'll be joining a flight of Lancasters, on a bombing raid as cover, but hanging some distance behind, so you should be able to sneak in without detection. Gerry will be concentrating on the bombers." Rutter told him. "You have a map of the drop area, a German map, but if I were you, I'd get rid of it once you have your bearings. It might be seen as suspicious if you're challenged and searched, an officer on foot with the need for direction."

"Right," Lawrence acknowledged, feeling the time closing in on him, as he had once before.

The crew had entered the aircraft and engineers were putting out the lights inside the hangar. Rutter held out a hand, and Lawrence responded with a tight grip, trying to ignore the strip of goose bumps climbing up his spine, so cold that he swallowed hard to dispel it.

"I can't think of anything else, except good luck, and good hunting," Rutter said. "Unless you...?"

Lawrence shook his head.

"Let's just get on with it, see what's next."

He nodded a farewell, turned and climbed the short ladder into the dark aircraft. It was a difficult entry due to the bulk of the parachute, but once aboard, he was shown to a tight alcove in the fuselage, where a small metal seat was hinged down, the parachute forming a cushion beneath him. The officer who had joked with him flopped down into a seat opposite, and grinned as he motioned Lawrence to put on a leather flight helmet which held headphones. Once they were on, the officer held up a thumb.

"OK?"

Lawrence responded with another thumb as the officer pointed to a hatch that lay between them on the floor of the fuselage. He grinned as he jerked the thumb to the small entry door, and then the hatch.

"That way in," he explained jovially, continuing his advice. "That way out."

The hangar doors slid aside and Lawrence heard the engines cough into life, then growl loud enough to vibrate the whole aircraft. Some seconds later he felt the plane begin to move forward and could just make out movement through the small port in the opposite side of the fuselage.

It seemed a short journey to the runway, where the aircraft turned into its departure attitude, the pilot gunning the engines ready for take-off. A cackle of conversation between the pilot and the controllers on the ground seemed distant, but Lawrence guessed that this was far from unusual. Another wide grin from the crewman opposite reassured him.

Engines whined and slowly the plane moved forward, bouncing up and down gently, until the wheels left the ground and a few moments later, hummed into their housings inside the fuselage.

Within minutes, low cloud flashed by the small port that was the only visual access to the outside world. Somehow, Lawrence felt calmer now that he was on his own, figuratively speaking. Now, he was his own man, making the decisions which he controlled. The dark interior of the aircraft seemed almost comforting, allowing him the time to think, to plan as best he could and go over all of the information that he had, mentally, at his disposal.

Not that the thought to just abandon the mission had not crossed his mind, especially now that he was totally free from the control of others, to just make the jump out of the plane and disappear. If he could make it to France, there were ways that he could ensure that he would never be found. But that was far from his way, he knew that. Word had been given, no matter how shallowly, and would be not be broken on his part. And then there were his boys, who he would never abandon to the chaos in their lives that he had created. He wondered where they were at that moment, and if they already hated him.

Lost in his thoughts, Lawrence rubbed the dressing covered scar on his face. He looked up at the still smiling face of the crewman, who pointed to the hidden disfigurement, pressing the microphone bulb to his lips in order to speak.

"She found you in the wrong bed, did she?" Came the question, squeaking through the intercom.

Lawrence raised one corner of his mouth, in an almost imperceptive smile. He configured the headset to reply.

"Something like that."

*

After an hour in the air, Lawrence was dozing, the wheel of thoughts revolving constantly through his mind, and disallowing any proper sleep. A motion from the front of the aircraft caught his attention, and the co-pilot appeared squeezing through the narrow access that led into the cockpit. He waved a hand at his passenger.

"We'll be linking up with the bombers soon." He advised through the intercom. "Dragging behind until we're almost at the drop point. Then when they begin their run in, we'll peel away and get you on your way."

Lawrence felt that the co-pilot was almost suggesting that it was something which should be looked forward to, as if it were some eagerly anticipated holiday activity, and was apologising for the wait before it started. The airman continued.

"We have tea in a flask if you need a drink." He said, jerking a thumb forward. "But remember we're up here for a few hours yet. We keep a couple of pop bottles for emergencies, but any more than that and I'm afraid you'll have to put up with it."

It was beginning to look like parting company with a perfectly sound aeroplane might be the better option. Lawrence waved a hand to avoid any further need or explanation.

*

Some hours later, it sounded like thunder, a distant rumble that faded away slowly. Lawrence was wide awake but the sound woke the crewman opposite, who had dropped off a half hour before.
Lawrence Stretched out his legs as best he could, finding the cramped conditions increasingly uncomfortable. A flash lit up the sky and he took it for lightening.

"Looks like a storm," Lawrence suggested.

The airman shook his head.

"Eighty-eights!" he said. "But don't worry, they're more interested in kicking hell out of the Lancasters." He looked at his watch and whistled, upending an index finger to identify the hatch in the floor between them. "Not long now."

Lawrence felt his heart beating faster. Something began to change internally, something he had not felt for some time, something he knew but could never quite understand. It was a shadow over his personality, something that had never failed him in a difficult moment, but had sometimes led him along paths that made him pay for the confidence of his own actions. He knew it was there, wating to rise to the occasion, whatever that was. He had always known it, and was always prepared to let it run, whatever the outcome.

The shocks of war thumped the sky all around them, but rarely coming close enough to cause concern. As the crewman said, the Germans were more interested in the bombers, and hardly were aware of a small dark shape trailing behind.

The plane banked to starboard and Lawrence obtained a good view of the ground below, shockwaves bursting out from the impact point of the bombs dropped by the Lancasters. Ack-ack tracer lines clawed skyward to find the perpetrators of the raid, and several appeared through the fuselage window, already in flames.

The pilot called back through the intercom.

"Around twenty minutes, jumper. Red light on. Better get yourself ready!"

The airman opposite Lawrence hurried into activity, clearing the space around the floor hatch. He slapped his passenger on the arm as a method of reassurance, then checked the static line from his parachute. Above the hatch, a bright red lamp announced that time to jump was imminent. A heavy leather helmet was given to replace Lawrence's flight headset.

Noise from the bombing runs slowly died out over fifteen minutes as the aircraft left them behind to continue their work. Turbulence increased as the plane dropped through cloud cover, until small calibre anti-aircraft guns reported their discovery.

"Looks like they know you're coming, boy," said the crewman, unlocking the hatch mechanism, a smile on his face.

"You think so?" Lawrence asked, nervously.

The airman shook his head, crackling through Lawrence's headset.

"I wouldn't worry, they fire on any damn noise in a bombing run. Even shoot their own damn planes if they get in the way. Paranoia, I guess."

"That's a relief," admitted Lawrence.

By the time the hatch was raised, the sky was almost clear. Wind rushed up into the fuselage along with the filaments of low cloud which remained. The light was still red. A thumb jerked skyward was the signal for Lawrence to stand. He struggled to comply through the discomfort of cramp from sitting so long, and stretched his body as best he could in the limited space.

The aircraft banked gently as it descended. The hatch was folded back to its maximum limit. A voice came through from the cockpit.

"Ready jumper, don't forget when you hit the ground, roll in the chute. If it's windy down there, it'll drag you back to blighty."

"Right."

"Green light on! Good luck jumper!" Came the instruction. "Go."

Lawrence looked down for a second, through the hatch and into the void. He could see nothing but the strands of cloud as they flashed by beneath the aircraft, then he was through before his brain had even demanded it, out into the night and the dark.

Engine noises diminished with the shadow of the aircraft, out into obscurity, and he was on his own, dropping like a stone for what seemed hours, wind in his face and his limbs flailing, until a sound like an eagle's wing arrested his fall, jerking him up as if on a spring until the inertia faded and he steadied.

He was aware of the chute strings and reached up to grab them, finding the tightening lines reassuring as the dark canopy flapped and unfolded above his head. His body swung like a pendulum, this way and that, until the parachute found its place in the sky and stabilised to a silent descent.

Lawrence looked down into the bleak night, with only the odd pinprick of light invading the darkness beneath his boots. A sudden relief overtook him, now that it had begun, with one direction left to go, one task to fulfil. He began to search for the ground below, surprised at how long he seemed to be in the air and dropping, concerned that he might not have the time to brace and land well. His eyes strained into the night, until obscure shapes formed below. He tightened his grip on the chute lines and prepared to roll as soon as he hit the ground, diffusing his weight against the impact.

Then, he could see it, a long hedge which appeared to line a field of some kind of crops, which were too much in shadow to identify. They rushed up toward him and he remembered the drill, to relax into it and not to tighten up, or broken limbs might be the result, and that was the last thing he needed.

'Flump', His feet hit the soft earth, and he let the chute take him for a moment. He thumped the round, flat button on his chest to release him from the parachute. Then, finding himself on his back and still being dragged by the canopy, he reached for the lines nearest the ground and hauled them in, taking the wind from the bloom of silk and flattening the parachute, and then pulling it toward himself and folding it into the tightest bundle that he could manage. Once he had achieved this, he wound the cords around the material and tied them off.

For the first time since he had landed, he realised that the ground was wet, either from recent rain, or a flooded field. He stood up and hastened through mud toward the cover of the hedgerow, hunkering down to listen for a few seconds. It was deathly quiet, only the far distant sound of the anti-aircraft guns popping off against some real or imagined enemy. Quickly, he thrust the parachute as far into the foliage of the hedge as he could reach, then divested himself of his flight suit and helmet and did the same with them. Broken branches and debris were pushed in as camouflage until he felt satisfied that no passing eyes could detect them.

Reaching into the pocket of his tunic, he pulled out the forage cap and put it on, straightening the German jacket until it felt right. On his back, he had a light knapsack, empty so that it flattened inside the flight suit, but gave an extra layer of plausibility to anyone who looked upon him.

His next priority was to get out of the wet, which rose to his ankles, so he squelched along the hedge until he found a gate and climbed over. He found himself on a narrow side road, with no indication of where he was, so he checked the compass that had been part of his equipment assignment and found south east, knowing that was the general direction of the station halt.

He squinted in the dark at the watch that he had been given, German service issue for officers, good quality and perfectly set to the correct time. Two hours until dawn, but it would soon start to get light, so he decided to start along in that general direction until there was enough light to check the map, and hopefully find signage along the way. But walking was hopeless in wet boots and socks, so he found a dry place and took them off, squeezing out as much moisture as he could from the socks and inclining the boots so that as much drained out as possible.

As he rubbed his feet with dry grass, the sound of an engine came out of the first distant twilight of morning, and a single slit of light appeared around a bend not far away. He knew that it was folly to try to run or hide, especially bare footed, and so just sat waiting to see what the day might bring.

Soon, he could see the light for what it was, a German military motor cycle and sidecar, with rider and passenger, doubling the odds against him, so he kept the Luger buttoned in its holster, and put his faith in bluff. Within seconds, the headlight had illuminated him and slowed down, stopping some yards away. Lawrence remains seated and waved lazily, as if pleased to see them.

The German rider set his feet on the ground. He raised his goggles and looked down the road, seeing the strange sight of an officer in the headlight, sitting on the grass verge with no boots on, his cap pushed back and scratching his bare feet. The officer waved casually again and sat back, his hands clasped, with his elbows resting upon his knees. The rider swung his machine pistol from his back and levelled it forward. Inside the sidecar, the passenger did likewise and began to disembark. Both wore long, leather coats, a little muddy, and boots of a similar disposition.

Once on the ground the passenger began to walk forward, presenting his own machine pistol, which was still hooked around his neck by a strap. The rider switched off the ignition and also dismounted, following a few yards behind his friend.

Lawrence watched them come, and just sat calmly, waiting for their approach. The passenger halted a few steps from him.

"Hände hoch! (Hands up)," he ordered, checking the officers rank. "Herr Oberleutnant."

Lawrence shrugged, as if unconcerned at the challenge. He casually raised one hand.

"Guten Morgen soldaten," he greeted in perfect German. "Do you happen to have a clean, dry pair of socks?"

The strange question was ignored by the rider. He kept the gun trained on the officer.

"What are you doing here?" he asked, looking out across the dark fields.

Lawrence made a look of disgust.

"Ach! I was on my way to Bei Schallenberg," he began. "To catch the Berlin train," he paused for a moment. "I have been granted leave to visit my mother, who is ill. And as you can see, I was wounded in Holland." He indicated the dressing over the scar, removing it to show the wound. "A passing truck promised me a lift, but there was a damn raid by the RAF, and we were ordered to look for a possible parachutist." He paused again to take a deep breath. "We found no parachutist but I was left behind, and ended up in some bloody flooded field, where as you can see, I now sit trying to redress the situation."

"Your name?" asked the German.

"Maas," answered Lawrence. "Kurt Maas. Oberleutnant Kurt Maas."

"Papers?" asked the other soldier.

Lawrence fished into his inside pocket and found them, presenting them over to the soldiers. He noted that the rider of the motorcycle began casually looking across the fields while his passenger checked his documents.

"Ja! We too were told to look for parachutists, but I think this is something the Luftwaffe do every raid," said the rider. "I think to cover their asses."

The other German handed back Lawrence's papers, and from the casual manner of the pair, he knew that he had cleared the first hurdle. He needed to keep up the façade.

"Are you by any chance going in my direction?" he asked. "I would appreciate a ride."

The rider shook his head.

"Apologies, Herr Obrleutnant, but we have orders to report to Sondersee, which is in the opposite direction, but there will be frequent traffic by morning. If we see any, we will tell them that we have seen you and hopefully you will get a ride."

The German turned and pointed back the way that they had come.

"Bei Schallenberg is about eight kilometres in that direction, about two hours walk, but I have no idea of the regularity of the trains." He dropped the machine pistol to hang on its leather strap. "But there is some kind of flap on at Schallenberg, so you may have a long wait when you get there."

Lawrence looked in that direction, then stood calmly and gave a normal salute.

"Then I shall enjoy the walk, and the wait," he said. "Thank you, gentlemen."

Almost in unison, the two soldiers clicked their boots and returned the salute.

"Herr Oberleutnant!"

They turned and walked back to the motorcycle which purred in the background, and a few moments later waved as they passed. Lawrence returned the gesture, then sat back down on the grass bank and began to pull on his damp socks. He looked down the road after them.

"Sloppy," he said to himself. "Are they all like that?

*

By first light, Lawrence had covered some distance toward his destination. There were occasional trucks moving along the road, and he considered waving one down, but decided that one successful challenge was quite enough, and upon hearing the motor, dropped behind the hedgerow and let them pass.

The morning dawned as bright as he could have hoped for, particularly as he carried no bad weather gear due to the limitations of his situation. He wondered what an inquisitive German might make of the fact that his back pack was empty, and resolved to rectify that as soon as possible. He had a few Deutschmarks in his pocket, but no more than a soldier might carry, in order not to raise suspicions. And he felt the need to eat something, so once at Bei Schallenberg, he would have to throw himself into the abyss and take what risks might be necessary.

As he walked, he began to think through the possibilities of finding his quarry. It was particularly hard to envisage a logical plan, as all he knew of the place was from the photographs that Denning had shown him. He decided to get a general feel of the place first, then pick out the spots where he would do the deed, and hoped that would lead to some kind of success. But there were so many variants that could discount his efforts.

Soon, all around, the forest began to close in, leaving the fields behind. Sunshine filtered through the branches and scattered puddles of light on the road ahead. The sound of another motor, somewhere behind alerted the passing of another vehicle, so Lawrence made himself scarce among the low branches and underbrush.

The previous truck had a covered cargo section behind the cab, but this one was open, with just the iron supports for a canopy visible. Lawrence peered through the branches and saw the seated figures of ramrod-backed SS men, remembering the times when he had interpreted in many an interrogation of such soldiers. He guessed that they were heading for Bei Schallenberg, and were part of the security for the Fuhrer later that day.

As Lawrence walked, he wondered what angst Colonel Denning would be feeling. Surely by now, he would be aware that he was in Germany, providing of course, the plane had returned safely. From thereon, he could only guess at Lawrence's condition and progress.

A two wheeled cart appeared down the road, going the opposite way, with one old man driving the old brown horse. It came steadily on, and Lawrence kept up his pace until within hailing distance. He halted and waved cheerily up to the driver.

"Guten Morgen," he smiled. "Schallenberg, Wie heit ist es?" (How far is Schallenberg?).

The old man pulled up the horse, and looked down from the seat.

"Schallenberg, zwei kilometre." He threw a thumb over his shoulder in the opposite direction to the one in which he travelled. "But they won't let you in today. Big security checks to anyone going into the damn place. SS all over the place, checking papers, searches. Damned SS turned me back. I'll have to come all of the way back tomorrow."

"Ah," replied Lawrence. "Must be some kind of crackdown. I heard there might have been a parachutist search last night."

The old man began to laugh. He slapped his knee and laughed louder, until it made him cough. He bent over and thrust his face into Lawrence's.

"Hitler is coming!" he cackled. "A big secret that everyone knows."

Lawrence raised his eyebrows, feigning surprise.

"What about those needing the train?" he asked.

"Too bad," the old man replied. "Those who were in before the SS came, stay in. Those who are outside, stay outside. If you are going for the train, don't hurry, you'll have to wait until tomorrow."

Lawrence made a gesture of disappointment.

"Ach! Then I must wait."

The old man reached over to the other side of the seat, turned back and threw a sausage down to Lawrence, who caught it in both hands. He nodded twice and urged the horse on once more.

Lawrence called after him.

"Danke! Watch out for the parachutists."

*

It was just before nine thirty and the morning sun climbed steadily behind the trees. Around a wooded bend, Lawrence had his first sighting of the small station halt of Bei Schallenberg. As the cart man had told him, there was considerable activity further down. He could clearly see people being turned away from entering the small hamlet, reinforced by light armoured vehicles and temporary machine gun posts on either side of the road. This, he thought, would not be as easy to confront as the motor cycle soldiers.

Lawrence slipped into the trees by the side of the road and ate the sausage. It was garlicky, but partly masked by onion. He hated garlic, but ate the sausage just the same. As he ate, he tried to think through the best way to get into Schallenberg, wondering if there might be a way further into the forest, where the trees would give him cover until he could find some kind of way in. But if there was no other possibility, unless he confronted the security point, it looked like his options were less than limited.

He checked his watch, nine forty-four. From what he had been told, Hitler was due to arrive sometime in mid-afternoon. That meant that time was closing in on him, and the longer it took him to get into the hamlet, the less time he had to find an assassin. It would be no easy task, knowing the rings of security that would be around the Fuhrer.

Eating the sausage made his face hurt. Lawrence rubbed it gently until the discomfort faded. He stood up and slipped on the light back pack, then made his way into the woods, listening intently for any sound of the numerous patrols that he knew would be around. He was right to take the precaution.

The sounds of the birds reminded him of his childhood, when he had spent so much time with his German grandparents. He had never concerned himself why his mother and father had found it so easy to disbar him from their company and leave him with others, and had just enjoyed the freedom it gave him, following the paths of the sparrows and other characters of the forest. Holidays had passed so quickly being a loner, either in the German woods or others in France with his relatives there. Both sets of grandparents came to understand his ways and how he was becoming different from his younger brother, who somehow seemed to fill the gap that he could not. But no matter, he thought, feeling no animosity, just the curiosity of why.

Somewhere ahead he noted a change in the bird sounds, moving from chant to warning. Lawrence paused for a moment to identify the direction, and then heard the first spoken voice, distant but definite. Now was his first important choice, knowing that another challenge might not be so easily dissuaded. A patrol would be made of many individuals, not all so effortlessly satisfied, and dealing with them not so simple, even if he followed Bull's welcome advice. He had the Luger, but that would only draw more attention, and make his task harder.

They were coming his way but not yet in sight. He slipped off the backpack and looked around for foliage that was easy to pull from the ground, but thick enough for what he wanted, finding several that fitted the bill. He had done this many times when he was a boy, making it easier to camouflage himself until deer or badgers passed close enough to almost touch, thrilled until fit to burst that he had fooled them until the wind changed and the game was over.

Lawrence pressed himself into a tree by the path he was following, away from the direction of the patrol, spreading the dead leaves away with his foot until they hid his boot marks, then he pulled the unearthed foliage around him until almost every part of his body was covered, as naturally as he could manage in the time he had at his disposal. He slowed his breathing, letting his natural calm take over, and waited. He followed the advice that he had been given to check the space that he found himself in, just in case, noting any fallen branch or stump that might be useful in his defence, should that situation arise.

For several minutes the voices increased until he could make out the words. Six of them, maybe seven, he guessed, involved in fairly idle chatter; wives, or someone else's, girlfriends or the shortcomings of officers, all valid subjects for bored soldiers.

They were close, words fleshed out with laughter, until Lawrence realised how close. The helmeted head of a leather coated soldier meandered into the corner of his eye as the man circumnavigated his tree, while the others were spread out on either side.

"Halt! Halt, halt, halt," one of the soldiers called, lazily. "Nehmen wir eine Pause. (Let's take a break)."

"About time," answered another.

Lawrence moved his head imperceptibly slowly, to take a look at where they all were. Those on his right were moving in toward the others, to squat on the ground only yards from where he was hidden. They passed so close to him that he could smell their after shave, or the gun oil that they used to clean their rifles.

For some minutes, the soldiers smoked and chattered to each other. Not once did any of the Germans have any idea that he was there, almost within touching distance, until one of them found the back pack that he had forgotten to pick up.

"Was zu Holle ist dieser? (What the hell is this?)" asked one of the soldiers, raising Lawrence's pack, and displaying it to the others.

"Ach! Some poor boot's going to be tongue whipped for leaving it behind," someone said. "Anything in it? Any smokes? See if there's a name. Maybe we can help him out."

The German shook his head.

"Keine name. Nichts."

"Let me see," came a voice of authority, that might be a corporal.

Lawrence heard the sound of the pack being thrown, and was glad that he had not used it for storing anything that might have been suspicious, but nothing was a suspicion of its own. Some moments passed.

"Schmidt! Take this back to the sergeant straight away. Tell him where we found it."

"Kann ich meine Zigarette zu ende bringen? (Can I finish my smoke?)." Schmidt asked.

"Nein!" The corporal demanded. "Gehst du. Nun!"

The sound of shuffle was the man rising, and with a curse that could not quite be heard, he made off back toward the checkpoint. Lawrence realised that he had made his first mistake, and scolded himself for it. The corporal called the rest to aural attention and told them to spread out, to search the area, unaware that he was less than a metre away from what he sought to find. The German blew away the last smoke from his cigarette and it wafted across Lawrence's face.

"Spread out!" ordered the corporal. "Vorwarts!"

Steadily, the line of soldiers moved away from where Lawrence hid within his improvised camouflage, thankful that it had worked. The thoughts of what might have followed if he had been discovered crossed his mind, and he resolved to be more careful of his survival. However, he knew that he had just increased the perceived threat level by his own carelessness. That the pack was completely empty offered no satisfaction to him, as an empty pack might have concealed something that fertile minds might imagine, and in this case, they were absolutely correct, but for all of the wrong reasons.

Lawrence waited for some time before leaving the cover of his camouflage, but he knew that the clock was ticking. The voices of the Germans had stopped almost completely as they moved away in their search. In their chatter, Lawrence had heard two of the soldiers discussing the arrival of Hitler that afternoon, and learned that he was due around three-thirty. He looked at his watch. It was ten-thirty-five. Schallenberg could only be a short distance away now, so he left the path that he had been following and cut through the woods in the direction that he knew it to be.

He was right, and within a short time he knew he was there, seeing activity through the trees. He had wondered what security he still might have to confront, knowing perfectly well that it would not just be a road block and a few roaming patrols.

Ahead, through the trees, he could see a high wire fence which marked the boundary of the station yard, filled with coal dumps, regular placed piles of wooden planks covered by tarpaulins, small workers huts and other familiar railway impedimenta. Beyond lay the station buildings. Lawrence was surprised how small the place was, and wondered if his task might be easier than he thought, if he could get in. Had it been a perfect world, he would have preferred to be moving in the dark of night, but that would mean dropping by parachute in the light, and a perfect world in 1944 was far from the case for most people.

Where there was passage to move around the yard, sentries plodded slowly in their boredom, occasionally crossing the path of another, and stopping for a few minutes to pass the time in talk. Beyond the yard, he could see the tracks, where there seemed to be more people milling around, including the helmeted guards, who seemed to be in tandem. It seemed to Lawrence that even if he managed to get in, he faced the same problems getting out, so maybe it was not as easy as it seemed.

His eyes roamed the area beyond the fence, and looking to his right, a few yards metres away, the branch of a big tree almost reached the fence, but it been cut off clean, and it would take a good effort to clear the metal links and make a good landing, with hopefully no broken bones. It was not the perfect entry, but he could see no better way, so he carefully moved toward the base of the tree, keeping an ear cocked in case of more soldiers.

The sky had darkened. It began to rain, just a few spots at first, but then heavier. Lawrence looked up at the gathering dark clouds, a surprise from the bright morning that it had been earlier, fooling him into thinking the day would be clear. Suddenly, his damp socks were not so much of an issue.

He reached the base of the tree and looked through the links of the fence. Just beyond, several wood piles lay side by side, covered part way down by faded green tarpaulins and weighted by ropes which were tied to stones. The timber was stacked about three metres high, so if he could clear the fence, they would give him a little cover on the opposite side. Lawrence took off his forage cap, despite the rain, not wishing to lose it, as he felt it formed an integral part of his uniform and helped him mingle in with other military characters within the station area.

The rain increased. Through the nearest canyon between the timber heaps, Lawrence saw several guards running toward the station buildings, wondering what had made them alert, but then he realised their hurry. One was dashing with a small piece of plank above his head, the rain running off in rivulets. They were running either for cover, or to get their foul weather gear, probably the latter.

Lawrence knew that his time was short if he wanted to capitalise on the convenient bad weather. He shinned up the tree, taking advantage of every small branch and foothold, careful to avoid the smaller ones that might break, or even give his passage away. Soon, he was at the big branch that might help him navigate inside the railway yard. He looked around, covering every angle that might hide a sentry. Climbing across, he came to the square cut where once the long branch had extended over the fence, but now ended a metre away. He crept out, inch by inch until he could go no further without attempting the jump. He would have preferred more space between the wood piles, but there was nothing else for it, he had to go, and go now, before any sentries returned. Shuffling slowly to firm his footing, he spread his arms a little for balance, took a breath and hoped that the big muscles in his legs were still as good as they used to be. Lawrence launched himself up and forward.

At first, it all went well. He felt the rain as he sailed over the top of the fence, almost as if in slow motion, lowering his feet and anticipating a landing, but as he did so, the heel of his right boot clipped the metal and he pitched forward. Impacting soft earth where the land beyond sloped down to meet the fence, it was still a jolt and knocked the breath from his lungs.

Lawrence rolled over onto his back, mentally checking every limb, every muscle, every bone, and was glad that it was only his cap that had become detached.

He pulled his senses together and bound them into a bundle, his own mental version of Roman fasces. Rain drove off some of the mud on his face but he helped it away with his hand, and finding his cap, used it to dispel the worst of the moisture.

Quickly he hauled himself back against the end of a pile of timber, facing the fence that he had just negotiated, and looked quickly around, checking that he had at least taken a step nearer without discovery. He had, and apart from his assault by the weather, remained whole, apart from a few bruises. A feeling of deep relief flashed over him, but his thoughts identified what still lay ahead, and his confidence in achieving his goals were far from firm. Lawrence knew that the guards would soon return, and the quicker that he could mingle with those around the station area the better, assuming that those within the secure perimeter would have already had their papers checked.

Lawrence reached up and pulled the end of the green

tarpaulin over his head to deflect the rain that had increased its force. He saw that there seemed to be more overlap on the sides of the pile, and so he edged around, intending to wait a few minutes for the rain to ease before moving. As he backed around the corner, keeping the tarpaulin above his head, he saw that he was virtually side by side with a German SS guard who had decided to follow his example, and instead of running for foul weather gear, would sit it out until the downpour stopped. The man was puffing hard on the last of a cigarette, the smoke dissipating into the weather.

They stared at each other for a few surprised seconds. Lawrence spoke first, hoping to bluff his way through as he had done before.

"Hallo, Haben Sie Zigaretten? (Have you a cigarette?)", he smiled cordially.

The guard froze, looking Lawrence up and down with his eyes, seeing the strange figure of a German officer, muddied down one side with a big patch on his cheek. Chances for the bluff had passed and Lawrence knew it. He wondered what to try next, but the other took the initiative first. He brought around a rifle, capped with a wicked bayonet, with his left hand, and levelled it before Lawrence had a chance to rise. Lawrence gave it one last try.

"Achtung! (Attention!)", he ordered. "Legen Sie Ihr Gewehr ab (Put down your rifle). Ich bin eiene Deuche Officier (I am a German Officer)".

That too failed to work. The guard abandoned his tarpaulin

umbrella and gripped his rifle harder, hauling back the bolt to chamber a round. Lawrence knew that he had got it all wrong, and no amount of linguistic deception was going to work. He did the only thing that seemed prudent, and rose to hold his hands high into the rain. The German hooked the barrel of the gun to indicate the direction that he wanted his prisoner to go, toward the station area, and probably reinforcements who might beat the living daylights out of him if he allowed it to happen. Even with good papers, he knew that he was not in a good situation, and must think quickly.

Lawrence smiled, a leering smile that he hoped would distract his captor, then snapped his right thumb and forefinger together as loudly as he could. It was just a fragment of a second, no more, that took the guard's eye from him to glance at what was causing the sound, a fragment that changed the odds.

Lawrence's hand came down and caught the rifle with one hand, pulling it toward him, while the other reached across and encompassed the rifle bolt, stalling the action, the bayonet sliding uncomfortably close to his ribs.

What happened next was one of those strange moments in his life that seemed to be lived by someone else. Another mind seemed to take over, oblivious of fear or desperation, often unaware of his own surroundings as his body worked to take out the offender with whatever means necessary. In these moments, neither pain or fear of it mattered, every sinew and muscle working toward subduing what his brain explained as delinquent to his own survival, his own benefit, his own advantage. Although Lawrence knew of its existence, he never challenged it, never questioned it, just living with the enigma that inhabited the same body as he for a brief time.

Thunder masked the alarm call of the guard, the sound

crushed in his throat as Lawrence released the barrel of the rifle and threw the whole weight of his fist into his opponent's throat, popping his eyes and ejecting his tongue. The German found his senses and fought back, trying to kick forward with his legs, to find a target for the heavy boots. He tried to call again, for help which would never come. Lawrence found a purchase on the man's jacket and pulled him inward, toward him, until his terrified face was near his own, finding his tongue with his teeth and biting down hard until it almost came away in a kiss of violence, leaving a stump behind his lips.

Lawrence spat it away, together with the blood that came with it, but the pain urged the German to fight harder, and Lawrence felt himself pushed over backwards, unbalanced by his enemy until the weight of the man pinned him into the mud. With a free hand, the Englishman reached around, and over the crown of the SS helmet, and finding the short peak, gripped it securely and hauled it backwards, the leather strap around the German's chin cutting deep into his throat as his head was pulled back to the point of almost snapping his spine. The man coughed and struggled, his fingers finding the dressing on Lawrence's face, his nails scraping along the scar as they found flesh beneath, and then tried to find the bayonet on the rifle that had been pressed between them.

Lawrence released his grip on the helmet, and found the button on his cuff, pulling hard to release the wire that it hid, and in a second, he had slipped a noose around the guard's neck and pulled hard, as hard as he could. The wire began to bite deep, but caught on the man's tunic collar. He coughed more blood as Lawrence pulled harder, the red spattering his face.

It was clear that there was to be only one outcome, so Lawrence pulled harder, until the German's eyes widened and his hands clutched at the wire noose around his neck his mouth frothing the blood that was present but unable to make any sound.

Then, what Lawrence feared most happened. Above the spattering rain, a voice called in German…

"Hans! Hans! Wo sind Sie?"

It was still some way off, but Lawrence knew that he must finish it quickly. With a maximum effort, he heaved the croaking German over to one side, trying to keep the strangle hold secure, but the movement made him release his grip and the guard managed to intake a little air.

As the German put up both hands to his neck to find the wire, Lawrence formed a fist and hit the man hard, square in the face. His nose burst like a ripe tomato, and the bone almost pierced the skin. Lawrence hit him again, and continued as the German pulled his head from one side to the other to avoid the blows, but it was too late, and the face became almost unrecognisable, and still.

Lawrence looked down at the man, wondering if he was indeed dead, and considered making sure by re-using the wire, but those looking for Hans were getting nearer. For a second, he was shocked by the brutality of his own actions, but the moment passed and he discarded the fleeting memory of guilt. More important was now his own secure integrity. He reached over and took the German's pistol from its black leather holster, deciding that the more firepower he had the better, mentally thanking the doctrine of Colour Sergeant Bull as he put the Walther into his own pocket. Then, he thought quickly of disposing of the German, finding it quick and easy to roll him into the shallow ditch by the fence, where weeds and nettles flourished, and all but hid the body. He stood and kicked the foliage over the grey uniform, making as good a job of it as he could, then made his way around the piles of timber, remembering to retrieve the dressing that had been pulled away from the scar on his face. It was now wet and bloody, but felt good as he replaced it, and held it there with one hand.

The effort of the encounter had drained him. He staggered along the perimeter of the fence, keeping behind several small huts and workshops, out of sight of any more sentries that might be around. Voices raised some distance away and he feared that the German had been found, but risking a look from his position, he saw only two long-coated sentries moving in the opposite direction, lost in some personal joke that made them laugh. Lawrence knew that it was only time before the man was found, and realised the state that he was in, muddied and blooded and an obvious target for scrutiny. There was no way that in his present condition he could move around the station area, and search for an assassin.

Passing one of the small huts, Lawrence looked through a small window into the gloom inside, verifying that there were no occupants. He also saw a small sink, served by one dripping tap, and slipped inside to try to clean himself up. This was no mean task, with what little was available to him, but clean water worked its magic and although still wet, Lawrence made himself as presentable as possible, even managing to replace the dressing, although it sometimes failed and he had to restore it with pressure from his palm.

He fell back against the door, jaded and exhausted, and as physically uncomfortable as any man could get, but he was still active and free, with one damn German behind him. He looked at his watch. Almost noon. Soon, he must begin his task of finding the potential killer of the most hated man in Europe, and do everything he could to keep him alive.

Chapter Five
En Passant

Despite his expectations, the rain seemed to have set in for the duration, and occasional peals of thunder added to the discomfort of the day. Lawrence left the hut and worked his way around toward the main station buildings, keeping his eyes skinned for any sign of a sniper. He identified the fact that the assassin must take position within the sealed area, as the outer fence would nullify any clear view of the Fuhrer.

Lawrence checked his watch again. Twelve fifteen, almost. The main station structure was what he had expected of the place, from the photographs that he had been shown. Surprisingly, the weather seemed to have sapped the enthusiasm of the guards, who he observed had found shelter in any covered spot that shielded them from the rain, to the detriment of knots of civilians who had found themselves confined in the compound until the passing of their leader. Whether any of them were aware of the reason for their quarantine, Lawrence knew not, and decided to take a look inside the main station building.

He stepped across the threshold as thunder followed the lightening that lit up the sky, taking off his cap and striking it against his thigh, as if his condition was wholly due to the weather. The space was crowded, with every seat taken, and children double parked on their parent's laps. Along one side of the room, a small counter sold coffee and other minor comestibles, the long queue evidencing a roaring trade among the

SS guards who often pushed their way ahead of the civilians waiting patiently in line.

Lawrence took a quick look around and made his way down toward the line of customers hoping for coffee before the supplies ran out. He had just passed the head of the line, when a guard reached out a hand toward him. Lawrence halted, and looked around to see a smiling face beneath a dark grey helmet.

"Herr Oberleutnant," the soldier said, his outspread arm indicating a space made in front of him, "bitte…"

Lawrence made a curt nod and stepped into the line. He tipped a finger to his forehead.

"Danke."

Lawrence took his coffee and offered paper Marks, unsure of the cost of such things at this stage of the war. He nodded his thanks once more to the soldier who let him into the line, then found a place on the wall nearest the door, where he could drink his coffee and take a look around at those within.

The coffee was just ersatz, a brew that took the place of the real stuff in wartime, but it mattered little for one who had nothing between his lips for some hours, except for the tongue of a German guard. Lawrence let his eyes take in the space and the people waiting there. Any one of them could be the one he was looking for, assuming that there may be only one. Nothing, and nobody caught his attention, but that perhaps showed that he was looking for a professional who just blended into the crowd, and would not risk revealing himself until necessary, if even then.

Lawrence finished the ersatz coffee to the last drop and was glad of it. He left the mug on the window sill and went outside, keeping under the cover of the canopy which stretched out to the nearest railway track. He guessed that in a couple of hours this was where Hitler would be ushered to board his train, and designated this for routine investigation. Here it seemed, was where the Fuhrer would be most covered by the security, and the overhang of the canopy, so perhaps he should also look further out, to where a sniper might shoot from some distance.

He considered the other side of the tracks, but decided that this was a doubtful direction as the entourage on the platform would then be covered by the train itself, not a good line of sight to give confidence of success.

People, hoping to board a train eventually, still milled around along the platform, the weather making negotiating the whole length of the structure somewhat difficult. No-one seemed to give Lawrence any second look, many being as wet and dishevelled as he was, and perhaps for the first time in his life, he praised a thunderstorm.

Occasionally, he noticed someone take a casual stare at his facial wound, but found that his best Teutonic frown deflected their eyes to any further glances. He slowly walked the length of the main station building, bearing in mind Sergeant Bull's constant advice to be aware of what his surroundings offered, in his own defence, should they be needed. Lawrence looked casually through every window and door, large and small, for any possible passage of a bullet, but found little to suspect.

At the end of the platform, he halted and looked around the corner, finding a park for all kinds of trolleys and carts, used by the railway staff to convey goods to and from the trains. This, he thought, may be worth investigating further. He raised his hand and looked at the dial of his wrist watch. Twelve fifty-five.

The thought crossed his mind as to how he would deal with the assassin, if and when he found him. It was something that he had thought about many times, but then it had all seemed so far away, but now that he was on the cusp of the action, he had decisions to make. Of course, it all depended upon where and how the killer was to set himself up to complete his mission. He had no doubt that the security around the Fuhrer had gone to every extreme to check the area, so either the shooter was good at his planning, or would wait until the last minute to take position. That meant that Lawrence would have little time to act, but how would he do that so silently that he could then walk calmly into the waiting room and wait to be approached by his partisan saviours? Shooting the assassin was a possibility, but only by using the noise reducer that Rutter had given him. Without that, his only options would have been more physical, and either way, he must do the job quietly in order not to be discovered and questioned. Suddenly, he felt that many of his chances were taking a deep dive into a dark place.

Standing upon the edge of the platform, Lawrence looked across through the passing people toward where several SS guards were converging toward an officer, who was stood in the rain, clad in a long, black leather coat, with rain dripping from his sharp cap. As he looked on, the officer appeared to be chastising his soldiers, but for what, Lawrence could not decide. Maybe they had found the guard that he had the confrontation with. But if that were the case, surely the whole station compound would be alerted. Still, the officer berated his men, speaking furiously and finally jerking a finger toward his face in some strange interpretation of anger at their failures.

Thunder boomed above, followed by a further lightening flash that took his attention from the drama down the track.

Lawrence looked up at the dark skies, and waited for another. When he looked back, the knot of soldiers had gone, lost in the host of railway workers who hurried from one dry place of work to another.

He wondered from which direction the Hitler entourage would arrive, and how they would progress to join the train. It mattered somewhat, as that would indicate far better the location of the shooter. Lawrence decided to work methodically from where he started, and made his way back along the platform, avoiding the milling civilians, but progressing unhurried and keeping his hat pulled well over his face, as best he could. Passing the open doors to the waiting room again, he found the situation unchanged, apart from the line for coffee which had disappeared, possibly due to exhaustion of ingredients. A sign on the counter top, advising 'abgeschlossen (closed)', confirmed it.

Reaching the opposite end of the platform, the place where he had ascended first, he looked out, his eyes following the track, to where it quickly disappeared around a bend where the forest closed in. He decided that this gave little recourse for a sniper, and all but discounted the possibility, although he did keep it in mind for a swift retreat if it came to that.

Slipping down the three steps back into the weather, Lawrence made his way around to the back of the station building, where long grass and thick foliage claimed the open ground that stretched over to the fence. He pulled his collar tighter around his neck and looked for anything that might lead to the roof, a place for the assassin to find a clear shot from above. He had noticed that along the length of the platform canopy there were small sections which had fallen away with time, and offered limited opportunity for a sniper, and any of these may have been pre-prepared by the shooter.

There was nothing to be found, but he surprised a long-coated guard relieving himself in the thick foliage, his rifle strung over his back. Lawrence could not resist the opportunity, he snapped his heels and saluted, amused as the soldier fumbled to return the gesture. He shook his head and smiled.

"At ease, soldier." He grinned in perfect German. "Carry on, please."

Lawrence walked by, but felt confident enough to turn back, his head inclined as he had seen haughty German officers do under interrogation.

"Have you seen anything back here? Anything?"

The soldier straightened and made himself presentable, unslinging his rifle.

"Nein! Herr Oberleutnant. Nichts!"

Lawrence walked away, somewhat pleased at his interaction with the soldier. He could have walked on, but that, he guessed, was not the manner of a German officer under such circumstances.

As he made his way around the building, he took particular interest in the roof, and any access to it, feeling that this would be the best position for a killing shot, possibly before the target reached the cover of the canopy. Nothing. Lawrence let the idea of a close up attempt to kill Hitler rattle around in his mind, but whichever way he examined the concept, it always came out as suicidal. He felt the chances of a successful mission beginning to fade, and tried to formulate a better plan.

As the rain ceased a little, he marched over to the trolley park, taking a good look at the equipment, but there was nothing which stood out as being suspicious, and much of it was broken and bent anyway. What ladders there were failed to be of any use, due to lack of length, broken rungs and general disrepair. As the rain stopped, more civilians began to abandon the smoky space of the waiting room, and splashed onto the platform. More guards appeared from their dry retreats and began to look more concerned with the security of the compound. Several began to check papers, even though they may have been checked before.

Lawrence felt confidence in the documentation that he had been given, but he knew the faults of overconfidence, and mentally went over his assumed story in his mind. He thought that now the weather had improved, that maybe the sniper would begin to seek out his position, if he had not already done so, and warned himself that now he must increase his scrutiny of the place. It was now ten past two in the afternoon, and the minutes were ticking away.

Down the track, opposite to the bend which Lawrence had identified as a possible escape route, on the other side of the station, the sound of steam escaping the boilers announced the arrival of the Fuhrer's personal train, the 'Fuhrersonderzug'. Lawrence pulled himself inside the entrance to the waiting room, and looked down the line, to where two powerful steam engines, double-headed, backed slowly closer to the station. Beyond the two engines, specialised coaches were being hauled, clicking and squealing over the track. Lawrence guessed that there might be fifteen or sixteen of them, the function of which, apart from two 88 flak-gun wagons, he had little idea.

The engines halted, still some distance from the platform and clouds of white hissed from the steam chests on either side of the front wheels, hiding the mighty steel machines. Some activity beyond the nearest track included a group of SS soldiers, and railway workers, who appeared to be preparing to uncouple the coaches and divert the locomotives into a siding, which after changing the points would allow them to move forward and take their place at the other end of the coaches. They would then be recoupled for the Journey to Berlin.

The deep squeal of steel upon steel accompanied the forward movement of the locomotives to the prepared positions. Lawrence watched with some interest, wondering if this might be another situation that he needed to monitor. But he doubted that it could be, as the engines, wagons and coaches provided a perfect shield on the opposite side. The advantage point had to be on the station side.

As Lawrence looked again for a shooter's nest, the heavy huff-chuff of the engines identified that the two huge machines were edging toward a situation where they could re-couple, ready for the return journey to Berlin, and eventually on to the Berghof, Hitler's mountain home.

It seemed a strange thought, that within the next two hours it would all be over. Either Hitler would be alive, and he might have a hell of a lot of talking to do to explain it to the Germans, or if Hitler died, and he, Lawrence, lived to tell the tale, then he might have to do the same to his masters in London. Almost a lose-lose, but perhaps not quite. Yet.

The heavy clank of shunted iron and screaming chains declared the final completion of the train, punctuated finally by a last release of white clouds from the steam chest. Then, almost imperceivably, the whole column of the 'Brandenburg' began to edge back toward the station platform, from where, soon, the most powerful man in Europe would embark. At any other time, it might be an exciting experience, but at that moment, Lawrence felt the pit of his stomach looking for escape.

It was almost a panic that began to take over his natural calm in moments of stress, but it was not a stress felt by most in such situations. Lawrence's issues were concerned with the pieces falling into place where his mind dictated, the need to plan several steps ahead so that each was prepared and ready, but not only that, each step must have their own series of possibilities, which must also be planned and nurtured until he could pick the best from the opportunities that were presented before him.

This situation, he knew, was nothing that he could formulate his mind around, and wondered how those in London could ever expect success from such a hastily cobbled scheme. Of course, it was a shot in the dark, he could see that, with a low value pawn such as himself thrown into the mix, as the best hope with the least loss. So, why did he feel obligated to try so hard to complete his work? His boys would be cared for and credited to some extent for what little he might achieve, even if he threw the towel into the ring and disappeared right then. But he knew why. Once committed to the game, the die was cast and the pieces were lined in their ranks and ready for battle. It was the way that his nature had always played him, usurping his brain for its own amusement and setting him into the fray, lined him up against the guns and close enough to see the match to the touch-hole. But while the pieces lined up and gave him the orders of attack, they gave nothing for retreat, or surrender.

And yet, Lawrence had come through the smoke many times, virtually unscathed, apart from the enforced scarring of recent days. He had even sidestepped the hangman, and now here he was once more looking up the skirts of the reaper, posted dead to all he knew, except the latter.

Men's lives depended in him, or so they told him. Surely that would be the incentive for any decent person, and the more he let it ramble through his mind, the images grew stronger, and mingled with those that he harboured from Dunkirk, the ones which refused to part from him and go on their way.

Two thirty. The engines lay waiting just beyond the platform, with their haulage parallel to its edge, hiding what lay beyond as he had guessed, but forming a perfect canyon, leaving only a few small spaces for anyone to make a sniper's nest. Lawrence put himself in the marksman's place and looked for his own preference, and knew it had to be high and with a clear sight of the Fuhrer. The canopy covered most of the overhead possibilities, so it had to be along the platform, from one of two directions.

He stood at the corner of the platform nearest the end of the train, on the ground near the steps, keeping his head low, and an eye on the movements of guards, who seemed to double with every blink. He rubbed the scar to ease the irritation that it had begun to cause him, finding that the dressing was losing its power to hold.

Lawrence decided to use the hour left him to check as far along the track in each direction as he could, and try to spot the gunman. First, he would use his position to make his way back to the fence, then keep low in the foliage and work his way along until satisfied that it was clear, or as satisfied as he could be. Then he would do the same on the other side, but the trees came closer there, so it would be quicker to complete his sweep. It began to rain again.

He would also need to cross in front of the main guard post, which he had seen before gaining entry to the station, and had been set up a hundred yards away, along the main road. Deciding that an overt stance was the more appropriate, he stood to his full height, walked into the centre of the muddy road and turned back the way that he had come, then waved furiously, as if ordering men to follow, as if he were some haughty Prussian officer, at the pinnacle of his arrogance.

It seemed to work, as no-one challenged him from down the road, puffs of blue smoke from some of the guards perhaps evidencing another urgency. He realised, however, that he dared not try the same thing twice. At a time like this, even German officers showed their papers.

Thoroughly soaked, he worked his way along the fence, the elastic of plants springing back in an attempt to wet him further. Stopping some distance from the trees, he looked intensely up into the foliage, trying not to miss anything that might suggest his quarry. He moved closer and looked for footprints in the mud, but there was nothing. Turning back, he saw the distance to the platform area and knew it was an impossible shot, the distance and the civilians who might be in between spoiling the possibilities. It had to be the opposite side. It was almost three.

Working back to the gap in the fence that led to the guard post, he kneeled and looked to see if there were any soldiers looking in his direction. The last thing he wanted was to make a run for it, and knew that it was his own paranoia that was wanting him to remain anonymous. His papers were good, hopefully, but caution was always a good companion.

Another peal of thunder cracked and lit up the sky with attendant lightening, so loud that the four guards recoiled and looked up into the sky. It was all that Lawrence needed and he thanked providence for a stormy day. Quickly, he leapt across the gap and back into the foliage on the other side. But now, he noticed many more guards, obviously searching for something. Several of them were coming toward him. Searching the long grasses, sweeping back and forth with a stick. Lawrence swallowed hard, wondering if this was where he tested whether Kurt Mass's papers were still in order, but he could not just jump out of the long grass in the rain.

They were coming closer, too close for comfort. He edged around to one side as the soldiers advanced, looking intensely into the shadows of the foliage, blinking away the rain that persisted. Two were coming close, to pass on either side of him. Lawrence tensed, and slowly let his hand drop to his pocket, where he had placed the Walther pistol belonging to the first guard that he had encountered, and felt the cold grip, his thumb searching for the safety…

*

A sound from the road marked the advance of traffic. He tried to look around, but there was too much of the long grass invading his vision. Through the rain and the grass, Lawrence could make out the nearest Germans, standing to attention for some reason, with their backs toward him. Quickly, he found a broken branch and followed their lead, stretching ramrod straight as a black Mercedes 770, converted with an extra axle, rolled through the fence opening, its six wheels splashing mud and rainwater in every direction. He edged slowly away from the guards, and as soon as the moment passed, and they began to return to their duties, Lawrence turned away and began to switch the grass as if he were one of them, involved in the search.

The black car pulled around the back of the station building, toward the area he had been intending as his last search, and he saw the swastika pennant flapping in the rain.

"God-damn!" Lawrence thought, in English. "The bloody man's early!"

He was about to break into a run, to do his best to get close enough to act as some kind of shield; one last throw of the dice, of the many that he had rolled successfully lately, maybe to finally join the ranks of those he could not save by failure in his task.

Guards formed a wall and Lawrence could only catch the briefest of glimpses of the one that he was tasked to protect, swaddled in black leather with a dark, flat military hat, suddenly shielded by a plethora of dark umbrellas to keep him from the rain.

Lawrence tried for the other direction, and made his way to the platform, where he just managed to reach the raised floor before SS managed to staunch the wave of admiring civilians who flocked to greet their leader. The people pressed ever closer to catch a glimpse of the man, kept secure in a ring of steel and leather. Hitler climbed the three steps up onto the platform, and paused briefly to return the greeting, before continuing along in the dry. SS guards pushed people away roughly, keeping a sterile ring around the man at all times. Someone fell and Lawrence used the space to advance further, beginning to wonder if London had got it all wrong, and perhaps someone in the crowd might after all be the assassin. He jerked his head one way, then the other, frantically trying to locate any possible killer among the bobbing heads and waving arms.

Somewhere among the jostle, he caught the brief sight of an officer, looking in his direction, as if the man recognised him and wished to maintain eye contact. The last thing Lawrence wanted was recognition of any kind, and wondered if perhaps Denning should have found a man less like the person he was portraying. All he needed right then was some-one who might wish to remake an old acquaintance. He dropped as low as he could while still able to observe the crowd around Hitler's entourage and edged forward.

Forcefully making their way down the side of the train, the group reached the main door to the waiting room, and Lawrence was almost up to them, his eyes flicking one way, then the other, dreading the sound of a gunshot. Rain battered the canopy above, when suddenly there was a commotion nearby. Lawrence turned to investigate the upheaval, noticing that there was a rear entrance to the waiting room at the far side of the building, and both doors had been flung open. Emerging from the dark interior was a pitiful sight, a man with his face blue and bloodied, and in a dreadful condition, trying to speak, with arms outstretched and lunging toward the Hitler group.

Lawrence recognised him immediately as the first guard that he had encountered, and left in that condition, and he had hoped dead. The crowd quietened and parted a little at the sight of the almost zombie like apparition, arms outstretched and pushing between them, toward the group surrounding the Fuhrer. Those unable to see the wounded guard continued cheering and pushing forward, making a maelstrom of people, bustling in all directions and against each other. The soldier was trying to speak, but was hindered by part of his tongue not being present, and so gurgled illegibly and physically protested with his arms flailing.

Still huddled to remain unseen, Lawrence was almost within touching distance as the man pressed through the tangle of people, trying to make contact with his fellows around Hitler. For one brief moment, the soldiers and the Fuhrer froze in astonishment at the commotion, then the bodyguard responded by contracting around their leader.

Lawrence sprang forward, formulating a plan of action, as pawn took pawn with the speed of a panther. As he leapt, his right hand reached for his pocket and the Walther pistol that he had taken from the man, in case he needed an increase in firepower. That time was now, but Lawrence had decided upon a riskier use for the gun. At any moment, he expected the sound of that single shot which would herald the failure of his mission, but non came.

Now committed to his own immediate survival, Lawrence took hold of the pistol and threw it to the ground, where it clattered amongst the feet of the crowd, its flight hidden by the press of bodies as they constantly changed position. The Englishman grabbed hold of the guard and became entangled in a vicious struggle as he was identified by his opponent. As they turned in a waltz of combat, the multitude parted, ebbed and flowed around them, scattering as both bodies fell to the ground and continued their struggle.

Lawrence rapidly put his mind through the lessons that Sergeant Bull had instilled in him, but this was no place to unfold the button noose again, and so used every muscle to avoid the blows and return them with as much force and speed as he could. The German was still suffering from his previous encounter with Lawrence, and turned to the defensive, but there was no let up, and the man on top of him rode the violence with little apparent mercy. It continued until several of the leader's bodyguards heaved a pathway through the upheaval of civilians and grabbed Lawrence roughly, two others heaving the bloodied tongue-less guard to his unsteady feet, on the verge of unconsciousness.

An SS major appeared between the antagonists.

"Was ist denn hier los?" he asked. "Was ist los?"

Lawrence pressed forward a little, still held by the SS bodyguard.

"This man tried to shoot the Fuhrer!" He rasped sharply. "I saw him, saw the pistol, aimed at the Fuhrer!"

The major twisted his face in disbelief. It all seemed so far away from two soldiers fighting.

"Was?"

The crowd were chattering excitedly amongst themselves, and the noise was increasing as the explanation spread.

"Silence!" shouted the officer, and the people around complied immediately.

He turned back to Lawrence, who made an effort to point at the pistol on the ground, and then flung his head in that direction to confirm the evidence.

"Sehen Sie! (Look)," he added. "Pistole."

A soldier picked up the gun and handed it to the major, who examined it, while the battered sentry tried to protest in a splash of blood from his mouth and half illegible words. The SS officer looked at him, then Lawrence.

"What has happened to him?" he asked, one eyebrow dancing above the other.

Lawrence feigned frustration with himself.

"I may have been a little over diligent, but he was trying to shoot the Fuhrer," he explained.

The pistol was shown to the unfortunate guard by the officer. He waved it in front of the man's face, he asked calmly…

"This is yours?"

Again. there was protest and a spattering of blood. The major found a handkerchief and wiped as off much red as he could from his grey tunic. Lawrence wanted to do as much damage as he could, and did not wait for any remonstration. He slapped his black leather holster.

"I still have mine," he declared. "You want to see?"

The officer shrugged, already knowing how this was due to end. Lawrence unclipped the button and folded back the flap, revealing the Luger's grip. A wry smile from the major to the guard revealed how he believed the incident had evolved. Someone in the crowd nearby called out, an unseen woman's voice that added to the narrative.

"Ja!" It called out. "Ja, I saw it" He tried to shoot the Fuhrer.

Someone else joined in the denunciation.

"I saw him too!" It confirmed, adding to the conviction for an unseen weapon, but allowing their judgement to take over their observations.

It became a condemnation of the innocent, the crowd swayed by their belief that others had actually experienced the outrage, and added their voices to the denunciation of the crime.

"Nein! Nein!" Came the burble of indistinct dissent from the beleaguered sentry.

Before any more could be said, another tall officer pushed through from behind the major. Lawrence noted the general's pips on his shoulders and the red and gold of his cap. His leather coat was draped over his shoulders, and he wore a pair of gold rimmed spectacles. He looked hard at Lawrence, then without any further conversation to the combatants, spoke to the other officer, nodding in the direction of the guard.

"Shoot him!" he ordered.

The major confirmed to order to his men with a flick of his head, and the screaming man was hauled away, a shot announcing his demise a short time later. In the confusion, Lawrence had glimpsed a stern face with a tight, dark moustache peering through the bobbing heads, just for a moment, before it was ushered away toward one of the carriages, and out of his sight. Still in the custody of the SS, a thought spread like a forest fire through his brain…

"Hah! God-damn! The bastards still alive!"

*

Within a very short time, the whole platform had been cleared, the civilians cast out into the open where they became victims of the storm; men, women and children left to the mercy of the rain without concern. Hitler was long gone, swept into the luxury of his personal car among the string of carriages that dominated the station.

Lawrence was still surrounded by SS officers and men, split into several groups and each lost in a different conversation. Just two guards shared the space close to him, and he wondered if this might be the time to make his exit, but it would be a risky attempt, and he knew it. Better just bluff it out and see where it led before throwing himself once more into that dark hole.

Lawrence felt no guilt over the executed German, but was pleased that his failure to do the job properly had paid a dividend of sorts. A kind of satisfaction came over him, the way that the pieces had co-ordinated to protect a mere pawn, a mere chancer, a late-comer to the game with no experience of the opponent. His problem was that he had no idea how far the game had progressed, or where the pieces of each side were situated, or whose turn to move was next. Pawns were often that way, stepping one square at a time across the board, sometimes isolated and prostrated to the enemy, and then eliminated with little interest from one side or the other. Or occasionally they moved with extended luck, hiding in the shadow of a rook or a knight, with their burrows always discovered as the game progresses, when a predatory bishop seeks them out.

What the hell was happening here, Lawrence wondered?

There had been no attempt at the life of the Fuhrer, unless a silenced bullet had missed, as well as another opportunity. There had been no confusion of his bodyguard in pursuit of an assassin, only the confusion he, Lawrence, had caused to save his own skin. Had that in itself put off the shooter, created enough upheaval to protect Hitler? How the hell did Lawrence know? He waited, his mind going through his options, and wondering what was next.

An officer dropped from the steps of one of the railway cars and hurried over to where Lawrence was held. He snapped the short distance down the platform and took him brusquely by the arm, leading him to where the rain managed to find a gap between the carriage and the canopy, in front of a darkened glass window. The two remained in the wet for a few moments, until the window slid slowly down, and a sallow face appeared from the gloom inside, still wearing a brown military cap.

Lawrence knew the face well, as everyone in the world might. He snapped to attention, the rain tracing the contours of his face and dampening his collar and shoulders.

"My Fuhrer!" Lawrence saluted.

Hitler halted at the window and looked down at him from the carriage, his face stern and serious. A trembling hand dashed from the window and offered it out. Lawrence grasped it firmly, thinking...

'Thank God. If they shoot him now, I'm in the clear with London'.

"Sir!" said Lawrence.

Hitler's demeanour changed a little.

"It appears that I owe you my thanks. I am told that you are the officer who confronted the assassin?" He looked at the rank. "Oberleutnant?"

"I am happy to do my duty, my Fuhrer," said Lawrence, wondering if he might be making a meal of it a little, but feeling somewhat apprehensive at the same time. "It happened so quickly."

Hitler withdrew his arm, aware that it was getting wet, but allowed others to stand in the rain. A thunderclap pealed and the leader's eyes danced slightly upward with no movement of his head.

"What's wrong with your face, soldier?" Hitler asked.

"British grenade, sir," replied Lawrence. "A little too close."

The Fuhrer nodded slowly.

"You received medical treatment for this wound?"

Lawrence touched his cheek, where the scar was revealed by the peeling dressing.

"Yes, sir," he confirmed. "But I think it needs looking at again. I will…"

Hitler turned slightly and spoke to someone behind him in the dark of the carriage, cutting off Lawrence in mid-sentence. There was a hushed conversation, then the leader looked back briefly.

"You are waiting for a train to Berlin, Oberleutnant?"

"Yes, sir. I have leave for another ten days, medical leave, and my mother is terminally ill, so I hope to…"

'Lay it on thick,' Lawrence thought.

Once again, Hitler cut into the reply, then looked back down at Lawrence, smiled and closed the window. Lawrence blew out a breath of relief and looked at the officer next to him. They stood there for a few moments, but that seemed to be the end of the interaction. They stood back from the rain slipping down beside the carriage.

"I was going to ask for his autograph." The Englishman grinned.

Another officer had left the train by the unfolded carriage steps and approached the two officers waiting by the window. Lawrence saw that his insignia was of a General of Division. He clicked to the salute. The General smiled.

"You can have more than his autograph," he imparted, "you are dining with him tonight."

Lawrence blustered at the suggestion.

"I... I have to... Berlin, I have to reach Berlin... my mother is..."

The General raised a hand and smiled deeper.

"Calm down, Oberleutnant. It is a great honour, and you will be in Berlin sooner, by the personal train of the Fuhrer."

"But, but..."

"Take it easy, soldier. You will have something to tell your grand-children, how you spent time with the Fuhrer on his personal train. Not many of your rank can claim this." He raised a hand to indicate a carriage further down the train. "Please. Let us get you out of these wet clothes, and see to your wound. The Fuhrer is concerned that you are cared for."

When a heart drops with a heavier impact than gravity against the stomach, the brain often admits that all is lost. So it was with Lawrence, already salivating at his good fortune and ready to join the anonymity of the waiting room to wait for salvation. It was not to be, and the great chess-master had once more advanced the pawn to one last vulnerable square, where every piece on the board envied its resilience, and determined to end it.

He tried not to look as he felt, urged triumphantly onward to the next move, and instead of the fleeting valour that he thought to take advantage of, found himself thrust into the very heart of the Reich, in the very cocoon of the Fuhrer himself, and hoped he could remember the order of cutlery when the time came.

Chapter Six
Giuoco Piano (A Quiet Game)

Lawrence was thrust onto the train, led down a corridor, and showed to a small compartment, where he sat in damp clothing and looked out onto the opposite side of the train from the platform. He could see part of the loop, where the locomotives could make a turn, ready to return to Berlin. Beyond were coaling slips and water cranes, and everything else that might service a steam locomotive, and beyond that the trees that surrounded the small station halt.

He chided himself for enjoying the sense of victory too much, knowing that he should have slipped away in the crowd before being backed into the limelight under the Fuhrer's moustache. But the margin for that had been slim, and in truth he had little means of escaping the results of his action.

A Major slipped the door and entered with a fresh uniform on a hangar, which looked about his size, new boots and socks and underwear. Lawrence was glad of the socks; he had walked on damp wool since the parachute drop.

He stood and saluted. The Major grinned and handed over the clothing.

"You are a Major, now," he said, as if it were a joke. "Someone will collect your wet things and see that they are cleaned. You will need to keep your papers and personal items. Someone will be along to bring you coffee and see to your medical needs. Perhaps later, something a little stronger." He mimicked the act of drinking alcohol. "I would wish to welcome you aboard the Fuhrersonderzug, 'Brandenburg'.

"Danke schön," Lawrence thanked him.

"Bitte." The Major answered, and left, locking the door behind him.

'Well, this was a hell of a turn up for the books that no-one had foreseen', Lawrence thought as he stripped and put on the new uniform, admiring the shoulder insignia in the small mirror opposite the long seat. Damn, the Germans had style in their uniforms, different from British khaki that still looked like it belonged in the Khyber Pass.

Shortly after, an orderly knocked, unlocked and delivered coffee. Not the mud in a cup that he was used to, but the real stuff, and cream, all served in silver with biscuits to make the illusion. Lord, this was living. But even the swallow of real coffee again could not dismiss the strange feelings of being in the wrong place at the wrong time. It was never meant to be like this, with nothing quite what it seemed, where everything appeared to be going right, but all for the wrong reasons. At the back of his mind, Lawrence never quite believed that he could succeed in this task, but always determined to try to see it through, if only for his own personal reasons. And so, here he was, praised by Adolf Hitler for an act of valour that he did not perform, by an assassin that he never found, and may not have even got one round away. Like the pawns in this whole, damn war, he was buffeted around by strangers, against those who were stranger still.

There was a slight knock on the door and Lawrence heard the key turn once more. The polished walnut slid open to reveal a smartly dressed woman of about his own age, dressed in a grey suit and dark cravat. She wore flat shoes and Lawrence noticed the small wristwatch with the swastika motif on the face. He could detect little make up and the most delicate shade of lipstick.

She seemed a little shy, and had trouble making eye contact, keeping focus mainly on the carpeted floor until Lawrence spoke first as she entered, carrying a tray of medicinal items. Standing, Lawrence addressed her, formally.

"Guten Abend, Fraulein."

She smiled awkwardly.

"Guten Abend, Herr Oberleutnant." She returned the greeting. "I have been asked to renew your dressing." She looked up. "Do you require surgical attention?"

He shrugged away the thought.

"Nein, danke," he confirmed. "I've had enough of medics pushing my face around. It's mainly just sore, and the rain did not help."

She told him to sit down and closed the door behind her, then walked over to the small table by the window and settled the tray there. From where Lawrence sat, he could see his own face in the oval mirror opposite. As the woman removed the dressing, he could see the twisted side of his face reflected there. She winced a little.

"I'm sorry," he said. "If you wish to leave it, I can manage myself."

She looked into his eyes for the first time, and shook her head.

"It's all right, I have seen wounds before."

There was an uneasy silence while she cleaned the injury, and he was surprised at the amount of dirt and grime that it had accumulated.

"You are a nurse?" Lawrence asked.

The woman shook her head, and kept working on his scars.

"I have been on the General's staff for a while, as a communications secretary, but I have general experience in medical aid. All of the secretaries have."

"The General?" Lawrence asked.

She looked at him, as if he had never heard of the rank of General before.

"General Muller. He is a tactical aid to the Fuhrer."

Lawrence smiled the smile of a seasoned soldier.

"I have seen Generals before."

The woman laughed.

"This train is full of Generals," she told him. "And Colonels, sometimes a Field Marshal, but rarely much below a Major, except for the Fuhrer's personal guard, but they are in another part of the train."

"Then I am a fish out of water," Lawrence admitted.

She finished and began drying his face.

"I think that you are in a rank of your own, Oberleutnant Maas, and respected by everyone on this train for your courage in saving the Fuhrer."

"Ah." He exclaimed, wearily, knowing the truth but playing the game.

The woman still seemed reserved and inward as she stood and gathered her things.

"May I know your name, Fraulein?"

She turned with a slightly coy expression.

"Elsa Schmidt."

Lawrence nodded his thanks.

"Thank you, Elsa Schmidt."

*

After Elsa had gone, Lawrence looked at himself in the mirror, turning his head to look at the clean dressing which hid the ugly scar that he had endured. His eyes moved slowly down to look at the crisp Major's uniform that he now wore, more green than grey and clasped at the waist by a polished black belt.

When they took his wet clothing, they also took his sidearm, and for a moment, he felt some concern over the small noise reduction cylinder that had been in his pocket, which fitted onto the barrel of the Luger, and which they were bound to find. However, it was not a standard issue piece of equipment, and could easily be mistaken for some random piece of tubing that could be found on any piece of military equipment, its purpose discovered only by close examination. He decided that if it was discovered, the circumstances being as they were, he had a good chance to invent some story to explain it.

Lawrence pulled the vents of the tunic, admiring the fit. Then, his gaze into the mirror froze, his mind working on something that concerned him, something that had assaulted his logic, just a small thing that irritated his reasoning like the Princess and the pea. He turned to look at the window, frosted against the bustle of people moving along the platform, and then reached down to the table where he had put his papers before removing the old tunic. Lawrence looked hard at the knot of worn documents and pressed his lips tightly together, trying to recall every second of the events of the last hour. It was just a small thing, infinitesimal in the scale of things, but important enough to trouble him. He put it into the files of his mind, and told himself not to be so alarmed.

He blinked it away, and told himself that he was paranoid, but who would not be under his circumstances? For once, he seemed to be on the better side of fortune, the subject of esteem and gratitude. Of course, it was undeserved and the figure offering these platitudes was the vilest man in history, but hell, beggars can't be choosers.

He sat and finished the last biscuit. The lock on the door clicked and slid open, to reveal a senior officer with General's pips, which set well against the grey and red stripes of his uniform. Behind the General were two SS guards at attention. A smile was offered as the door closed, and shut out the guards, followed by a curt nod as Lawrence rose quickly to his feet and came to attention.

"Please. At ease, Oberleutnant," said the General, apparently forgetting his promotion. "I hope that you have been looked after quite well. You will understand that we have certain duties to perform concerning the welfare and safety of the Fuhrer, and after such an incident as that which has just occurred, we must ensure that all security checks are carried out before we leave for Berlin."

Before he could reply, the General held out a hand, which Lawrence took, nervously. The officer was surprisingly young for such a rank, but then, many of Hitler's senior ranks were, the older ones perhaps thinned by the length of the war. He was good looking, with deep brown eyes and regular features, and exuded authority.

"Thank you, sir. I have had real coffee, for the first time for many months." Lawrence returned the goodwill in his own way.

The General grinned.

"I think that you will have as much coffee as you wish, at least while you are on this train." He almost whispered, his eyes widening to emphasise the statement. "What you did out there will not be forgotten. The Fuhrer does not treat such loyalty lightly."

He straightened.

"Now," he declared. "We must deal with a few formalities, after which, you are free to move around this section of the train. This will be your personal space until we reach Berlin, by direct sanction of the Fuhrer. You may request anything at any time." He levelled a hand toward the engine end of the train. "This evening, you will dine with the Fuhrer, and his staff. The train will be leaving in the next twenty minutes, and we should reach Berlin by eight thirty, the day after tomorrow."

The General could see the unease in Lawrence's eyes.

"Do not worry. The Fuhrer is at his best when socialising, and you will be briefed before you attend the meal, so be not concerned. I am certain that second to the Fuhrer, you will be the guest of honour, so to speak. Now, I should formally check your papers."

The General reached over and took the documents that Lawrence handed over. He opened the army paybook and briefly looked into it. After a moment, he handed them back, and saluted.

"Oberleutnant Maas. It is a pleasure to meet you. Is there anyone you wish us to contact for you in Berlin, to perhaps inform them of your arrival in two days? We have connection points along the tracks for regular communications."

Lawrence's heart sank a little, picturing so many scenarios where this might betray him when they reached Berlin, if those aboard the train took matters into their own hands, young Frauleins with flowers, or an elderly woman, puzzled by the man who stood before her, posturing as her son. Apart from the mother, he had little further knowledge of Maas's extended family. There had not been time enough.

"Oh, no, thank you, General," Lawrence garbled. "I would prefer to surprise those at home."

The General cast the offer aside with a wave of his hand.

"Ach. As you wish."

There was a sharp whistle from the front of the train, and a brief shunt as the double locomotive took up the slack of the carriages and wagons. Lawrence could hear the staccato huff of the steam valves, gaining slowly in acceleration, and see the animated blur of steam through the frosted window.

"Ah!" the general said, as he turned toward the door. "We are moving, a little late, which will annoy the Fuhrer, but better late than never," he paused. "I am General Muller, by the way. We will meet later, but tell me, Maas, are you a card player?"

Lawrence shook his head.

"Chess is my game, sir," he admitted.

Muller clapped his hands.

"Better still, an intelligent game! Not sullied by the invasion of alcohol and tobacco as so many of this train's pastimes tend to be. Journeys on the Brandenburg can be tedious, so when you feel ready, please join us in the rear dining car. The guard will show you the way." He smiled again. "Would you like more coffee? It is the least we can do for a hero."

*

Accepting more coffee seemed the better idea, allowing a little time to think it through. He had no wish to be transported to Berlin; in fact, if there was anywhere on the planet that he would prefer not to be induced to see the sights, it was Berlin. He looked at the window, then pressed his face to the design where he could peer through the open sections of the frosted glass, seeing only forest passing by, with the occasional open area by the tracks. Now and then the figure of a sentry at the present arms passed by near the edge of the tracks, guarding the way as he had been informed by Denning and Rutter. And somewhere up the track, he knew that there was a decoy train rolling ahead of Brandenburg in case of attack.

Lawrence considered breaking the window and leaping out, and that might still be an option, should he be willing to break his neck. Perhaps Brandenburg might halt for coal or water, giving him the chance to slip away before he was found missing. 'Shame to miss the Fuhrer's evening bash, but needs must', he thought. He wondered what the most hated man in Europe was doing right now? Perhaps scrutinising the maps for some small part of England that he had forgotten to bomb, or sending his U-boats to deny the people of Britain oranges and bananas, and other foods that they had all but forgotten the taste of.

But whatever Lawrence's plan of escape was to be, the longer he delayed it, the further away its success seemed to be. And sitting in that compartment was moving him no closer to it, so he bit the bullet and decided to merge with the enemy.

He slipped the door open, now finding it unlocked, and saw that only one guard was now outside. The soldier clicked to attention and Lawrence gave him the nod, tapping an index finger on his temple as seemed to be the routine response by German officers. In the British Army, it was known as the 'tennis elbow' salute.

"Er, the rear dining car?" he asked of the SS guard.

The way was indicated and he turned left, moving along the carriage to the intersection with the next one, rolling gently with the motion of the train. When he reached the end of the corridor, he turned back, and when he saw that the grey clad guard was looking in the opposite direction, he tried the outer door of the coach. It was locked. He slipped across to the other side, past where the intersection doors bobbed slightly out of synchronisation, and tried the other. Locked. His options diminished.

With nowhere else to go, Lawrence grasped the metal and went through to the next carriage. It appeared to be a bathing carriage, lined with several opulent and well fitted bathrooms. He moved along until he came to the junction with the next car and tried the connecting door, finding it open and populated with top German brass of all ranks, higher than Major. For a second, there was almost a silence as his presence was noticed, and then a concerted toast from those with alcoholic drinks, and those without. It became a roar of appreciation. Lord, this was becoming embarrassing.

Lawrence slapped his hands by his sides and clicked his neck, trying to be formal, and still appreciative. Muller appeared and led him forward, halting at a large, polished oak table near one long window.

In true 'Bull' tradition, Lawrence quickly took in the space, checking to see where anything of use in a scrap might be found. Chairs, lamps, and all of the usual items, including trays of cutlery which were some distance away, and which he might find difficulty reaching if it came to it, there being so many Germans in between. The one good thing was that there appeared to be a lack of personal arms for passengers aboard the Fuhrersonderzug, no doubt due to Hitler's paranoia, and rightly so if recent history was to be considered. Lawrence was to learn later that no-one on the train was allowed weapons except the twenty-two men of Hitler's personal bodyguard, stationed in their own carriage further forward.

"Gentlemen!" Muller announced, loudly. "I give you, Oberleutnant Kurt Maas, soon to be raised to Major, and saviour of the Fuhrer." He grinned. "And our opportunity to still win the War."

Lawrence tried as best as he could to look happy. 'Well,

well', he thought, 'if Denning could see me now'.

Muller went through the names in the room, informally putting a face to each one with an outstretched arm, but Lawrence's head spun so much with the impossibility of his situation, that he all but missed every one, recognising only the fact that there seemed to be none of the other names so recognisable in the entourage such as Himmler or Goering. 'Shame', he thought, 'it would be nice to get the set'.

A Colonel blustered forward and grabbed Lawrence by the shoulder, shaking his hand roughly until his head wobbled. Others followed, eager to congratulate him. At the back of the coach were several women, all in grey suits, and he recognised Elsa Schmidt. He tried to smile through the moving heads, but failed the contact.

"Kommen Sie Maas," said the Colonel, pulling him across the coach floor, where the carpet was so thick, it was hard to walk. "Have a drink with us. Tell us how you got that damn wound on your face. Do you need treatment?"

"Nein, danke," answered Lawrence, to the Colonel, whose name he quickly found was Kalmer. "Fraulein Schmidt kindly replaced the dressing. It had been on for some time, and I was most grateful for the attention."

Kalmer, who was already a drink ahead, nudged him in the ribs with his elbow.

"Wouldn't we all like attention from Fraulein Schmidt, yes?"

Lawrence pretended not to have understood. Kalmer was a little shorter than Lawrence and he shuffled around, to look the other directly in the face, speaking with one hand upon his hip. He waved a finger at the hidden scar on Lawrence's face.

"And how did you come by this memento?" he asked. "May I see it?"

Lawrence shrugged and peeled away the dressing to display the wound. Kalmer grimaced and took a sip of his beverage.

"Ah," he said, "with a duelling scar like that, you will have your choice to dance with every pretty woman in Berlin. Yes?"

Lawrence laughed and replaced the linen dressing.

"I doubt that, sir. I doubt it very much."

"And how did you receive such a magnificent trophy?"

"Dancing too close with a British grenade in Holland." Lawrence replied, hoping the scar did him justice and that the surgeon had done his work well.

Another officer, whose name he quickly forgot pulled him into his little knot and the same questions were answered again, each time with Lawrence trying to remember the formula that he had memorised, never overstating his own false part in the action.

As Lawrence was pulled from one group to another, he took care not to drink too much, sipping the drinks he was given slowly to avoid loose talk that might inevitably come with alcohol. Any contradiction that he let slip might easily come back to haunt him, or worse, and it was hard enough to remember the lies sober. Where he could, he disposed of a half glass into someone else's, and from the condition of such early drinkers, he wondered how some of them would be in a good enough state to face the Fuhrer later. He was to be surprised.

When his fame faded, and the cacophony of praise had died down, Lawrence migrated to the less smoky section of the carriage, where he found General Muller and another officer engrossed in a game of chess.

"Ah, Maas," Muller greeted him. "Join us. You will enjoy this game."

Muller was sitting sideways to the oak table. The other officer was staring into the board, but turned to look at Lawrence. He was older, and quite portly, but with a fresh complexion. Muller flattened a palm toward his opponent.

"Maas," Revealed Muller. "This is General Elster."

Lawrence snapped to attention, making it look a little sloppy, as if he had drunk more than he had. Muller downgraded the gesture.

"Ach Maas! We are all friends here. And for you, a salute is un-necessary. Your subservience is no good here, you are one of us."

General Elster returned to his game, only giving the slightest gesture of recognition. Muller shrugged.

"We are avoiding the better part of the proceedings." He explained, jerking a thumb toward the others inside the cigarette smoke. "I do not drink, and Elster here has a heart condition, so we are looked upon as outcasts, and must fill our time with the pastimes of sobriety."

Lawrence smiled hollowly. Muller explained the situation.

"Our little celebrations are…" he paused. "… Quite selective. The Fuhrer likes a little nap once he is on the train; he disapproves of alcohol, and he hates smoking of all kinds, so we have our little gatherings well away from the Fuhrerwagen, but only when Goebels and Himmler are not aboard. When Goering is aboard, he enjoys our little 'get togethers'."

"I see," said Lawrence, looking back down at the game. "May I watch?"

"Of course," Muller answered. "Elster has put himself in a situation where he has a big decision to make. He is desperate to chase me into a check situation, but if he does so, I have the better choices. He sees this, but thinks that this will result in him entering a dark place from which there is no escape."

Lawrence relaxed a little and leaned against the wall of the coach, his eyes dancing across the pieces. A countenance of recognition crossed the open half of his face.

"He is of course correct, General Muller."

General Elster sat back and looked up at Lawrence, slipping a gold monocle into his left eye, and squinting intensely. He looked back at Muller and spread his hands.

"Do you see?" He looked back at Lawrence. "The bastard lets me win occasionally, to keep my interest, but takes the utmost pleasure in my downfall." You know this game?"

Lawrence nodded.

"I think so," he confirmed. "It is a game between a Turk and an Armenian, I think in 1927…"

"1928, in Istanbul," corrected the smiling Muller.

"Yes, 1928," agreed Lawrence. "Both white and black sought to develop quickly, forming a pawn centre, around which the game developed. Basically, white followed black, with black eventually forming the best defence and drawing white into a false security and…" He stopped mid-sentence. "I'm sorry, I do not wish to spoil the game."

Muller laughed aloud. Elster pushed himself back into his chair.

"And how did this game end?" he asked.

Lawrence raised a wistful expression.

"The Armenian, white, failed to see the deception. He kept

pressing for the checkmate that seemed to be developing for him. Two moves later, black castled and the trap closed, with mate in another two moves. For all of his experience, the Armenian failed to see it, and it haunted him for the rest of his life, which was quite short as he hanged himself nine months later. A sad ending to an interesting game."

Lawrence risked a glance at the rear of the coach, where the women were gathered in a group. For a moment he found Elsa Schmidt glancing over at him, but it was over before he could risk a smile. Maybe he was wrong. After all, what woman in her right mind would look twice at someone as grotesque as he? It was an embarrassing moment, and he looked back into the chess game. General Elster slapped the table and leaning away from him, looked up at Lawrence.

"Here!" He exclaimed. "You take over the damn game. So long as you don't hang yourself if you lose!"

Lawrence protested, too busy working a way out to want to play against Muller. General Elster rose from his seat and walked over to the others.

"But I wouldn't…"

Muller cut him off.

"Yes, of course! It would make a welcome change to have a new opponent." He indicated Elster's now vacant chair. "Please."

Lawrence sat and surveyed his white pieces.

"Your move," Muller told him, hooking his chin onto the back of his right hand.

The white attack of Elster's was confident, not as he would play with someone like Muller, but competent. Unfortunately, it was far from creative, and developed poorly, a situation that his opponent was bound to observe. Lawrence saw the obvious move to rectify the situation, but was convinced that Muller would see it also. He offered sacrifice to a bishop, for no other reason than to confound black. Muller hesitated, and stared into the game for some minutes. He uplifted his eyes without moving his head and smiled.

"Very well," Muller finally agreed. "I shall remove your impudent bishop."

He moved a rook toward Lawrence's offer of his piece, but stopped before releasing his fingers and completing the move.

"And yet..." he murmured, freezing his position and staring intently at the board.

Lawrence allowed an expression of innocent impatience, then touched the dressing over his scar, as if it was causing him pain. Muller sat back, as if needing the reprieve of time.

"Perhaps I am thinking like the Armenian," he said, realising that several others had discovered interest in the game, and had gathered around.

Muller returned the rook to its original place. He glanced at the onlookers with an air of surprise, then gave Lawrence a wink.

"Perhaps we should finish this game later," he suggested. "Time to make ready to dine with the Fuhrer. He hates impunctuality. We can offer you a bathroom?"

Lawrence's mind was upon the passing miles, when he should by now have been contacted in the waiting room at Schallenberg. He wondered what those back there would make of the situation, and the confusion caused by his disappearance. A confusion matched by his own. Dining with Hitler had been the last thing on his mind, but how to avoid it now that fate had become his opponent, when only a few days ago it seemed to be on his side.

"Thank you, General Muller," Lawrence replied. "I would like very much to clean up."

*

The long steel caterpillar wound through the German countryside, all four hundred and thirty metres of it, with two huge B52 locomotives coughing their clouds of steam across the fields and through the spaces between the trees.

Behind the locomotives came the first flak car, an armoured anti-aircraft flatbed wagon converted to hold two quadruple 20mm batteries, one at each end of the vehicle. It also had quarters for the officers and men who manned it, usually Luftwaffe Regiment 9, designated as 'Regiment, 'General Goering'.

Behind the first flak car came a baggage car, and next came the 'Fuhrerwagen', Hitler's personal carriage, which was centrally strengthened to include its own bathroom, complete with marble bath.

Then came the 'Benefiswagen', the Command Car, which held a communications centre and a small conference room. Next, was the 'Kommandowagen', which housed Hitler's personal bodyguard of a twenty-two-man SS security force. The forward dining car followed, and then two carriages for guests, after which was the bathing car, and then the second dining car where Lawrence had played chess with General Muller.

Two sleeping cars followed for general personnel, and then a press carriage where Otto Dietrich and his staff were sometimes employed, but not on this occasion. Finally came a second baggage car and then the second flak car, similar to the first, to complete what was normally a fifteen or sixteen section train.

Lawrence had been shown back down to the bathing car that he had passed through earlier, and into one of the ample cubicles, where he took advantage of the facilities to clean up to a standard that matched his new uniform. He decided that if the Germans insisted on giving him a Major's image, then he was damn well going to look the part, and try not to smell like something that had passed through a horse. However, he went sparingly with the cologne and other personal products that were available, not wishing the Fuhrer to get the wrong idea of his saviour.

He looked at himself in the mirror before putting on his tunic, seeing how the disfigurement of his face had changed him, and thanked Heaven that it was for others to witness such a sight and not he, unless he looked into a mirror of course. He re-fixed the surgical dressing, and was thankful for it, then pulled on the tunic.

To say that Lawrence was balanced upon the edge of being frantic about his situation was something of an understatement, but in truth, some kind of limbo had overtaken his fears. Although he was speeding toward Berlin in the midst of the German hierarchy, and away from his designated route of escape, he could not have wished for a more elevated position. And yet, the anticipation of dinner with Adolf Hitler did little to ease his concerns.

He opened the door that led into the corridor of the bath car and found it empty. Taking the opportunity, he checked the windows, to see if there might be a way of escaping the train, but all were secure, with only a small ventilator above each allowing fresh air to enter. Every window in the corridor was almost fully frosted, with only a few small places in the design to peek through and enable him to see outside, across the passing countryside. The sun was going down, and in a half-hour it would be dark.

Lawrence decided to return to the dining car, where he had left the others, trying the doors at the end of each carriage, just in case. They were locked securely. However, the window in the exit door was clear, and he caught a glimpse of sentries, standing to attention along the track at regular intervals, presumably to dissuade any attempt to de-rail the train. The discovery added little to his chances of disembarking before Berlin.

Pressing down the polished handles of the connecting doors, Lawrence entered the dining car, to find it changed completely. Gone were the uniformed revellers, to be replaced by white-jacketed waiters, who had moved the furniture to the centre of the room and were placing cutlery, crockery and other items pertaining to a potential meal.

Seeing him enter, the waiters snapped briefly to attention

and acknowledged him, then continued with their work. He stood for a moment rocking gently with the movement of the train and decided not to engage them, but to carry on down into the next carriage, where hopefully he would find someone who would advise him of the times and protocols of his upcoming ordeal with the Fuhrer.

Reaching the other end of the carriage and avoiding the busy waiters, Lawrence moved quickly across into the next, allowing the door to close behind him. He was now in what looked like a sleeping car, and from the design of the vehicle, it was segmented into several sections, with the corridor changing sides as he moved along. Each section had three compartments, with drop-down bunks and Lawrence guessed that these were for lower ranked passengers. Some were occupied and he received acknowledgement as he passed.

Somewhere toward the front of the train, he heard the shrill call of a steam whistle, and he wondered what it was for. He guessed that the 'Brandenburg' must stop at regular intervals to either refuel the engines, or change them completely to avoid delay, and guessed at the latter.

Hoping to find Muller, Lawrence moved along the carriage, glancing into each compartment, but found that after the second, they were empty, and guessed that the duties of the higher ranked officers took them further toward the front of the train, where Hitler was. Never-the-less, he decided to complete his search of the last section, moving slowly down the corridor with one hand steadying himself on the brass rail as he negotiated the crossover to the other side of the car.

The first compartment on his left was empty, as was the second, but the third had the blinds pulled completely down. Lawrence braced himself against the window and looked to see if there might be a small gap which he could peer through in his search for Muller, and he was in luck. A small corner had caught on a fitted ash tray and gave just enough space to peek in if he dropped onto his haunches.

Keeping his hand on the rail, and rolling with the movement of the train, he squinted into the window and aligned one eye with the upturned blind. What he saw was the last thing that he expected.

Chapter Seven
The Berlin Defence

The eye that invaded the small space beneath the blind widened as it followed the sharp, shiny brown knee length-boots upward to where red-striped trousers hung around the tops. Lawrence recalled that the last time that he saw anything like it, he had shot the participants. That it was Muller was quickly confirmed as he changed his angle of view, but the recipient of his amorous attention was more difficult to determine, until the passion intensified. Lawrence swallowed and tried to relieve his dry throat.

It was Elsa Schmidt, and he decided from the height at which she had hitched her skirt, that she was far from as shy as she pretended.

Lawrence's mind intervened and took him back to that night when he had taken the law into his own hands, when he had felt no constraint in the action that he had taken, and even now felt no tinge of guilt or remorse. He wondered, why he was not like others, who could just allow their betrayal to vent in a tirade of anger and assume the mantle of being a victim, and be thankful in not being the guilty. But his mind did not work that way, and to forgive and forget were not his to evoke; that was the prerogative of the brain that he was born with. Nor did vengeance play any part in his actions. It was far more clinical than that, a kind of justice that was his to impart to return his imbalance to a level which satisfied him. But fate had played a game with him that night, and while he only sought to punish the man, and allow her to remain the mother of his children, the passion of the moment interfered and put them both in his line of sight, and the single bullet finished them both.

A door opened further along the carriage. Lawrence shook off the sepia replay in his memory and regained his feet, and as quietly as he could, made his way back through the chicane of corridors until he met with General Elster.

"Maas!" said the general. "I was looking to…"

Lawrence saluted. A voice came from behind in the limited space and he found Muller, back in parade ground order. The General reached to grasp the brass safety bar as the train rolled.

"Ah! Maas," Muller echoed.

"I was looking for someone to explain the protocols," Lawrence explained, nervously "how to address the Fuhrer, where to sit, that kind of thing. I'm a little anxious."

Muller slapped him on the back and grinned.

"Ja, of course, you are, who would not be?" he agreed. "But you have nothing to worry about, you are after all, the guest of honour. He will be pleased to see you, to thank you properly for your courage this afternoon."

Elsa Schmidt appeared from around the bend in the corridor. She showed no signs of her recent athletics. Muller turned as he heard her footsteps.

"Ah! Elsa. Please inform Maas of everything he needs to understand before we dine with the Fuhrer." Muller said, then gave a curt nod. "He prefers to eat at eight-fifteen when he is aboard the Brandenburg, prompt."

Muller glanced at General Elster and returned the way he had come, back to the compartment. Lawrence and Schmidt pressed themselves into the window to allow Elster to pass, and there was little space to spare. After he had negotiated his way around them, Elsa beckoned Lawrence to follow, and they made their way steadily toward the front of the train. The Englishman found it hard to compare the almost timid manner of the woman with what he had observed a short time before.

"When you enter the Fuhrerwagen," she began, "it will be on the stroke of eight-fifteen, no earlier, and certainly no later. A waiter will open the door at the appropriate time. You will enter after General Muller and General Elster, halt when they do, and salute the Fuhrer with the party salute." She looked back at him. "You will not click your heels, he does not like that. He also does not allow smoking in his presence."

"All right," Lawrence affirmed.

"You will not speak until the Fuhrer speaks to you, but under the circumstances, I am certain that he will greet you warmly himself."

Lawrence nodded his understanding.

"And how do I know where to sit?" he asked.

"There will be name tickets, but General Muller will indicate your seat. You will move to your position immediately, but you will under no circumstances go around the back of the Fuhrer. You understand? You must go around the opposite end of the table."

"Ja."

"You will then wait until everyone has found their seat, and only sit after the Fuhrer, and Generals Muller and Elster, have taken their places. Clear?"

"Ja," Lawrence acknowledged. "Will there be anyone else there? Will you be there?"

Schmidt shook her head.

"The women do not eat with the Fuhrer on the train, unless specifically invited, and rarely when Fraulein Braun is not accompanying the Fuhrer. But Colonel Mennerheim and Major Schwarz are to attend the dinner, and also Obergruppenfuhrer Schaub, the Fuhrer's adjutant." She made a matter-of-fact expression. "Usually, Borman accompanies the Fuhrer, but while he has been convalescing, the Reichsminister has been in Berlin. He will be waiting to greet the Fuhrer when we arrive at Friedrichstrasse."

Lawrence shook himself, and spread his hands, inviting inspection.

"Am I presentable now, for appearing before the Fuhrer? I don't think there is much more that I can do to improve my appearance, and this scarred face is hardly an improvement."

Elsa Schmidt avoided eye contact and looked away, as if embarrassed by the question. She smiled gently, almost coyly, and evaded an honest answer, keeping to a general narrative.

"I think that the Fuhrer will not be too critical. It is an honour to be invited to dine with him, which indicates his gratitude at your service this afternoon. If the Fuhrer indulges you in small-talk, you will reply in the most general terms, and ask no questions, this is very important. If he asks you a question, you will answer honestly and briefly. You will not burden him with personal or military problems, or ask a favour of any kind."

"I understand," Lawrence confirmed. "What am I to do until eight-fifteen?"

"I will return you to the guest compartment. It will be your place until we reach Berlin, on instruction from the Fuhrer." She told him. "At eight, General Muller and the others will collect you, and escort you to the Fuhrerwagen. From there you will follow the instructions that I have given you. Come!"

She turned abruptly and led him along the narrow corridors, through the dining car that he was familiar with, via the bathing carriage, and into the first of two guest wagons in which five plush compartments had been established, his being one of them. Schmidt slid open the door and bade him enter. Once inside,

Lawrence turned and made the accepted military dip bob of gratitude.

"Danke Schon, Fraulein Schmidt."

She returned a half smile, with a curt slant of her head.

"Bitte. You must remain here until General Muller comes at eight. If you require anything, there is a bell to press for a waiter. You understand? You must not leave the compartment until it is time to meet the Fuhrer."

"Ja. Ja, I understand, Lawrence confirmed. "Perhaps I will see you later, before we reach Berlin?"

"Perhaps," she answered."

He thought he was being polite, but she turned with a flourish and returned the way that they had come. As he slid the compartment door closed, he risked a quick look after her, noting the confident rocking of her shoulders while her head remained remarkably stable. Lawrence wondered what to make of her, but decided that was speculation best known to others.

*

His compartment was neither opulent nor spartan, certainly comfortable and elegantly outfitted in the finest art nouveau, the hard lines of which gave a confined feeling, which he guessed might be intentional. There was a small toilet with an added wash basin and the thickest towels that he had ever seen, at least within the last week or so. Two subtle electric wall lamps gave a nice overall ambiance, and at the far wall, the usual frosted window, with an additional blind which could be pulled down to cover it.

This window, however, had the addition of a small vent which could be opened to allow fresh air to circulate. Lawrence opened it slowly and looked through the letterbox space. It was getting quite dark. He looked at his watch and found that he had just over an hour to wait before his ordeal with Hitler, wishing it might be cancelled, or that the Fuhrer had found it below him to have a mere Oberleutnant at his table.

Lawrence fell back into the long seat and flipped down the arm rest, wondering how the hell he was going to get off this metal trap. It crossed his mind that they might wire ahead to check his papers with Berlin, doubtful that his luck would continue. Already, he had pushed the limits of what any normal murderer could expect and still be breathing, not to mention one more hapless unfortunate whose demise had been down to him.

A whistle from one of the engines accompanied a definite reduction in speed. Lawrence rose quickly from his seat and looked out into the evening, where a name board passed too quickly for him to read. A few workmen stood by the tracks, lined like toy soldiers in a Nazi salute. Then, SS guardsmen could be seen running toward the slowing train and lining up, along with the workers.

Lawrence struggled to see more through the ventilator, and realised that they were coming up to a station yard, where coal and watering facilities were situated by the tracks, ready to refuel the engines, which could exhaust their tenders every one hundred and twenty miles or so.

The two locomotives came to a halt, the carriages squealing behind them. Cylinder cocks expelled their water content and the boilers vented steam in a satisfying exhale, like huge creatures breathing, catching their wind after a long run. Soon, the noise of workers doing their jobs filled the evening air, and Lawrence wondered if this might be his chance to escape. He changed position and looked back down the train, and saw several officers descending from a carriage further down.

Quickly, he slid open his compartment door and found the corridor empty, so he slipped through and made his way toward the rear of the carriage. He negotiated the connecting double doors between the cars and entered the bath carriage, then found refuge in the first cubical when he heard voices coming in his direction, all but closing the door behind him, but leaving enough space to peer through.

As the conversation neared his hiding place, he recognised one voice as that of General Elster, but could not see the other, and he slid the cubicle door closed before they passed, flipping the lock. Allowing them time to move into the next carriage, Lawrence checked that it was clear before vacating the bathroom, then hurried along to where the corridor ended and veered to the left, where there was a limited space which allowed exit through the access door to the outside.

Steam and smoke filtered past the half open door and Lawrence pushed it a little further and took a step down, until he could see General Muller twenty yards away, talking to another officer beneath a station lamp, whose rank it was hard to discern. Perhaps he should make a run for it, but if he did, and was caught, his credibility would be totally blown. The idea balanced like a see-saw, until something discarded the thought.

As Lawrence looked on, he saw the officer with whom Muller conversed put his hand into his tunic jacket and hand over what looked like a pistol, and in the illumination of the lamp it was obviously not a standard German army issue. It was something that Lawrence was perfectly familiar with, a mark four Webley, the outline clear even at twenty yards. The weapon was now somewhat obsolete, recently replaced by the new Enfield, mark one, but still used and valued within the British officer corps. Why Muller needed such a firearm baffled him, until a stern voice from behind shook him back into reality.

"Oberleutnant Maas! You were instructed to remain in your compartment. Did I not make that clear?"

Lawrence turned abruptly, to find Elsa Schmidt looking down him, her face having lost the coyness that had been there previously. He fought for words to defend himself.

"I apologise," Lawrence blurted, for a second losing his poise. "As the train had stopped, I thought it no matter if I went outside to get some air. I saw that others had disembarked. I didn't think…"

"Ah, Maas!" It was Muller, who had returned to the train and stood a few steps away. He looked up at Elsa.

"My dear Fraulein," he smiled up at her, "do not be so harsh with the Oberleutnant. Do not forget the service that he has done for the fatherland today. If he wishes to breathe in fresh air, then we must accommodate him. What would the Fuhrer think if we denied him such a simple request?"

Elsa Schmidt's expression changed quickly. Her eyes betrayed her discomfiture and she fidgeted slightly on the step above him.

"Herr Oberleutnant, please forgive me, I did not mean…"

"Ach! It is finished," Muller interjected, seeing her embarrassment. "Mass, please come down and see the Fuhrer's wonderful Brandenburg. You will never see another like it, although there are many in the party who strive to copy it." He paused as Lawrence stepped down onto the gravel to join him. "Field Marshal Goering for one, and Goebbels, and so on, and so forth."

Muller led Lawrence toward the lamp where he had spoken with the mysterious officer, who had walked off into the night. He halted, turned and looked directly at his companion with that friendly expression that always seemed to be hovering behind a conversation. Muller leaned forward, with a straight back, in a manner that inferred that he was about to whisper some interesting but forbidden secret.

"Did you know that Reichsmarshal Goering, at his estate of Karinhall, has a huge model train exhibit, just like the real thing, electrically controlled with signals, and trees and, well, everything that you can imagine?"

Lawrence was nervous. He feigned interest.

"Er, no. I did not."

Muller's hands danced in a kind of excitement, as if the subject was close to his heart.

"Of course, I have not seen this wonder personally, but it has been widely reported. Even the Fuhrer was impressed. And, as the trains are rushing to their destinations, British bombers on wires streak across the miniature countryside and drop their ordnance, all worked by electrical current, but there are heroic miniature German guns to shoot them down." Muller paused and smiled. "Would you not like to see it?"

"It must be a sight to see," lied Lawrence. "But I imagine it is nothing like the experience of riding the Fuhrersonderzug."

Muller guided him gently by the arm, toward the front of the train, where several carriages ahead, the locomotives were being serviced for the next part of the journey. He pointed at the first flak wagon.

"See how the Fuhrer is protected, even when travelling. Nothing is left to chance. And travelling in such style, although the Fuhrer declines too much extravagance, preferring more artistic themes."

They halted, and Muller continued with his descriptions.

"Each carriage weighs over sixty tons, and there are often sixteen of them, all with their own specific purpose, from the Fuhrer's own personal car, to dining cars, sleeping cars, baggage cars, and even a press car, although this is not used so much when he is travelling. Next to the Fuhrer's personal carriage is a conference and communications vehicle, and also there is the Kommando car, where twenty-two SS men of the Fuhrer's closest bodyguard watch over him," Muller looked at Lawrence. "They are the only armed people within the Brandenburg," he said, "for obvious reasons."

"Quite something, isn't it?" Lawrence declared.

Something did not seem right. It felt like there was an undercurrent of probing, but for what, Lawrence had no idea. It was as if everyone knew something that he did not. Even now, he might have made a break for it into the night, but knowing that Muller carried a British revolver, he thought better of it. He turned, to look back down toward the rear of the train.

"So!" Muller advised. "It will soon be time for you to meet the Fuhrer in a calmer location. Do not be afraid, he just a man, as we are, but there are protocols which we must observe…"

"Fraulein Schmidt has advised me of how I must behave when with the Fuhrer," Lawrence said.

"Ah! Then all is good. Fraulein Schmidt is always to be relied upon," Muller confirmed.

Lawrence nodded and raised his brows.

"I had already formulated that opinion."

*

At the appropriate time, there was a knock on the door of Lawrence's compartment. He swallowed hard and opened it to find General Muller and the others come to find him, ready for the formal dinner with the Fuhrer. Muller slapped him on the upper arm.

"Do not look so serious, Maas. It is a great honour for an Oberleutnant to dine with the leader." The General looked him up and down. "Come! We do not want to be late."

Lawrence followed as the officers moved forward along the corridor. He was told that there had been a change in arrangements, that the Fuhrer had decided to eat in the command car, just one carriage ahead. Low lighting lit their way as they moved along, with blurred smoke from the locomotives flashing by the frosted windows.

A waiter in a short white jacket waited outside the door, waiting for the bell which would beckon them in. Lawrence felt his head swimming, wondering what fate still had in store for him, his head rolling with the regular clack of the carriage wheels across the tracks.

'Ding! Ding!' Eight-fifteen on the mark.

The waiter bowed gently to the officers, opened the door wide, and Lawrence followed the others inside.

The first thing that he noticed was the increase in illumination, a stark white luminosity that brushed the soft light of the corridor away. Through the moving figures in front of him, Lawrence caught quick glimpses of the most despised man in Europe, his face quite stern and composed, a black lock of hair racing others that competed to cover his forehead and the cartoon-like dark moustache that seemed to be his trademark, for good or bad.

Blithely, something in the inherent sense of humour of the Englishman compromised Lawrence, and for a moment, he fought off the uncontrollable urge to laugh. But soon, the moment passed as he re-established his own sensitive situation in his mind.

There was a brief show of recognition and welcome toward the German officers that Lawrence failed to hear. He put his hands behind his back and cast one eye around the table to identify his place, but failed to find it. Then, as the individuals spread out and formally gave the party salute, Lawrence had his first full observation of Hitler.

The man seemed taller than he had expected, with his hands clasped together in front of him, occasionally raising himself by his toes, his heels leaving the floor temporarily. Only when speaking directly to one of his senior officers or another did his features show any change. Hitler's head suddenly bobbed in agreement at something that Muller told him, like a child's toy that someone had nudged.

Hitler froze, and his head moved, his eyes searching in the direction of the nervous Lawrence, who was absorbed in following the teachings of Sergeant Major Bull and locating items of use, just in case.

"Maas!" Hitler's voice was almost shrill, and surprisingly feminine.

Lawrence felt himself jump at the uttering of his false name, and worked hard to retain his balance, both physically and mentally. He raised his right arm sharply, and remembered not to click his heels.

"My Fuhrer!" He voiced, a little too loudly.

Hitler was already navigating the end of the table and outstretching his hand toward him. Lawrence anxiously stepped forward and took it, finding the grip stronger than he expected. Hitler covered the first hand with a second, in what seemed like genuine emotion. His deep blue eyes narrowed and the demeanour softened.

"What I owe you, Maas, will not be forgotten. We owe you a great thanks."

For Lawrence, it was as if he were some ham actor, living through the final act, one in which it all would be revealed and he would be seen for what he was. But it was a play in which he must remain in character until the very end, for if the finale was revealed to the audience too soon, they would tear him limb from limb, and perhaps ask for their admittance returned.

Hitler kept hold of Lawrence's hand and pulled him gently to the table, swapping name tags until he was on the Fuhrer's left hand.

"You will sit by me, Maas," Hitler ordered. "And tell me of the struggle in the west. You were involved in the Dutch theatre of war, were you not?" He turned to Muller. "What did the British call the operation, garden something?"

Muller smiled and leaned forward over the snow-white table covering.

"Market-Garden, sir. They named it Market Garden, their name for a minor agricultural prospect."

Hitler for a moment seemed to reflect upon something internally, as if the subject had made him think deeply. Lawrence sat quite still, wondering if this was a regular occurrence, and glanced at the others, who seemed not to notice. The Fuhrer returned to the present.

"We beat them, Maas," he said, sternly. "We beat them, and we shall do so again. Mark my word, before 1945, we shall push them back into the sea. Let them have France for now, but they will not keep it." Hitler paused, as if looking for the first course. "Market Garden?" He was thoughtful once more. "They cannot even think of a sensible name for such an operation. 'Market Garden', as if they wish to sell us potatoes."

Lawrence looked at the others around the table, and they all seemed to hang on every word that Hitler said. Elster was sitting next to him, on the opposite side to the Fuhrer, and his lips were pursed in a determined twist. As the first course appeared, served by two waiters, Hitler turned suddenly once more to Lawrence. The motion made him jump, but he hid it.

"Now, tell us of this 'Market Garden', Maas. And your involvement in it."

Muller sat back as a soup was put in front of him, a pea consommé that looked anything but appetising.

"Yes, Maas. We are all waiting to hear of your exploits in

the defence of the Ruhr," Muller interjected, almost mockingly.

Lawrence felt it again, that he was put on the spot, for reasons that he could not explain to himself, an uncoordinated feeling of unease. Quickly, he tried to remember every aspect of Maas's files, and began the biggest bunch of lies that he could ever remember telling in his whole life. He tried not to make it too much like an Errol Flynn saga, introducing other characters, and giving them huge chunks of the heroic actions, so as to make it more believable. Hitler seemed to gobble it up as much as the pea consommé, which in Lawrence's opinion was the more palatable.

As the story continued, Lawrence felt the need to calm it slightly, becoming quite taken as being the narrator who beguiled the Fuhrer. Now and again, Hitler and others around the table interposed with questions, which Lawrence found fairly easy to parry, but as main course of fish arrived, Muller asked...

"So, you must have known Colonel Kruger, he was in charge of engineers in that sector?"

Lawrence paused awkwardly, his brow furrowing.

"Colonel Kruger, I didn't know him personally... I..."

"Nein! Nein" Nein!" Interrupted Hitler's Orderly. "Kruger was transferred to the eastern front, two weeks before the attack in Holland. Meinhart took over command of engineers, but he was killed on the second day, you know that, Muller."

"Ach! Of course, I forgot," he smiled. "This fish is good,

no?"

"I think Colonel Meinhart's second in command was also slightly wounded," Lawrence added, making up the fact, to sound convincing, and hoping no one knew better."

Muller looked at him and nodded slowly as he ate. He waved his cutlery in a gentle motion.

"Ah, war is war."

Hitler ate quickly, and finished the main course before the others. Elster was next and as he pushed away the plate, he addressed the Fuhrer.

"Maas is an excellent player of chess, sir. In our short acquaintance with him we have found this. His strategy is most impressive, is it not, Muller?"

Muller leaned forward and clasped his hands, with his elbows upon the edge of the table. He raised his eyebrows in agreement.

"Absolutely, I can see the shadow of an accomplished player, an ability to think ahead, with the face of a poker player, an admirable opponent, with whom I must finish the game."

Lawrence made a motion of surprise. He fidgeted a little.

"I play when I can, General, but the war gives little opportunity, and of poker, I have not the slightest idea. I have never played."

"Then we must teach you," Muller replied.

Hitler spoke, a little tetchily.

"I am not a chess player," he said, with those around the table paying respectful attention until he had made the comment. "But in my younger days, I enjoyed backgammon. However, I have not played for some time."

"Poker is like chess in many ways, Maas." The General explained, almost sardonically, looking away from Hitler to the man next to him. "A game of bluff, and forward thinking, but one of great reward, or great loss, if you are willing to engage in the psychology of the challenge."

"Like the Armenian?" Ventured Lawrence.

"The Armenian?" Which Armenian?" Hitler asked, unaware of the context.

Muller gathered his thoughts quickly, and qualified the question with the answer.

"A chess master in 1927, my Fuhrer..."

"1928," corrected Lawrence, who finally realised that he had engaged in a verbal contest with Muller, but why, he could not understand.

"Ah, yes," Muller conceded, "1928." He turned back to Hitler to finish his answer. "The Armenian failed to observe a sequence of moves in an important game and lost to a Turk. He hung himself shortly after, in despair."

Hitler waved his hands erratically. He shook his head and twisted his face irritably.

"We have hanged many Armenians," he looked around impatiently at a waiter. "Where is the desert?" Then he looked at Lawrence. "You like strudel, Maas?"

"Very much, sir," Lawrence replied. "My grandmother made wonderful strudel." This was actually true, one minor fact that he did not need to lie about.

"And they have looked after you since our acquaintance this afternoon?" Hitler asked.

"Wonderfully, my Fuhrer," he confirmed, nervously. "Everyone has been so kind, especially General Muller and Fraulein Schmidt."

"And what are your plans when we reach Berlin?"

"To see my mother, sir, and see that she is cared for, then return to my unit in Holland."

Hitler nodded, almost solemnly.

"When you return, you will have the rank of Major, Maas." Hitler looked Lawrence directly in the eye, his head a little tilted but without the benefit of a smile. "It is the least that I can do for your service, and if I can do anything for your mother, you must ask."

Lawrence pursed his lips, as if to confirm that his fictional mother was beyond help, as he also felt at that moment. 'Just let me off this bloody train,' was another thought that crossed his mind.

The strudel came and it was good, although not as good as his grandmother's. But he let it go and made all of the signs that it was. When it was finished, and more small talk had passed, Hitler tapped a spoon on the white tablecloth, then stood up as the talk subsided. He glanced at Muller, who produced a flat box of dark red leather with gold piping. On the top was the gold eagle of the Nazi Party grasping a lightning bolt. Muller stood and passed the box to Hitler, who also stood, and beckoned Lawrence to do likewise. Lawrence did so, and the others around the table did so too.

Hitler held out the box with his left hand and offered the right to Lawrence, who took it, his face a picture of surprise.

"In thanks, and gratitude for your actions for the Fatherland." Hitler smiled tight-lipped. "Maas, I award you the Iron Cross, with oak leaf cluster, and the promotion to Major." He nodded curtly as Lawrence took the red box and opened it to view the contents.

His promotion had been hinted at before, but he never imagined such adoration from those whose lives he had spent the last five years trying so hard to end. So many thoughts contradicted their way through the pathways of his mind. How could he have foreseen this when a hessian hood so recently masked his view of a world that he thought he would never see again? It was so comically remarkable that he felt on the verge of breaking into laughter at the absurdity of it, but he shut out the urge to follow through. It seemed prudent.

"Well Maas?" asked General Muller, leaning forward like a domineering schoolteacher. "Have you nothing to say?"

"I... I... er... I didn't expect such a..."

He really was quite taken aback, as the Iron Cross with oak cluster was certainly not the usual decoration given to a British officer serving in the field, even under such strange circumstances. Elster slapped him on the back and instigated a round of applause, which seemed to go on for far longer than it should have, even in the presence of the Fuhrer. Lawrence looked to his left, at the stern face of Hitler.

"Thank you, sir." Was all that he could think of to say, at least all that he could think of that would not have him shot, or facing a noose again.

Coffee completed the meal, the real stuff again, to which he was becoming quite fond of once more, but what might one expect when in the company of the man who invaded Poland, France, and Russia? You would at least expect the villain to drink real coffee and travel in the Fuhrersonderzug, the steel caterpillar on rails that had the resources of a small town.

Then, somehow without direction, it was over, and as one person the officers around the table stood, bowed slightly to Hitler and bade their 'good evenings'. Lawrence followed suit, a little behind as he was unfamiliar with the routine. He felt that he should say something, and eased himself into character again.

"My Fuhrer," he uttered nervously. "Once more I must thank you for your kindness…"

Hitler stood and once more held out a hand, covering Lawrence's with the other as it was shaken.

"Major Maas. It is I who must thank you, for your timely action of this afternoon. When we reach Berlin, I will arrange a formal presentation in the Reichstag," the leader said.

Lawrence twisted his mouth away from the scar to form his best smile. 'Not bloody likely,' he thought, 'once off this train, I'm gone for good and any presentation you want to make'.

As he followed the others, past the waiters at the door and toward the next carriage, he wondered who the hell would ever believe him? At that moment, whatever happened, William Lawrence decided never to recount the story of the day that Hitler awarded him the Iron Cross, oak leaves or otherwise. Doubtless they would get the wrong end of the stick and accuse him of all kinds of wrong doing. The events that led to his almost being hanged were bad enough, but he was certainly no traitor, nor would he be accused of it, so he set his mind to say no more about it.

It was by now just after nine forty-five and as they reached Lawrence's compartment, he began to slide open the door when General Muller, who was just ahead, turned and put a hand on the polished rosewood to stop it. General Elster disappeared into his compartment at the opposite end of the carriage.

"Not so fast, Major Maas. You must show off your new decoration to the others, presented by the Fuhrer himself, and well deserved if I may so," he said.

Lawrence stalled.

"Sir, I was hoping for an early night's sleep. It has been a very long day."

Muller straightened.

"Nonsense, Maas. Make the most of this special day, you will have something to tell your grandchildren. Everyone is waiting to congratulate you. To toast your courage. You want me to make it an order?"

Lawrence hesitated, but knew he had little choice other than to continue the act. A pang of guilt stepped up to be counted over the German soldier who had been shot to cover his present situation, but he dismissed it immediately. Everyone plays the game at his own risk.

"Of course not, sir. I will be happy to come."

They walked down the narrow corridor, past Elster's room.

"Is General Elster not joining us?" Lawrence asked.

Muller turned and put a finger to his mouth, and spoke

gently.

"The General has not been well for some time. I think he is better resting. And he witnessed the Fuhrer giving the decoration to you at dinner, so let him have his sleep."

General Muller led through to the next carriage, the bath car, then, the second dining car, then two sleeping cars with ample bunks where several personnel were engaged in their evening endeavours, then on through the unused press carriage where, at the opposite end, he opened the double doors for Lawrence to walk through.

Having entered, Lawrence found it dimly lit, and from the randomly stacked piles of boxes, deduced it as some kind of baggage car. It seemed as if they must go further to the reception. Then the lights went out.

Chapter Eight
The Reti Manoeuvre

Through what seemed like waves of mist overflowing across him, Lawrence saw the critical face of Colour Sergeant Bull, bending over and pointing an accusatory finger, overtaken by Officer Willoughby pushing away the unpolished cupboard that led to the big drop and eternity. William George Lawrence sucked in a breath and felt the pounding hammering at the back of his head, as a pretty woman asked questions about his childhood in both French and German languages, to which he answered in English. He groaned.

Dull, blurred shadows moved across the space in front of him as he tried to focus and recall how he came to be in such a state of anguish and lost control. Had he experienced the drop, and was this his final breath? Was he dreaming, and would the next few moments clarify into sometime before the hallucinations of sleep took over his mind? But the pain in his head resolved the doubts and slowly he came around to the fact that he had failed to respect every lesson that Bull had taught him, and the false security of an Iron Cross seduced him into some kind of physical and mental sanctuary.

Lawrence forced open his eyes. Trying to move, he found himself restricted by some kind of ties that bound him to a wooden chair, his hands behind him. General Muller sat on the edge of a small table, his arms crossed, bare headed with that casual smile twisting one side of his mouth. His manner was supercilious and knowing.

"Ah, Maas!" he remarked, as if Lawrence had just casually walked into the room. "You are with us once again."

Lawrence groggily looked around, to find Colonel Kalmer standing some way to one side. He pushed his head around to look at Muller again.

"Wha..." He almost spoke in English in his hazy grasp of reality, but checked himself, and returned to German. "Was? (What). General, what is happening? Are we...?"

Muller continued his comedy of control.

"Calm yourself, Maas. No harm will come to you." He acted as if reconsidering the statement. "Well, not yet."

Lawrence was coming back, the perils of his situation at last clearing in his mind, but why he had no idea, and tried quickly to search into the recent past to identify the mistake that he had made to put himself there. But it would be literal suicide to offer too much defence until he was sure what was happening. As Lawrence's head dropped onto his chest, Muller bent over and stared up at him, speaking as a benevolent teacher might scold a child for its own good.

"No doubt Maas, you will be considering what has forced you from the dizzy heights of heroism, to the situation in which you now find yourself?"

Muller laughed aloud.

"Oh, would you prefer to continue our conversation in English?" he asked, changing language. "My English is excellent, as you can see. I have no objection to English."

Lawrence held out in German, his voice croaking a little at the exertion.

"General Muller, I don't understand why you are treating me this way, I…"

The General laughed again, keeping to English.

"Maas. Let us be cordial, and do away with the repartee of interrogation that we both know is pointless. I guarantee you that I can make this easier for you if we can, how do the Americans call it? 'Talk Turkey'."

"General, I…"

Muller looked sternly at Lawrence, an air of disappointment on his face. He cut into Lawrence's protest in German.

"What is your real name by the way?" he asked. "Not that it matters, but just out of curiosity."

"I am Oberleutnant…" Lawrence paused before continuing. "Now, Major Kurt Maas, promoted personally by the Fuhrer, and…"

Muller held up the red box, containing the Iron Cross.

"This piece of junk?" he uttered. "Obsolete, like the one who awarded it."

Lawrence formed words that were never spoken. Whatever was going on here was becoming stranger by the second. He kept in character, fearful of leaving it behind. As his senses began to return, he scanned the space within the gently rocking carriage, looking for those things which might help him, just as Bull had told him, and cursed himself for forgetting. Muller stepped toward him, with his arms still folded.

"You are a British agent, assuming the identity of a German officer," Muller growled in English. "We were looking for you, and you handed yourself to us on a plate," he grinned. "How you managed such a dramatic introduction was pure genius, but look at you now, promoted to Major and decorated by Hitler. I hand it to you, English, I have only admiration for your creativity."

"Sir, I must…" Began Lawrence in German, but he was cut short again by Muller, who addressed Kalmer, aided by a beckoning motion with his hand.

"Give me them!"

Kalmer brought over items which he put onto the table. Muller turned to them, holding up Lawrence's old tunic.

"And these amusing little toys of yours," he said, using the button to extend the wire.

Muller's eyes widened and he looked down at Lawrence as if they were questioning him. A moment later, he casually threw the jacket back onto the table and picked up the short bayonette, twisting the handle until the second blade popped. Finally, Muller held up the Luger pistol, and paused for a second before pulling back eight times on the slider to eject the rounds. Lawrence noted immediately that the General had not discovered the change in calibre that allowed one extra. Instead, the German slipped on the small silencer and twisted it into place. He then pointed the weapon at Lawrence's chest, as if to discharge it.

Lawrence saw the finger tighten slightly on the trigger. He swallowed hard and waited for the detonation of the last round and wondered who would be the most surprised. Muller pushed the Luger menacingly toward him.

"Bang!" The word made Lawrence jump involuntarily, and his eyes twitched.

Muller stepped back, admiring the noise suppression attachment.

"Wonderful," he approved. "You might even think that we Germans manufactured such a piece of engineering." He looked back at his prisoner. "You have nothing to say?"

Lawrence knew that the game was up. How could he defend his possession of such items? He gently tested the bonds that held him, but there was no give in them.

"You say that you were looking for me?" he asked in

English.

Muller smiled and nodded slowly, tapping his own cheek, which mimicked the scar on Lawrence's.

Lawrence realised that it had all been for nothing. He had been a worthless pawn in the game from the beginning, but why had they played such a complicated drama when one bullet could have finished it? Why had he been allowed to sit next to their Fuhrer, when he could easily have stuck a fish fork in the man's neck? He thought back to Muller's words, that 'the Iron Cross he had been given was as obsolete as the man that awarded it'. What the hell?

"It is a pity that we will not finish the game, I have so little opportunity to find a chess player of your knowledge and skill." Muller said.

"Untie me," answered Lawrence, "I can beat you in five more moves, maybe four."

Muller smiled.

"Alas, I cannot indulge myself in your tempting offer." He rested an elbow on one hand and clasped his chin between forefinger and thumb. "Our situation reminds me of the Reti manoeuvre," he said, "you recall this from 1921?"

Lawrence nodded.

"An end game scenario," he replied. "Kings and pawns."

"Ah! Exactly." Muller found satisfaction in Lawrence's knowledge, and he musingly repeated the words. "Kings and pawns. There is more significance to this than you might ever know."

Lawrence's mind was clearing enough to investigate his surroundings more clearly. He determined not to make the same mistake twice, and if he could just find a way to break free of his bindings, he would need to know where his best opportunities lay. Now that the light was better, he could see that this was obviously a baggage car, also used for storage. Windows were covered with latticed blinds which swayed slowly with the motion of the carriage, which he guessed was somewhere around sixty feet in length.

Among the pyramids of boxes were personal luggage and equipment, much he guessed belonging to Hitler, and needed in his travels. Lawrence's eyes discarded the useless and he tried remember where anything that could be utilised as a weapon was situated. Of course, he would need the opportunity, and hoped that at some stage he might be left alone to make exertions that could free him from the chair. There seemed little, apart from the baggage, that might be useful, but in at least two places, there was a brass fire extinguisher,

Kalmer moved closer to General Muller, giving Lawrence the shortest of glances.

"Have you seen the time?" he asked, tapping his wristwatch. "What about Elster? And where is Feldmann? We can do nothing without Feldmann."

Muller looked at Kalmer.

"Relax. We have plenty of time. Feldmann has his duties, and I will take care of Elster when the time comes, and anyone else if necessary."

Kalmer looked at Lawrence.

"And him?"

"Providence will deal with Maas. You know that," Muller answered.

'Three of them I need to be aware of'. Thought Lawrence. "Whatever their intentions for me are, Muller, Kalmer, and Feldmann, whoever he is'.

"Am I to be executed?" Lawrence asked, deciding it best to just come out and get it said.

Muller smiled, insincerely.

"My dear Maas, do not worry. While you are on this train, no-one will harm one hair of your head. I guarantee it." He thought for a moment. "Once we are in Berlin, however, I would not take bet one Mark on how long you will survive.

Lawrence grinned back, just as insincerely.

"It's not my hair that I'm concerned about."

General Muller cast a hand over to Lawrence but addressed

Kalmer.

"You see, my dear Kalmer, how the British retain their sense of humour in the direst of consequences. Now, why can you not be so relaxed, and behave in such a manner?"

But Lawrence's thoughts were already elsewhere. In trying to understand what was happening to him, and how his fortunes had suddenly turned over, he reflected on what little information had slipped by before him. He remembered Muller's remark about the Reti Manoeuvre, and how he had brought it up so casually, and more important, why. The theory concerned a closing game with each king having only one pawn, each pawn striving to promote to a queen, a case of multiple threats and multiple paths to a given location. Whatever the implication, Muller was unlikely to explain it to him, but the suggestion certainly made him think. Whatever the scene that Muller was enjoying painting, it was certain that Lawrence was looked upon as a pawn, and it appeared that it was of no importance which one.

There was a brief knock on the carriage door. Kalmer rushed to open it and an officer slipped through after checking back the way that he had come. Lawrence identified him as the man that Muller spoke to while the engines were being refuelled. So, this, he guessed, was Feldmann. Now, he knew that whatever was going on, that there were three of them.

"How much longer?" asked Kalmer of Feldmann.

The other looked at his watch.

"One hour, forty minutes or so. It will be an extended stop as the engines will be changed for new ones."

"You will have plenty of time?"

"Of course, I can uncouple the carriages while you take him up to the command car. I will make sure that the doors are unlocked, but keep your heads down as you move down the train, and make sure he cannot call out."

"Just make sure that you disengage from the rest of the train!" Muller growled angrily. "And see that your people stay in this section. We will do the rest. But wait until the last moment before you do anything, in case he decides that he wants a full security check. You know how he is."

"Or how he was." Joked Kalmer, nervously.

Only then did Lawrence have a glimmer of what was to happen. They were going to kill Hitler on the train, not in the station. There could be no other explanation, bearing in mind the pieces that he was beginning to put together. So, he was just like the Reti pawn, provisionally useless and the only path to a given location for either himself or Hitler was far from desirable.

There was another sharp rap on the door and Muller walked across and opened it slightly, engaging in low conversation with someone. Lawrence leaned to one side, but could neither see the new face, or hear anything of the conversation. 'So, he thought, now there are four of them'.

Feldmann left shortly after, leaving only Muller and Kalmer in the baggage car with Lawrence. General Muller reached into the inside pocket of his tunic and pulled a handful of documents. He looked over at Kalmer.

"Now I must go to implicate the poor Elster while he is asleep," he said. "A shame, he was a rather good fellow, but well past his potential as a soldier, or a politician." He glanced back at Lawrence and grinned. "Or, as we both know, anything like a decent chess opponent. But I will miss him."

General Muller straightened and looked down at the bound Lawrence. He put his hands on his hips and leaned back a little.

"So, you see, Maas, how lucky you are to be at a crossroads in history, at the demise of one regime, and the rise of another, for I am certain by now that you have... how do you say in English? Put two and two together."

To Lawrence it still seemed 'five', but he hoped that his arithmetic might improve soon.

"You know, General" the Englishman spoke up, "I might be able to help you in your endeavours, I suppose theoretically that we are just about on the same side." Lawrence sat back in the chair that he was bound to. "I gather that we are concerned with the well-being of your Fuhrer?"

Muller laughed aloud and Kalmer, in a sinister manner, smiled along.

"My dear Maas, you are helping far more than you could ever know, but not in the way that you might understand. Before this night is over, you will be the hero to some, and the villain to others. But I hope that you know that I bear you no animosity or ill will. However, you must play your part like the unfortunate Elster." He looked at his watch. "Ah! Speaking of which, I must for a short period, bid you 'au revoir'."

Without further discussion, Muller walked toward the door of the carriage and glanced through the small glass window that allowed one person to avoid bumping into someone coming in the opposite direction. Satisfied, he opened the door and slipped through, closing it firmly behind him.

*

General Muller moved purposely through the unused press car, sidestepping the desks and chairs and other equipment utilised on occasion by the propaganda brigade who sometimes rode the Fuhrersonderzug with Hitler. He then made his way through the two sleeping cars, in which there was the usual flurry of personnel, engaged in all manner of conversation and activity.

Muller's rank broke a path for him as he worked his way through, acknowledging the salutes but returning few, and keeping his gait to a steady walk, as if in no great hurry to pass. The rear dining car still contained a few late drinkers, including some of the female administration workers, most of which did not even see Muller pass by. Next, he paced along the bathing carriage, where one or two cubicles were engaged, and finally made his way into the rearmost of the guest cars.

Muller knew that Elster had commandeered the last compartment in that section, as he always did, preferring the quiet for sleep that this place often gave him. There was no-one in the narrow corridor, Muller had made sure of that, and he put an ear to the glass of the sliding door, down which the blind had been pulled. He hoped that the door had not been locked, but it was of no consequence as he had a duplicate skeleton key to all of the guest staterooms. He hoped that he had given enough time for Elster to fall asleep, knowing that he often read for a while before finally retiring for the night. Old German prose that could put anyone to sleep.

No sounds could he hear from inside Elster's compartment, so gently pulling on the handle, Muller slid it gently open a little until he could see inside without being observed himself. Elster was laying on the long seat, which was opposite the pull-down bed, a book lying open on his chest, and his head propped up a little on the arm rest. As Muller entered, there was no response from the prone man, so he closed the sliding door behind him.

Moving to the window, the General took a gold cord from one of the curtains that held them back. It was about a metre long and ended in a tassel. Muller bent over and slipped the cord underneath his victim's neck and slowly eased it across his chest, then knotted it loosely, so that the tassel became the secure part of the noose. Elster made a muffled noise but remined asleep, but Muller kept motionless for a few seconds until sure that he was not waking. He spoke slowly, almost melancholy.

"Goodbye, old friend. You die for the Fatherland."

Muller pulled the knot tight and heaved upwards, finding enough slack to reach the metal baggage rack above Elster's head and use it as a fulcrum to haul the waking man into a sitting position, and then higher, his weight choking the words of indignant surprise that he fought to expel from a gasping mouth.

Muller braced his feet on the edge of the seat and heaved with all of his might until the choking Elster was pulled above him and fighting for life, his eyes popping out almost as far as his tongue. Elster groped at the gold cord around his thick neck but there was not enough space to force his fingers through. A squeak of breath escaped between his lips, the best that a strangled man could make as a cry for help.

Muller held Elster's weight for several minutes, until certain that the man was dead, and not just unconscious. He waited until he saw the blue tinge in Elster's skin spread to his lips. Slowly, Muller let the body drop back onto the long seat, the dead man's limbs flopping lifelessly. He paused for a while to retrieve his composure from the effort. It had not been an easy kill.

Standing, General Muller pulled a sheaf of papers from his pocket and pressed them into that of the deceased. They were false proof of Elster's commitment to the plan, and somewhat discharged the guilt of the true conspirators, just as they were supposed to do.

Satisfied that his work was done here, Muller once again hauled Elster into a position which gave the impression that the General had committed suicide. He took a bottle from the small bar and poured a little into Elster's mouth, enough for whoever found him to smell the effect, then took a drop himself, before emptying half of the contents through the small ventilator window. The scene would give credence to the picture that Muller was working to create.

Straightening his jacket, Muller took another check around the compartment, and prepared to return to the baggage car. He slipped open the door and stepped into the corridor.

There was the sound of footsteps coming from behind him. Muller turned to look back into the compartment.

"So, goodnight Elster," he said, beginning to slide the door closed. "I will see you at breakfast."

General Muller turned to see who was coming along the corridor.

"Ah! Fraulein Schmidt."

He bowed slightly, and smiled.

*

Lawrence knew that this might be his best chance. One on one, as the situation now was, at least gave some possibilities of escape, if he could only think quick enough to solve the problem. He had already shamed himself in the memory of Colour Sergeant Bull's teachings, allowing himself to be compromised in the worst possible way, and now he must exonerate himself, if not by immediate force, then by stealth.

"So, your master has given you a little responsibility?" he said, returning to perfect German. "He didn't trust you enough to kill the old General?"

Kalmer raised one side of his face in a smirk. He spoke slowly and confidently.

"There will be time enough for such indulgences."

"Perhaps he will let you practice on a Fraulein, before

dealing with men." Lawrence went on.

The smirk lessened a little. Kalmer picked up Lawrence's bayonette, and flipped the second blade.

"If was not that we needed you unmarked, you would find out who is the Fraulein, and who is the man, Maas."

Lawrence laughed aloud.

As you can see, I am already marked, by far better than a 'kotzbrocken'
like you!" Lawrence retorted, comparing Kalmer to a lump of puke.

Kalmer waved the blade in a threatening manner and came a little closer to Lawrence to intimidate him. Lawrence laughed again, mockingly.

"What are you going to do?" he asked. "You have your orders not to lay a finger on me. What have I to fear from such an organism?"

The German officer reached forward and grasped Lawrence by the throat, tightening his grip until he gasped. He poised the tip of the blade close to Lawrence's eye, but the Englishman let him have his moment. Not yet. Not yet. Let him feel superior, until it became his undoing.
Coughing as Kalmer took away his hand, Lawrence looked contemptuously back at him. He spat on the floor.

"As I thought, the grip of a woman. Which German whore taught you that?"

Kalmer's eyes widened in anger. He slammed the bayonette onto the table and moved forward on Lawrence again, both hands groping for another, more powerful attempt. Now. As the German came close, Lawrence's knees pivoted sharply, both toecaps finding their mark in Kalmer's groin, forcing the breath from his lungs. As the man bent over from the power of the blow, Lawrence brought his forehead forward, like a hammer, into the centre of the officer's face, spreading his nose and sending him staggering backwards until halted by the edge of the table.

Lawrence was already on his feet, but still bound to the chair, his movements were limited. Kalmer had slipped onto his back. Turning, Lawrence took quick aim, and slammed one lower leg of the chair into Kalmer's windpipe, feeling the satisfactory crunch of damage, if not death.

The German officer spat red and pressed both hands to his throat, sucking for breath through the blood that blocked it. Lawrence twisted to see the extent of his attack, then bent over and pressed one knee into Kalmer's neck, allowing his whole weight to come down upon it.

It was one of those moments when justice felt good to be done, and he was the one to be executing it. There was no right or wrong, just the satisfaction of a successful outcome, no guilt or regret, just the eradication of something in his mind that had to be fulfilled to its conclusion. Lawrence had felt it many times, but seldom as now, when physical violence demanded his attention. On active service he had felt the challenge of survival, but that had nothing to do with this system of aggression that his nature demanded of him.

Kalmer expired and reality claimed Lawrence's attention. He looked for the blade, which had fallen to the floor, so he thrust himself over the body of the German and onto his back, where he could forage for the bayonette. Once found, it took but a moment to cut the bonds behind him and free himself. Now what? Just as he stood up, the carriage door opened and the face of general Muller appeared. Lawrence went for the Luger, still lying on the table where the General had left it, the silencer attached, but the bullets had scattered as Kalmer struck the table in his fall.

Knowing that there should still be one round left undischarged and undiscovered, Lawrence raised the pistol and fired as the door was slammed shut, and the jamb splintered. He had no time to chase ammunition, and threw the Luger as far down the car as he could. Had Muller realised this, the situation might have been different.

Lawrence was stiff and sore from his time bound to the chair, but there was no time to waste. He had already decided that his best chance was to escape the baggage car, and find some escape outside, so pulling the brass fire extinguisher from the wall, he pulled up the blind and shattered the large window, blinking as the smoke and steam rushed in. For a moment, he was showered with glass shards as the pressure drove them inwards, and shielded himself with a hooked arm, then he used the extinguisher to clear the jagged window frame and threw a leg over.

In the darkness, it was hard to see any handholds, but looking up he saw the narrow guttering above him, and reaching for it found that he could just grasp the edge. With a little stretching, and ignoring the rush of air and smoke from the moving train, Lawrence managed a grip. With difficulty, he managed to get a foot onto the edge of the window and hauled himself up until he could support himself, then looked for a better route of escape.

As the train negotiated a curve, Lawrence could see the connection point of the next carriage, and part of the flexible joint that allowed access. Also, there was a narrow ladder to the roof of the carriage, which engineers would use for servicing and repairs. With a little care, he found that he could almost reach the ladder by keeping one foot on the lower frame of the window, but even with the best effort, it was still six inches too far to grasp.

He thought about jumping from the train, but knew that his chances at the speed that it was travelling were slim. Only when it slowed down could he risk such an attempt, and he doubted that he could remain in his present situation for much longer without Muller's intervention in some way. Even now, he knew how lucky he was that few on the train carried weapons, but had little knowledge of what might be put against him in the next minutes. But Lawrence also knew now that the conspiracy needed him alive and unharmed, for what purpose he had yet to clarify.

As the force of the airflow caused by the passage of the train pushed him back and made vision difficult, he decided to make one huge effort to reach the narrow ladder as his best route of escape. A distant noise from inside the carriage told him that it was now or never. Holding on to the edge of the window frame with his right hand, and ignoring the glass shards that cut it, Lawrence swung his left side out and prepared to jump, as through the smoke and steam ahead, the boiler lamp of an oncoming locomotive on the other line blinked its growing aggression at him. 'Now or never, and damn the world'. Lawrence pushed hard with his right foot and reaching out with his left hand, launched himself into the smoking void.

*

General Muller had seen the Luger pointing at him and immediately pulled back sharply on the handle of the baggage car door. He heard the impact as the bullet slammed into the polished wooden frame, and unaware of the extra round so wonderfully engineered by the British security establishment, waited for the next one that Lawrence might have reloaded, and wondered how he might rectify the situation to his own personal benefit.

Muller kept a firm hand upon the brass handle of the door, so that Lawrence could not pursue him. Thinking that his only means of escaping the train would be toward the rear, he knew that the next car in line was the last, the flak wagon, and felt for the British revolver in his pocket. Then, Muller heard the sound of breaking glass. He risked a glance through the small port in the door and could just make out Lawrence's foot disappearing through the incoming smoke from the broken window.

He released his grip and entered the baggage car, cautiously, seeing the dead Kalmer, and the state of the man's injuries. Luger ammunition rolled around the floor with the rocking of the train, and the pistol lay where Lawrence had thrown it. Then, Muller hurried toward the broken window, and with his left arm raised the blind, edging his head around the side of the frame as a locomotive on the other line roared by and shrouded him with smoke and spent steam, forcing him to shield his eyes.

In the seconds that it took for the train to pass, Muller retrieved the Luger and loaded the pistol, pulling back the spring to enter a round into the chamber, then rushed back to the broken window and looked out, wondering why a perfectly serviceable gun had been abandoned, and not reloaded, a mystery he would never solve.

As the smoke died away, Muller could see by the first of the lamps in the station yard that they were reaching the halt where the locomotives were to be replaced. The Brandenburg was already reducing speed. Of Lawrence there was no sign, and the General looked back at the disappearing train that had passed on the other line, knowing that a vital part of his endeavours had been lost.

*

A thundering steel giant flashed its single yellow eye through the cloak of steam as it closed with Brandenburg, doubling the speed of the passing trains.

Lawrence felt the cold steel of the ladder and pulled himself up and into it, pressing himself tightly against the rungs as the oncoming engine screamed closer. He edged around the curve of the end of the carriage, changing hands to secure a grip and finding a better place to survive the proximity of the leviathans by placing one foot on a buffer.

The deafening roar of the passing elapsed, and Lawrence allowed himself a moment to recover his senses. As he felt the train reducing speed, he saw the yellow light of a railway yard lamp, then another, then water bowsers and coal dumps, timber props in neat piles covered in tarpaulins, and the occasional worker going about their business.

This was his chance, his gateway to freedom. A huge feeling of relief passed over him. If he could only disappear into the darkness before discovery, he was home and dry, in a manner of speaking. He risked slipping his head around the curve of the carriage and saw the lights ahead, and the adjoining loop in the distance where the two new locomotives waited to replace the current ones.

It was then that the dilemma in his sigma brain disallowed his escape. Like some constant obsessive-compulsive disorder that was forever his master, Lawrence found the scales of his condition forcing his conduct. He had been just a passenger in this game, and not the player. If he allowed whatever conspiracy that Muller pursued to happen, then he had failed his obligation, not only to himself, but to the thousands that might die needlessly, according to the explanation that Denning had given, should another take over the reins of the Reich.

Lawrence fell back against the cold metal of the carriage, weighing his options and what must be done. He knew that Hitler had a bodyguard up in the cars ahead, and perhaps by now his true identity would be known throughout the train and he was now the priority fox. The engines ahead squealed as steel upon steel dampened their speed, valve gear and drain cocks performing their functions to slowing giants.

The Englishman found the narrow ladder on the next carriage, and before the yard lamps made it too light, he stepped across and shinned up and onto the roof of the unused press wagon, pushing himself into the roof and crawling forward along the rough surface. Soon, the train halted along a short platform, with the Brandenburg locomotives extending beyond it. Immediately, a host of German uniforms began to disembark from several carriages ahead and begin to search along the extent of the train, especially in the wheel bogies and under-piping. He wondered how long it would be before they searched the rooves of the carriages.

Quickly and silently, Lawrence made his way up the

sequence of coaches, before anyone had the idea to look along the rooves, over the guest cars, the dining car, the commando-wagon, over Hitler's personal car and another baggage wagon, and found himself at the forward flak wagon.

Looking over the edge, Lawrence saw two men manning each double, eighty-eight-millimetre anti-aircraft cannon, and wondered how he was going to get over it. But the providence that snips one cord knotted another, and an officer appeared to speak to the crews through a central hatch that led to an enclosed space beneath.

"All right men, you've been up here in the open for long enough." he told them. "Go get something to eat while they change the engines."

The four Germans did not need to be told twice. Immediately they followed the officer back down into what appeared to Lawrence to be living quarters beneath the gun platform, leaving a clear route across to the locomotives. Once the hatch closed, Lawrence slipped down and across to the tender of the rearmost locomotive, jumping the short distance to the rim of the coal pit. Beneath him, an alert engineer was uncoupling the engine, and heard the scuff of boots, but when he looked up, there were only the stars and Lawrence had already dropped down into what remained of the black anthracite.

The engineer called back along the train and shouted for men to check the tender before the old locomotive left the train. Soon, two of Hitler's SS men climbed up and one of them shone a small hand torch into the pit, rolling the beam over the coal.

"Nein! Nein!" he said after a minute or so.

They jumped down and returned to their duties, while inside the tender, under a layer of coal and black dust, two white almond shapes popped open, contrasting against the dark. Lawrence spat away the grime from his mouth and rose far enough to see over the edge of the tender as the engines coughed from a hiss of inactivity to a gentle chuff forward and away from the carriages that they had been linked to for the first section of the journey to Berlin. The new locomotives had already joined the main line ahead of them, leaving space for the old ones to clear the points and reverse into the evacuated loop. This gave Lawrence a new problem, as he was now on the wrong train.

*

Feldmann hurried up to General Muller as his men were engaged in the search for Lawrence. Muller looked around to ensure that no-one could hear their conversation.

"Is the englishman dead?" asked Feldmann.

Muller shook his head.

"I don't know, but to everyone on this train, he is alive. You understand?" he replied earnestly. "Everything depends upon it. Dead, he is no use to us."

"And Elster?" Feldmann asked.

"Oh, I am quite sure that he is dead, quite dead, and primed with the documentation that exonerates us all, providing that the English agent remains alive and at large." Muller smiled. "At least for the moment." He rolled his head to one side. "And how is our leader? Not too alarmed, I hope, at another attempt upon his person."

"He can't believe it," said Feldmann. "After the man was decorated by him personally. He raved that he could have been eviscerated with a fish fork, or worse."

Muller raised his eyebrows.

"As last time, in Poland, when the bomb failed to kill him and took others in the room, you remember? How providence was shielding him, protecting his genius, for the good of the Fatherland? Well, Feldmann, not for much longer, we shall see to that soon. Then, we who remain loyal to Germany will prosecute the war properly, successfully, victorious over our enemies."

"Or conclude this madness with a compromise?" Feldmann added.

Muller looked at him, no agreement in his eyes.

"Perhaps," he said.

*

The locomotives to be replaced huffed away in a cloud of steam, slowly passing the connecting points to the siding. Some way ahead of them, the new engines were already on the same track and had already made space for them to move past the place where the two lines were connected. Once the nearby signal box had made the switch, and the old engines had moved out of the way, it would be clear for the new locomotives to reverse and be coupled to the Brandenburg.

As the tender of the rearmost original engine began its journey onto the siding, Lawrence looked furtively over the edge. He had made the decision to carry out his objective, but it seemed that now luck was against him, and soon the Brandenburg would leave him behind.

Between the junction of the mainline with the siding, there was a water crane, a device to pump water up the central pipe, via a support davit which could revolve to service either line. At the end of the rotating arm was a hose which was the final connection to whichever locomotive tender needed filling. Now that the moving engines cast their shadows over the crane, Lawrence decided it was his best chance to return to the Brandenburg.

In the poor light, and camouflaged by the steam of several locomotives, Lawrence, a dark shadow of coal dust, heaved himself up onto the edge of the tender and made the leap to the arm of the water crane, the impact of his weight shaking it a little. He pressed his body into the metal and pulled himself along toward the central pivot, narrowing his eyes to see better through the smoke and steam. He constantly looked to his right, where he knew that dark forces were searching the Brandenburg for him, and whenever he felt that he might be uncovered through clearing smoke, he hugged the metal and remained quite still until once more it enshrouded him.

Lawrence could hear the orders from an officer to direct his men to places where they might find him aboard the Brandenburg, oblivious to the fact that he was now elsewhere, but trying to return and risk the possibility of discovery. It crossed his mind once more, how strange the sinews of fate were playing this game with him, one moment snipping the strings of life which supported him, but the next, securing the frayed ends as the stretched sinew parted. And yet, something in his brain drove him on, and would not be denied.

Reaching the centre of the crane, he looked across to where the counterweight faded into the smoke and steam, and hoped that it reached far enough for him to transfer to the other track, the main line on which Brandenburg was waiting to depart.

Some way down the track, General Muller was pacing the harsh ballast that secured the sleepers and the steel rails beneath the train, while the SS men of Hitler's bodyguard were urged to investigate every dark place between the wheels and below the carriages. He looked at his watch and began to feel the pressures of time.

Feldmann, the SS commander, strode up and down the train slowly, hands clasped behind his back, at any moment expecting one of his men to call out that the fugitive had been found, and was becoming increasingly frustrated at the prospect of leaving him at large.

The new locomotives were in the process of being coupled to the Brandenburg, and the heavy clank of steel made Muller glance toward the sounds. As he did so, a dark shadow in the smoke attracted his attention as it dropped onto the baggage car that was linked between the forward flak wagon and Hitler's personal carriage. The figure dropped quickly, to flatten against the roof.

As Feldmann stepped close to Muller, the General smiled.

"Call off your men, Feldmann," he told the officer. "I think our fox has broken cover."

Feldmann looked around but was too late to see Lawrence's leap of faith. He looked quizzically into the face of the General.

"Tell your men to surround the locomotives on the other line," Muller ordered. "And tell them to remain there, as the assassin is somewhere aboard. The Fuhrer is safe so long as they keep it isolated," he laughed. "Our fox has just solved our greatest problem."

General Muller stood for a moment and observed the SS bodyguard follow the order to isolate the old engines, the soldiers spreading out to enter the steam and encircle the two engines. In Muller's strategy, this part of the plan was always going to be the most difficult. Dealing with the loyal men of the SS bodyguard was the hinge pin of the whole operation, and he had put all of his faith in the hope that they would obey Feldmann's orders without question. Unknown to Lawrence, he had now given Muller the relief that he had hoped for, and made the General's undertaking much easier. Muller turned back to Feldmann.

"Get the train moving. Maas is on the roof of the baggage car." He pointed up ahead to ensure that Feldmann knew which carriage was indicated. "Once we are out of the station yard, go up and take him." He grasped Feldmann by the arm. "But we need him alive, you understand? Alive."

Feldmann seemed unsure.

"But...?"

"You are armed, man. He is not. And he does not know that you will not shoot. Get him to the forward flak wagon, and I will join you there."

Feldmann's doubts were reassured by the General's words. He knew the importance of the plan, and now committed, he must follow Muller's orders to the fullest. As the commanding officer of the Hitler's bodyguard, he and his men alone, besides the Fuhrer, were allowed to be armed aboard the train, a trust obviously misjudged. And with the SS soldiers now somewhere in the poor light of the station yard behind them, the odds were favouring the conspirators.

Once the Brandenburg began to move, Muller jumped up onto the step of the door that he had exited by some time before and climbed aboard, now being on the leading part of the command car. Stepping over the connecting link, he knocked on the door, and waited until Hitler's aide answered.

"General Muller?" the man said. "What is going on? The Fuhrer is very concerned that..."

"I must see the Fuhrer immediately," Muller demanded. "It is vital for the security of the train."

Muller decided to keep it as concise as possible, to enlarge upon the perceived situation might not only bring more risk into the success of his plans, but perhaps also put doubt into the mind of the Fuhrer. His need now was to secure the British agent until the time came to complete his plan, and it looked like it was progressing remarkably well.

He pushed through past the aid, to where Hitler stood before a large picture of Frederick, the Great, the Fuhrer's hands rubbing nervously together. His lips were tightly pressed together, his frown indicative of his lack of composure.

"Sir!" Muller raised his voice to elaborate upon the situation. "We have uncovered an assassin who managed to conceal himself aboard the train, but Feldmann's men have him cornered in the locomotives which we left behind." He stood to attention and clicked his heels, to Hitler's contempt. "I am pleased to inform you that the situation is completely under control and the threat is completely eradicated."

Muller could see that the explanation did not please Hitler. His face darkened in anger and a cold prelude to a rebuke. Muller had not long to wait for it. Hitler exploded.

"Where is Feldmann? Why is he not here?" The tirade began.

For some minutes, Muller felt the weight of the Fuhrer's discontent, something that he had experienced before, but hoped that he would not again after the train reached Berlin. The thought strengthened his resolve to accept it, just one more time, and enjoy the dream of what he hoped was in store. As the Fuhrer's anger abated a little, he asked…

"Where is General Elster? Why is he not here?"

General Muller took on a sad expression.

"Sir," he said, slowly. "I am sorry to inform you that it was General Elster who was in league with the assassination conspiracy. When he knew that we had uncovered his intrigue, he attempted to hang himself. We tried to save him for interrogation, but I fear we were not soon enough. His heart was not strong, and even now may have succumbed to his own suicide."

Hitler turned to his aide, who stood in amazement by the door.

"Go and see if Elster is alive!" he ordered. "If so, keep him alive. He may hang, but not until we can watch the traitor struggle, and beg for his life."

*

As the aide left, on the outside of the train, Feldmann had found the narrow inspection ladder that led to the roof of each carriage. He reached down and unclipped the brass pin on his holster and felt the satisfying grip of the Walther PPK pistol. The ladder was partly shielded by the curve of the carriage, but some smoke from the engine was sucked into the space by the draught of speed.

As the new pair of locomotives began to pick up the pace and the train made the familiar clack along the rails, Feldmann climbed slowly upward, beginning to feel the cold of the night. A brief howl from the whistle of one of the locomotives surprised him a little, and he paused to regain his composure before taking off his forage cap and dropping his hand to find the Walther.

He was now close to the edge of the roof, close to where the weather extension hung over the side wall of the coach. Hooking his free hand under the last rung of the ladder, he looked over, squinting in the darkness and the rolling smoke.

Feldmann was not disappointed, for there, pressed against the roof of the forward baggage car, some metres ahead, was the grimy face of Lawrence, the whites of his eyes glaring back toward him, one arm around a ventilation outlet to steady himself. The German officer took the final rung and climbed onto the rolling roof of the carriage, keeping to his knees for balance. He held out the pistol with an outstretched arm and motioned Lawrence to stand.

It looked as if here finally, was the last sinew to be snipped, and the pawn was at last to be stopped in its path across the board.

*

Hitler's personal aide made his way down past the command car, and then the now empty carriage reserved for the SS bodyguard, through to the forward dining car, where a few confused personnel looked at him for clarification that was ignored. He carried on into the first guest car, where again, a few heads were emerging, seeking information about what was going on around them, and found the same lack of response.

Finally, he entered the second of the guest coaches, the last compartment of which he knew to be General Elster's. In this coach, there was nothing but closed, unoccupied compartments and he moved down, steadying himself by the polished brass bars along the windows. As in other carriages, the blinds were down, and had been for some time.

Reaching the end compartment, he found the sliding door

closed and the screen pulled down. He knocked, but there was no reply, and he wondered if the General had been moved to less salubrious accommodation, considering his crimes. He knocked again, and heard the merest sound from inside. He placed his head close to the glass.

"Hallo!"

There was no reply. He knocked again and waited a few moments before trying the door. It moved slightly.

"Hallo!"

He pulled the door ajar and found the lights turned off. Looking into the gloom, he saw Elster immediately, his face blue and bloated, his eyes popped and red rimmed, the lips parted and his tongue visible, a cord next to him on the long seat. He was not alone.

Opposite Elster, a familiar figure appeared, and a Luger with a small silencer emerged from the dark in an outstretched arm. It immediately discharged twice, once to the chest, and once to the head. The fourth conspirator had entered the game and waited for the next move that might lead to a checkmate.

*

Lawrence felt wretched. Blackened with grime and sweat and coal dust, and with only the whites of his eyes contrasting, he looked hard at the silhouette of Feldmann, his outline marked against the night sky and the deflected smoke behind him, and knew that he had nowhere to go. Thoughts of a frying pan and a fire crossed his mind.

Feldmann's Walther jerked upward, a sign for him to show his hands reaching for the sky. Lawrence got to his knees and complied with the sign, and the weariness of his efforts took over. It was not enough, and Feldmann motioned him to rise, and he did so, shaking gently with fatigue and the motion of the train. His eyes blinked sluggishly. The German officer shook the Walther, signalling him to turn back toward the forward flak wagon, which was unmanned for the night.

Lawrence started to shuffle his tired legs in the direction that the pistol was urging him, but as he turned, something ahead caught the attention of tired eyes, emerging through the night, through the smoke and steam of the double headed engines drawing the Brandenburg. At first, it was a pinprick of light, a pinprick that grew in size and headed toward them. Lawrence at first thought it to be just a trackside lamp, but as it closed and reflected the glow from the firebox against the tender. As the fireman shovelled in coal, he saw it for what it was, another oncoming locomotive on the other track, drawing its own line of coaches toward them.

Brandenburg had not yet begun to settle into an optimum speed, due to the continuous tight curves in this section of the line, and neither had the oncoming train, although they would pass quite quickly. Lawrence felt those sinews jangling and wondered if it might be another knot, or a blade, to extend the game a little longer, and squeeze a little more torture juice to test the opponents.

The engine on the other line growled by and enshrouded Brandenburg's double-headed locomotives in smoke from its chimney, coughing ash and boiler debris in its wake, extending down the whole of the train as it passed, with each man on the roof losing sight of the other for some moments. Lawrence summoned every muscle to his support, steadied himself and thrust his whole body across the gap to land flat on the roof of one of the carriages of the passing train. He rolled over and almost slipped between the moving trains, but managed to grasp one of the ventilator boxes and hung on. But his business was elsewhere.

Forcing himself up onto his haunches, Lawrence waited until sure that the moving coach had carried him past the German. Hoping to find a way back down into the Fuhrerzonderzug before being seen through the fading smoke, he launched himself back over the gap and squarely onto the roof of the command car, immediately aware that he had once more been located by Feldmann, who was advancing toward the gap that separated their coaches, his pistol still in his hand.

Feldmann jumped the gap easily, and grinned at Lawrence, once more under his control. They had now changed direction, with Lawrence facing forward toward the engines, and Feldmann facing the rear of the train.

Lawrence was damned if he would die on his knees, and stood, at that moment recalling what Muller had said when he was bound to the chair in the baggage car, that he was safe for the moment. Was this the moment when he was not?

Brandenburg picked up speed. Lawrence could now clearly see the line ahead over wider curves glinting in what moonlight there was. He could see quite a lot that Feldmann now could not.

Lawrence fell to his knees and clasped his hands together in the manner of a begging man. His face belied one who thought his life was to end in the next moment and he pressed his fists into his cheeks. He looked up into the face of Feldmann.

"Please! Please! I beg you. Please don't shoot me!" He pleaded. "Look, I have money, gold coins, take them…"

It was an amazing contradiction to Feldmann. Here was this Britisher, who had endured much in the last day, shown so much tenacity, now so beaten and broken, and thinking he was to be shot, begging for his life. He had no idea that they needed him alive. But the paradox was not lost on the German officer, and he enjoyed the moment, pulling back the slider of the Walther so that Lawrence could hear the bullet chambered. Lawrence's face took on the image of a man in distress, marked for death in the next instant. He pressed his hands together and his voice timbred and cried for his life, falling forward, still on his knees, almost to the point of kissing the feet of the German.

Feldmann twisted his lip in a smile of superiority. He laughed aloud and enjoyed an insult, wanting the moment to last a little longer, but his head was no match for the low bridge as the Brandenburg thundered through, the arc of brick funnelling smoke from the chimney over the mass of meat that was once a brain.

Lawrence coughed away the smoke and felt the weight of Feldmann as he fell over him and rolled away, or what was left of him. For a split second, the body teetered on the edge of the carriage as the train cleared the bridge, and before it disappeared over the side, Lawrence managed to retrieve the Walther, slipping it into his pocket.

He grasped the moment and dropped his head, shielding it with one arm against the wind and the smoke and the steam, trying to regain some strength to continue, as he knew that he must. How he desperately looked forward to close his eyes and sleep, hoping that when he awoke, it would all reveal itself as a just a dream. The thought of just giving up again entered his mind, and he knew that it would be so easy to just disembark from the train at the first opportunity, abandon Hitler to his fate and damn the man, as many already did. Was he not deserving of such a destiny? Why should he still strive to keep the bastard alive, when so many had died because of him? But then, he remembered why. If more able strategists took over the reins of Germany, what might be the cost in allied lives? What might be the cost in wasted lives and widows, and all down to William George Lawrence, who failed to keep the man alive for a few more hours?

The stoic voices in Lawrence's brain which dictated his actions once more stood him to attention and demanded his obedience. Slowly, he rose to his knees once more, his hands braced against the roof of the carriage, allowing the movement of the train to sway him a little. It was almost remedial, and he wondered how he had managed to stay alive for so long, when so many did not give a damn so long as he did their bidding.

*

General Muller spent a little time with Hitler, reassuring him, and with the British revolver still in his pocket, could have done the deed right then and there, but he had to have the Britisher alive and in the palm of his hand, so that all blame would be heaped upon him. And here was the proof, a British agent, and the weapon that he used to kill the Fuhrer, captured alive and ready to be torn to pieces by the nationalist mob. A killer who had killed before, the well-liked General Elster, and others, un-named. Anything that could be attributed to this man would be believed, and further the fanatical cause of a new regime.

Confirmation that the British had assassinated their Fuhrer would harden the most anti-Nazi of the German population and secure their loyalty to a new government, one whose subversive attempts to seize the leadership of Germany had at last succeeded. And all of those faceless supporters of the real assassins, those who Hitler had failed to identify on previous attempts on his life, would be rewarded for their encouragement.

Now, all that Muller had to do was make his way to the forward flak wagon, where surely by now, Feldmann had Maas under his control. Then, he would return, bid Hitler a reverent 'good evening', and then put a bullet in his brain. But Hitler was still agitated and isolated, now that his aide had not returned, and only General Muller seemed able to keep him informed.

"Where is Feldmann?" Hitler demanded, his hand shaking. "Where is He?"

Muller turned a little toward the door connecting with the rest of the train.

"My Fuhrer, Feldmann is dealing with the late General Elster, and investigating his compartment for information concerning any more who might be connected with this conspiracy."

Hitler clasped a hand down upon the other that was shaking. He shook his head and grimaced, one dark lock of hair falling over his forehead.

"Elster, of all people that I would have trusted." He shook his head more vigorously. "Elster." He looked squarely and darkly at Muller. "I should have liked to have seen him struggling on a meat hook."

Muller nodded in false agreement. His face took on a thoughtful presence, as if he too was shocked at the possibility.

"Yes, sir. I too found the possibility so alarming." He allowed a significant pause. "My Fuhrer, if I may, I would like to inspect the forward flak wagon. I think it would be prudent to ensure the alertness of all aboard the Brandenburg until we reach Berlin. Security there will be beyond reproach, and I apologise for any risk to your safety aboard the train."

Hitler abruptly nodded his agreement for Muller to continue.

"You must not reproach yourself, Muller," he said as the other began to walk across to the door that led to the small anti-room, and on to the first baggage car, and then the forward flak wagon, "your actions have kept me safe, and I will not forget it."

Muller halted and stood to a formal attention, the irony of the situation not lost upon him.

"My Fuhrer. It is my duty as a loyal German."

When Muller had left the Fuhrer's personal space, Hitler locked the door behind him, then went over to the opposite end of the carriage and did the same to the one there. His anxiety was at a peak, and not unreasonably so, considering the recent events. He rang the bell for the waiter's attendance, but there was no reply. By this time in the evenings, they were always stood down and had retired to their berths in the personnel sleeping cars, many carriages back along the train. Apart from the conspirators, the drama of the day was still largely unknown, and most were either dreaming, or deceased. Only when Muller's checkmate had been played would he enlighten others aboard, of how a British agent had assassinated their leader while they slept. And he had the proof to confirm it.

Muller rolled with the motion of the train, through the baggage car and across the flexible passage that opened into the flak wagon. A small metal door was the last obstacle to entering. He slipped the iron bar that held it closed, and swung it open.

Stepping inside, he found several SS men, alert but stood down for the night. Two played cards while another two were on their bunks. The space was a retreat from the double flak anti-aircraft guns above. Two men were always on duty in case of an alarm at night, while two could sleep.

In the centre of the wagon was a hatch which led up onto the gun deck above and could be accessed by a short ladder. A sergeant stood up and clicked to attention as Muller entered. The General looked around the limited space. The other soldiers followed their sergeant to attention.

"Where is Feldmann?" he asked.

The sergeant looked confused.

"He is not here, sir."

Muller looked inward for a moment, suddenly having the feeling that things might not be going to plan. He pulled himself back.

"Open the hatch," he ordered.

"Sir?"

"Open the hatch! Now!" Muller demanded without explanation.

Quickly, the sergeant complied, reaching up and partly opening the round metal hatch enough for a man to climb through. Muller pushed him aside and climbed the ladder, allowing smoke to infiltrate the lower deck of the flak wagon.

The gun deck was lower than the roof of the other carriages, to allow the guns to clear low bridges, and once there, Muller took off his cap and slowly raised his head until able to see over. There, a short distance away, he could see the form of Lawrence, his prone, weary form lying low against the roof of the command car.

Muller dropped down and with a wave of his hand summoned the sergeant to come up to the gun deck. At that moment, he weighed his options and decided that even dead, Lawrence could be useful as a scapegoat and an assassin. The man had become an irritating thorn in his side, and it was time to remove it. He put his mouth close to the ear of the sergeant and told him to initiate the cannon, ready to fire, pointing in the direction of the unfortunate Lawrence.

The sergeant began to protest, but Muller could hardly hear his words over the noise of the engines. The General took hold of the soldier's tunic and made it clear that there would be no excuses not to comply. The sergeant climbed onto the small spade-shaped seat and began to rotate the double barrels of the

'88'.

Back down the train, Lawrence could not make out what was happening through the smoke, only aware that there was enshrouded movement ahead. He stood, tiredly, and made every effort to maintain his balance.

"Shoot Man!" Muller ordered. "Shoot!"

The sergeant triggered the mechanism and the double stream of bullets, intermixed with tracer shells, lit up the sky and began to find their way toward the target a short distance away. Lawrence dropped to the roof of the carriage again and tried to crawl to the limited safety of one of the ventilator boxes, but progress was slow, and each moment he expected to be hit.

"Lower! Lower!" ordered Muller, watching the tracer fall closer to Lawrence.

But the line of bullets would drop no further. It was clear that the ordnance was made to defend against air attack, and an excited gunner might allow his aim to fall and hit the Brandenburg, creating Heaven knows what catastrophe. Lawrence looked up and realised that his continuing luck was holding.

"Under the bloody guns!" he told himself. "Under the bloody guns!"

Muller was beside himself, and fumbled for the British revolver in his pocket, coughing away the smoke that continually harassed his view of Lawrence. Finding the pistol, he pointed it into the passing smoke, only occasionally having a decent target. He fired and the sergeant dropped from the flak gun onto the deck, unsure of what might be firing back.

As the bullet skimmed the roof close to him, Lawrence pulled out Feldmann's Walther and fired blindly. Muller had no intention of risking being hit and dipped below the end of the flak wagon, where there was an armoured shield.

The short fire fight gave Lawrence the time to slip over the edge of the command carriage and grab the first rung of the maintenance ladder, letting himself down to where he could reach the entry door, but found it locked. He reached across the flexible connection between coaches and found the narrow ladder that led to the roof of the next carriage, Hitler's personal car. It too was locked.

Lawrence wondered how long he could keep this up, leaping about Hitler's Fuhrerzonderzug like a demented gibbon. His strength was fading and he need to find some kind of refuge, a place where he could defend himself with a decent chance of not becoming a colander. He was now totally aware that whatever reason had promoted Muller to keep him alive had changed, and all bets were now off. He risked a look ahead, toward where the locomotives would be, somewhere in the steam clouds. The windows of Hitler's carriage emanated a strange glow out into the night. They were partly frosted and any illumination from inside was dampened by inner blinds.

Lawrence looked up at the edge of the coach roof, to where the overhang was fringed by a disperser, a narrow rail that allowed snow and ice to slip through in the winter to avoid accumulation. He thought for a moment, wondering if what was forming in his mind was a good idea. For all he knew, the tyrant might already have an ounce of lead in his brain, but what the hell? And what if the dispersal rail would not hold him? A broken neck or a bullet? It was hardly a good outcome either way.

Reaching up and out, Lawrence's hand found the curved end of the rail and gave it a tug. It felt all right, and he suddenly appreciated the weight that he had lost while in prison, waiting for the man with the rope. Kicking off, and swinging from the rail, he knew that the least time that he was in such a vulnerable position the better. If someone began to target him again, he was a sitting duck.

Lawrence edged along the rail, inch by inch, fighting against the wind and the smoke, until he was in line with the first window. He paused for a moment and hoped that the damn thing would not break, knowing that his limited strength might not allow a second chance. He brought up his tired legs and braced them against the lower edge of the window frame as the rail began to give and sag a little, the bolts bending, but holding.

He stretched out his legs tipping his toes to get the best momentum that he could muster, as something like a signal pole flashed by and back into the night, brushing against the back of his tunic with inches to spare. Lawrence closed his eyes and made the final shove of a desperate man, his hands gripping the rail and using it as a fulcrum, while his body swung out and then forward, and crashing through a shower of broken glass and torn blinds, to struggle blindly in the debris on a dark red carpet, flushed with golden eagles of the Reich.

He opened his eyes to see the small motif of a gold swastika, aligned with others that formed the border of the carpet. Lawrence rolled over and tried to extricate himself from the glass and the ivory blinds that had wrapped themselves about him. He looked around the simple but opulent room that he knew was Hitler's personal retreat on the train. Quickly, he pulled the

Walther from his pocket, but realised that he was quite alone. Had he been too late, and now placed himself in jeopardy once more for nothing?

A toilet flushed, and from a door across the other side of the compartment, a jacketless Hitler entered, his face contorted in concern and surprise at the commotion of Lawrence's rather unconventional arrival. He looked at Lawrence with wide eyes and open mouth, the small moustache quivering above his top lip and his hands fumbling to slip light brown braces over his shoulders, and adjust the swastika motif grips. Seeing the pistol in Lawrence's hand, his hands left the braces and stretched toward the ceiling.

Lawrence pulled himself to his feet and leaned against a section of the wall, away from the noise from the locomotives, and the passing winds caused by them, blowing what remained of the blinds inward. He took a deep breath and the moment of silence seemed to last forever, one man thankful that he had arrived in time to perhaps save the other, and the other certain that he was to die. Suddenly, the Britisher saw the humour of the situation, but there was hardly time to laugh.

"For Heaven's sake, man." Lawrence said in English, forgetting himself. "Put your bloody hands down."

"Was? (What!)," asked Hitler, knowing little of the English language.

Lawrence coughed away the smoke coming at him through the window.

"Ah! Entschuldige bitte." Lawrence excused himself for his

slip into English, then reverted to an easier method of communication between the two. "Hands down, please."

Hitler complied but remained shocked and nervous about what might be happening. He stood, trembling, his arms crossed in an odd manner.

"Maas?" It was more a statement than a question. "Sie sind ein Englander?"

There was a hint of irritation in Hitler's voice, and Lawrence wondered for a moment if he was about to ask for his iron cross back. There was a carafe of water on a small table nearby, and he reached over and took a long draught. Replacing it, he looked back at the man on the other side of the carriage.

"Do you have a pistol?" Lawrence asked.

"Ja."

"Where is it?"

Hitler pointed to the brown jacket flung over the back of a chair. Lawrence jerked a thumb in its direction.

"Then I suggest you take it out," he said, nodding toward the door leading toward the front of the train, the one which Muller had exited by when he went forward to the flak wagon. "And shoot anything that comes through it. You understand? They are coming for you, not me." He thoughtfully revised his explanation. "Well, perhaps we both have an incentive to protect this space."

Hitler cautiously walked across to where his jacket lay, and pulled it on. Keeping Lawrence's eye contact, he slowly put one hand in his pocket and took out a Walther PPK, similar to the one that Lawrence had. For a brief second, the Britisher saw doubt in Hitler's eyes and wondered if there might be a problem, but quickly it passed, and the German pulled a chair closer to the locked door and sat with his arms crossed, the pistol resting in the crook of his elbow. Lawrence followed suit and pulling a chair of his own, sat backward and rested his chin on the back rest. It was good to sit, and not have any thoughts or demands, other than wait for something on the other side of that door. There was silent vigil for some minutes, which Hitler broke. They conversed in German.

"I take it that your name is not Maas?"

"Nein." Lawrence answered. "But my name is not important."

"Then I shall call you, Maas."

"Call me anything you like. Many have."

"Then why is a Britisher defending his greatest enemy?"

Lawrence laughed.

"It's a long story, just be thankful that someone is."

Hitler fell silent in thought for a while.

"It is hard to understand this situation, but I think at this moment you may be my best hope of survival. Many things have not seemed rational since I left Poland. You know that an assassination attempt happened there?"

"The world knows. And now you have another to bleat about."

Lawrence's tone sounded offensive, and Hitler turned to look at him.

"And yet, here we are, enemies protecting each other."

Lawrence laughed again.

"And why do I have the distinct feeling that even after all of this, you would have little compunction in having me shot?"

Hitler ignored the remark.

"It is very confusing," he admitted. "But I suspect that heads that should have rolled before, will certainly roll now."

Lawrence was growing tired of the conversation. In fact, he was just tired.

*

Muller heard the crash of glass above the live steam of the

engines. Taking a chance, he glanced around the side of the train and saw the blinds of the Fuhrer's carriage flapping in and out of the broken window. He looked at his watch. Soon they would be in Berlin, and the situation demanded careful timing. His fox was cornered and the plan was still viable. The conspirators were now reduced to just two, and he was certain that the other would have taken the initiative to seal off the rest of the train.

The sergeant of the flak wagon asked what was happening on the Fuhrerzonderzug, what was causing so much commotion, and the men from below appeared at the hatch, expecting it to be a night raid by the Americans.

There had been much activity by the American Air Force in this area recently. Muller calmed the concern, assuring that everything was under control, and an assassin was cornered, omitting the fact that the Fuhrer was in a similar position. He told the crew to stand down, but remain alert. The last thing he wanted was witnesses to the execution when the time came. Muller gathered his thoughts and went back through the flak wagon to the forward baggage car, and then to the connecting space to Hitler's carriage, finding the door locked. He tapped twice.

"My Fuhrer." He put his head close to the polished walnut and spoke loud enough to be heard on the other side. "Are you safe?"

*

Lawrence awoke with a start. The tap on his shoulder had been heavy and he still felt the shock of it as he opened his eyes, wondering how long he had been asleep. Damn, it was the last thing he wanted to do.

Immediately, he looked around, and saw the smiling face of General Muller, a British revolver and a Walther PPK in each hand. Hitler sat on the same chair, his hands in his lap, but had been moved against the wall of the carriage. His face was grey and drawn. Lawrence's stomach fell through the floor. So near, yet so far, and to fall asleep on the job.

"I told you to shoot him," Lawrence said. "I told you to shoot anyone who comes through the door."

It was as if Lawrence's words had triggered some indignance in the Fuhrer. His expression changed to one of disgust and it precluded a tirade of disappointment and disloyalty interspersed with insults of the worst kind, aimed at Muller and not him. Muller ignored it. He motioned Lawrence to stand and kicked his chair away, then stood where he could control the compartment.

"Well, Maas. So, we have come to the end of our little game." He smiled. "You have played well, but in the end, the odds were against you. But do not feel too disappointed. A better opponent has predicted your moves from the first pawn."

Lawrence dropped his head to one side.

"I have heard it said that a pawn is the most powerful piece on the board, because it has nothing to lose," he replied.

Muller shrugged.

"Reviewing our present situation," he parried, "I am certain that you would not prescribe to that theory."

There was a gentle tap on the door leading back into the train. Muller motioned Lawrence to move, so that he could keep him in his view while answering.

"Ja?" Muller asked, his ear close to the wood.

Lawrence could not hear nothing of what was said when Muller unlocked the door and opened it slightly and listened. A moment later, the door was closed and locked once more. Muller stepped back into the carriage space.

"It appears that the time is short." He explained. "Soon, everyone on the train will awake to find that our dear Fuhrer has succumbed to a British assassin, aided by traitors who have taken their own lives rather than pay for their crimes. Proof of the conspiracy will be the live assassin, who in due course will hang, after his trial, of course. Further proof will be the actual weapon that was used."

Hitler cut into Muller's words with another tirade of disgust, but it was clear that Muller was enjoying the moment.

"When I shoot you in…" he looked at his watch, "… fifteen minutes or so, I will remember the insults that you have thrown at me, the cold mornings in Russia that I endured at your order, and all of the other small things that have irritated me." He was thoughtful for a moment. "And be assured that your whore at the Berchtesgaden will be suitably consoled."

Hitler sat, his hands on his knees, a man resolved to his fate.

"Do you have any last requests?" Muller asked of him, mockingly, but there was no reply. "Or you, Maas? Perhaps we might play another game before you are hanged?"

"Maybe your man on the other side of the door could bring a couple of beers?" Lawrence said, trying to think this through. "And you could send my Iron Cross to my relatives, I'm sure they would be impressed."

"Ah!" Muller declared. "I had forgotten." He laughed. "It would be insane to find a British assassin with the Fuhrer's decoration." He inclined his head forward a little in mock salute. "Thank you, Maas, where is it?"

"In my pocket." He inclined his head to the left pocket of his grimy tunic.

Muller held out a hand.

"If you please, Maas."

Lawrence threw a look of contempt across his face.

"Get the damn thing yourself."

Muller looked seriously at him for a moment. He put the revolver into his pocket and levelled the Walther at him, motioning him to stand.

"Arms out, stretched out," he ordered.

Lawrence did as he was told. Muller stepped forward and put the end of the barrel directly into the centre of Lawrence's chest.

"The slightest move, and you will be a dead assassin." The German warned as he moved his other hand toward Lawrence's tunic pocket.

Lawrence sighed.

"Sorry Adolf," he said in plain English, glancing toward Hitler "but we've had a grand time, haven't we?"

In the split second that Muller's eyes glanced sideways to where the Fuhrer sat, Lawrence's hand dropped to grasp the barrel of the Walther, not to take the weapon but to jerk it upwards and back, as Bull had taught him. Muller reacted to the action and tightened his grip, but his trigger finger was encased firmly in the guard and as the business end of the barrel found the space beneath his jaw, anatomy had nowhere to go but react.

The bullet spattered teeth and blood over Lawrence's face, pierced the roof of Muller's mouth and entered the brain, ejecting most of it onto the ceiling above. In a heartbeat, the sinews of fate had been snipped again, and knotted in Lawrence's favour, thanks to the advice of one Colour Sergeant Bull, and once again the Gods of the game had allowed another pawn to survive a little longer.

Lawrence could see that it was getting light outside. He looked over at the startled face of Hitler, his mouth open in surprise at the idea that he might just live. Berlin must be close, and he had no wish to talk through the outcome of his presence there.

"Berlin soon," he told Hitler. "And for Heaven's sake keep the damn doors locked until you get there, this time." He stooped and found the British revolver in Muller's pocket, then tossed it over to the man with the silly moustache. "Here, a souvenir for you."

Hitler caught it and said nothing, remaining seated and confused. The train began to decelerate and a whistle from one of the locomotives announced its presence. Lawrence took a look outside and saw railway yards and stationary engines and wagons. He kicked over the blooded body of Muller and found the Walther, slipping it into his pocket as he went over to the broken window. He took one last look at the dictator and tipped a farewell, then pulled the blind down to cover the glass shards on the window frame and slipped over. He rolled on the sharp ballast stones next to the tracks and was careful to avoid the wheels of the carriages as they squealed past. It was a strange sight, a grimy figure emerging from the smoke after the Fuhrerzonderzug had passed, moving across the railway yards and through the wagons as the first light of a new day dawned.

Chapter Nine
The London System

Approaching London Airport (Soon to be Heathrow, July 1966)

It had been a tediously long flight and he had read the book again, for the third time since he had purchased it. Nothing made sense, and the frayed ends rattled in his mind, demanding to be tied.

Passport check went without incident and he collected what little luggage he had brought with him with little delay. English money seemed strange and he struggled with the demand from the taxi driver, unprepared due to his eyes constantly on the passing city and trying to remember.

Some parts of London remained clear in his mind, but when he tried to find them again, many had gone, and he felt a strange disappointment that part of his story had been eradicated. These places were of more importance than the major tourist attractions, but it mattered little. He was not here as a tourist.

Wembley, July 30 1966

He pulled the England scarf around his neck, happy to be seen to be supporting them. The World Cup Final was a major event and the stadium was full to capacity. It neared the end of the game and looked like the old country had something to celebrate.

Binoculars followed the players, but his interest was more on a particular section of the crowd, and he constantly checked, noting also the nearest exit point for the individual that he was observing. With seconds to go, and the English supporters already roaring their appreciation, he left his seat and with the walking sick in his hand, he made for the exit before the crowds might hinder his progress. Finding the appropriate exit port, he drew a soft hat from his pocket and pulled it down over his eyes, and leaned against the white glossy brick to wait.

The increased roar of the multitudes told him that it was a win for England, and maybe there might be longer to wait as the Queen presented the cup. He could hardly blame them on such an occasion. Moving toward the entry to where the crowd could be observed, he used the binoculars again to confirm that the man was still there, and had not left early. He was.

Soon, the early leavers began to appear and make their way home. He had chosen his spot wisely and few could pass without him observing them. Minutes went by and despite several who looked similar to his man, he was certain that he had not yet gone by.

Then, the moment came, and he recognised him easily, despite the years. He was wearing a sports jacket, and light slacks, open necked white shirt and carried a programme of the game. It was quite easy to follow and remain unseen due to the volume of English supporters all heading toward the underground. He followed down to the Wembley Park Station and took the same train when it arrived, disembarking two stops away, at Baker Street.

He followed a little way further, until his quarry halted at traffic lights and waited to cross. Stepping closer he assumed a London accent, for no other reason than the intrigue of the moment.

"Don't I know you, sir?"

The man checked the lights but they were still against crossing. He turned to see a man with a soft hat pulled over his face, and an England scarf pulled high across his face, despite the warmth of the day.

"I don't know, do you?" Came the casual reply.

He looked away, waiting for his chance to cross.

"I think so, sir. During the war. I remember you sir. You were very kind to me, you bought me something to eat, and I remember it very well."

A certain interest formed. He briefly looked again at the man.

"Oh, and where was that?" he asked.

"On the Embankment, sir," the man said. "Fish and chips if I recall."

Suddenly the past re-entered his life. The lights changed but he did not cross. He looked hard at the person by his side as the other removed the hat and unwound the scarf that revealed the remains of a large scar.

"Good God. I thought you were dead," said Rutter.

"I am," replied Lawrence. "Don't you remember?" He smiled. "Can I buy you a coffee, or should I say tea?"

*

They sat in a corner of the small café as London traffic hooted by and the volume of happy football supporters continued on their way home.

"So where have you been all of these years?" Rutter asked.

Lawrence shrugged and toyed with his cup.

"Oh, here and there. By the way…" he said, "… it's actually not Lawrence any more. And anyway, Denning crossed that name off the books years ago, didn't he?"

"I don't know what to say." Rutter admitted. "After you dropped into Germany, we heard no more from you. We just assumed that you were dead or taken, which amounts to the same thing, I suppose."

"Hitler's survival told you nothing?" Lawrence asked.

Rutter shook his head.

"I think we just put it down to the luck of the draw, that his security overcame another attempt on his life. They did plenty of times, you know?"

Lawrence thought for a moment.

"Have you read the book that was just published? The one about an attempt on his life on the train?"

"Only the bits in the papers. I try to avoid any war stuff. They get a bit tedious. Don't they?"

Lawrence let it pass.

"And Denning? Is he still breathing?"

"Absolutely, he was seconded to MI5 after the war, and helped shape it until he retired."

"And you?"

"Nothing so glamorous, I'm afraid," he admitted. "Luxury car market's my game. Had enough cloak and dagger stuff to last me a lifetime."

Lawrence finished his coffee and placed the cup back onto the saucer.

"What about your family?" Rutter asked. "Did you ever see your boys again?"

Lawrence inclined his head.

"Oh, I see them from time to time, but they never see me." He raised an eyebrow. "Why would they want to? They're doing well on the money that was given them. Denning kept his word on that one."

"I'm glad," Rutter said, asking a passing waitress for two more coffees.

He looked over at Lawrence.

"What did happen after you were dropped into Germany?"

"Damned if I know," the other answered. "But nothing happened as it was supposed to. That's why I'm here."

Rutter leaned forward and placed his elbows on the table. He looked directly at Lawrence.

"So, I take it that it was no accident that you found me today? What is it? Revenge, money, retribution?"

Lawrence shook his head. He waited until the second coffee arrived and the waitress had gone. How much to respond to his question was difficult. There were things he felt that should be kept until the right time, and maybe the right person, but who that person was, it was difficult to decide. He had to begin somewhere.

"Just trying to make sense of it all. I had the distinct impression that I was expected," he explained. "Used, manipulated, whatever you want to call it. Most of the instructions that were given to me turned out to be a complete waste of effort. I found no sniper waiting to take out Hitler, but ended up swept along with the current anyway." He thought for a moment. "Did you trust Denning?"

The coffee was still hot and Rutter blew over the liquid to cool it. He looked up, as if someone had accused him of something.

"Good Heavens, of course, man. He was my senior officer; he gave me a promotion. And it was twenty years ago."

"Twenty-two." He was corrected. "Denning mentioned an agent already on the ground in Germany, and that they would organise my escape after I found the sniper, providing I wasn't captured. Did he ever divulge the man's name to you? Or anything else?"

Rutter shook his head.

"It was a strange time in the cloak and dagger world in those days, it had to be because of the war. Many agents had been embedded since long before the war began, to wheedle their way into Hitler's inner circle, or the German Army, or the security services. They were the deep divers, the ones who took most risks, known only by their code names, even to Denning. It had to be that way, or they were worthless."

"But Denning communicated with these people? He had to, and he certainly did in my case."

"By a complicated and diverse system to protect their lives." Rutter told him. "Any dealings I had with agents was on a far different level, like you, set to achieve a specific objective."

"And the 'deep divers' couldn't be put at risk by something as mundane as saving the life of one of the worst dictators in history?" Lawrence offered. "And in the process, save allied lives?"

"Sorry, old man." Rutter admitted. "I'm afraid that was the way it was. What information they could provide was ongoing, and far more valuable."

Lawrence finished his coffee quickly. He smiled across the table. Rutter looked concerned.

"If your intention is retribution, I have to be honest with you and tell you that I intend to inform the authorities. I cannot stand by and see murder." He imparted. "I know you were convicted as such, and perhaps might be again, and will not stand by and watch it happen. I should also inform Denning of our little reunion. I see it as my duty to a senior officer, and a friend, even though we are both no longer in the service."

Lawrence laughed.

"You forget, Major Rutter, that I am a dead man, convicted and hanged, and there are papers filed to prove it. My name is no longer one that you can identify. You have no idea of my place of domicile or my occupation, either in this country or another. In another place, and another time, I might have considered the actions that you fear, and perhaps there are those that deserve it, but I will give you this undertaking. My intentions are to harm no-one, and I give you my word on it, so long as they do not intend to harm me. All I ask is that you remain silent for seven days, and say nothing about our meeting. After that, you can do as you feel fit."

Rutter felt uncomfortable. It had grown considerably since the conversation had begun. There was a silence in which he looked out at the street and watched the population go by. After so many years, it began to come back in more detail, images that he had not thought of in years.

He recalled a conversation with Denning, during Lawrence's time with Sergeant Bull, a conversation where Denning told him of Lawrence's condition, a strange condition of the mind known as a 'sigma male'. While much of the actual words were lost to time, he remembered the general line of recall. Such men were camouflaged in normality in everyday life, but were subject to their own interpretations of behaviour, of right and wrong, and the pursuit of it. Under the right conditions, such men could be extremely dangerous.

And yet, there was a trust that Rutter felt automatically for the man. Something in the way he spoke, in the way that after so many years his sense of apparent justice and determination to straighten things in his own mind was still so strong. Or was it the camouflage of the sigma male?

Rutter looked across the table once more, undecided. He saw the scar on Lawrence's left cheek that they had inflicted upon him. Time had healed and smoothed the skin, but it was still there, and he felt a shame that he had not felt at the time. He tapped a finger to his own face.

"How is it?"

"Oh," Lawrence replied. "So-so, I don't much dwell on it any more. Had a little surgery on it, years ago, and it improved a lot, but it never improved my standing with the ladies." He pressed his lips together in a smile. "The good thing is I don't need to shave that side any more, so I guess I save on razor blades. I don't dwell on it any more."

"I'm sorry," Rutter said, but Lawrence just shrugged it away.

Another short silence passed.

"So, why now, after all these years," Rutter asked. "Why would you leave it so long?"

"Because of the book." Lawrence told him. "Something so right, and something so wrong came back to haunt me, with questions that I have wanted answers to for years. But it just meant more questions, and I cannot let it lay until I know."

"I wish I could help you more, to rest the ghosts of the past. Lord knows you deserve that at least."

Lawrence looked hard across the table.

"Seven days?"

They left the café and stood in the street for a moment, both satisfied that their undertaking to each other would be fulfilled. Shaking hands, they parted and were about to go in different directions, when Rutter half turned back and called after

Lawrence, who faced him.

"For what it's worth, whatever happened back then, it saved thousands of lives. I want you to know that. The war might have gone on for another two years."

Lawrence just smiled back and raised a hand in farewell.

"Good day to you." he said.

*

In the days before Lawrence located Rutter, he had spent much time in Somerset House, the more substantial libraries in London, places of reference, and also purchased a second-hand typewriter from a pawnshop.

He had found a reasonable place to stay, and had begun to reference on paper as much as he could remember of those times in 1944. It helped remarkably, and returned much detail that he had almost forgotten, but which added to the volume of questions that he needed answering. He flipped through the book again, and tried to cross reference his memories.

A day after his meeting with Rutter, he took the underground to the north of London. Emerging from the station, he asked directions from a newspaper kiosk, and followed the advice that they gave him, fifteen minutes later finding himself at the entry gate to a small, run-down church. Opening the creaky gate, he went in and began his search, moving through the mis-aligned gravestones until he found the one that he sought.

Lawrence looked down at the faded engraving, moss covered and neglected. He put his hands in his pockets and stood for some time, then kneeled and began to clear away the moss, until he could read the inscription clearly.

    Colour Sergeant Stanley Bull
    HM Black Watch
    1898 – 1951

He had little more knowledge of the details of the man beneath the stone, and kind of liked it that way. And it was none of his business, anyway. But he always felt that he owed something to Colour Sergeant Bull.

Looking down again at the inscription, Lawrence spoke to the past.

'Well, Colour Sergeant,' he said, more to himself, 'I'm not sure that I did your advice justice, and I probably forgot more than I remembered, but it certainly helped to keep me alive all of those years ago. And I just felt that I should thank you personally.'

Lawrence stood there for a minute, remembering, then retraced his steps and made his way back, the way he had come.

*

It was raining. He thought of buying an umbrella but decided against it, preferring to skip under the canopies until he found the shop that he wanted. Once inside, he closed the door behind him and looked around. The toy shop owner asked politely if he could help, but Lawrence declined, and he took on the role of someone looking for the right thing for a birthday.

Finding what he wanted, Lawrence placed it on the long counter and offered a one-pound note, waiting patiently until the item was wrapped and the change given. He looked at his watch. It was still early, so he found a café and killed the time with bacon and eggs, toast and coffee. Today was an important day, and he hoped that he had been diligent with his research. It had not been easy.

He was half way through his second coffee, and he thought deeply of what he must do, what he should say, and what he should ask. He knew instinctively that upon this day might revolve everything that haunted him, and how he approached it would be important. Lawrence looked out of the window, and although still overcast, the rain had stopped. He wondered how the day would evolve.

But what if his research had been wrong? He would have to go back and start again, look at the dates, look at the times, go through all of those filmstrip readers at the libraries, phone books and the tedious hours of search and enquiry.

Lawrence once again took the underground to the closest station to his destination. He took the stairway to street level and navigated to an expensive row of houses in central London. Keeping to the opposite side of the street, he walked along until he found the number he wanted, then kept walking for some distance, until he found an appropriate place to wait without being too obvious.

A shade after ten fifteen, he saw the door of the three-story house open, and a portly man exit. He seemed quite elderly, wearing a dark raincoat and bowler hat, complete with rolled umbrella. He strode down the three steps that led to the street level, and began to walk in the opposite direction to where Lawrence waited.

At the end of the smart street, the man turned right. Lawrence was already hastening after him, and followed at a reasonable distance, waiting his opportunity. He had not long to wait. Concrete and brick began to change to a more verdant cityscape, with trees on either side of the road, and a park appeared, in which the dark raincoat entered by the first available gate, and followed the narrow path to a small lake.

Lawrence enjoyed the scent of foliage after the rain; it felt cleansing and fresh and reminded him of home, wondering when how long it would be before he completed his undertaking and saw it again. He had a large brown paper bag in his hand and widened the open end a little.

Opposite the lake was a park bench, made of metal, with wooden strips for the seat, and the elderly man took a cloth from his pocket and wiped it down before sitting. Lawrence strolled along as casually as he could, and reaching the bench, asked politely…

"Do you mind?" he asked, casting a hand over to the bench.

The man looked up at him, and Lawrence recognised the face immediately, a little older, considerably more portly but definitely Denning.

"Oh, please…" came the answer, offering the cloth for Lawrence to wipe the seat as a flurry of ducks began to appear around him.

Lawrence thanked him as the portly man pulled a bag from his other raincoat pocket and began issuing bread to the birds, casting it wide so that most would have a share.

"You're not very good at this, you know," said Denning while keeping his eyes upon the ducks, "I spotted you almost immediately." He sniffed, as if expecting a winter cold. "Rutter said you were back, although God knows why after all of this time."

Lawrence smiled.

"I thought he might not be able to hold to his word."

It appeared to incite a certain indignation in Denning. He turned slowly to look Lawrence in the eye, and spoke sharply, with a certain reserve.

"He's a British officer, or was, and as such commits to the obligation of who you give it to!"

Denning continued his popularity with the ducks.

"You know that we assumed you dead?" he confirmed. "And there was little that we could do to confirm one way or the other, but we did adhere to our agreement for the support of your children. Are you aware of that?"

"Yes," answered Lawrence. "And I am grateful for it."

"Then, what do you want?" Denning asked abruptly.

Lawrence put his hand inside the paper bag and drew out a hardback book, placing it on the seat between them. Denning glanced at it.

"Why did you write a forward to this book?" he asked.

"Because I was asked." Denning replied. "As I have composed several others that related to the period in which I was a part."

"And the substance inside? Did you see verification of the facts?"

"Of course, the author sent copies of documentation, and personal testimony, years ago."

Lawrence reached down and flipped through the pages, almost absent-mindedly, knowing that Denning had been misled. But he said nothing. He had to keep his own council until certain of the truth."

"But it was only recently published. Why so long?" Lawrence asked.

Denning sighed.

"Yours was a truly unusual undertaking, even during the war, and It had the highest clearance to go ahead, it had to have." He turned to look at Lawrence. "And I mean the highest. In order for us to proceed, I had to confirm to Churchill that nothing of this would be made public in his lifetime, and that the files would be destroyed. In both of these, I kept to my word."

"And he died last year. So, you didn't object to the book."

"Yes."

"But what was he afraid of, Churchill?"

Denning sighed again and took a tiresome attitude."

"My dear fellow," he began, "if the British public became aware that the Prime Minister had sanctioned the preservation of Hitler, they would have torn him to pieces at the first sight of his silly cigar. He needed to preserve his appointment as PM, and his reputation."

"But he was voted out."

"But he preserved his reputation." Denning confirmed, his words slow, and defined. "And he was back in office again in 1951, was he not?"

The food for the ducks was exhausted. Lawrence considered this new element in his analysis. Denning looked at the ground as they dispersed.

"What did happen? Were you taken by the Germans?" He asked.

Lawrence wondered how much to impart, in the interest of finding the truth.

"No," he said. "I was not taken, not by a long shot, although

I could have been. It was a cock-up from the start, and everything I expected was upside down. But I survived it."

"But you failed your assignment, essentially." Denning remarked.

"No. I did not." Growled Lawrence, irritated a little but understanding. "He survived, didn't he, Hitler I mean?"

"No thanks to you." Denning quipped. "Not according to the damn book?"

Lawrence shook his head, but said nothing.

"And you got away? From Germany?"

"Eventually. It took a long time, but I crossed the border into France. My grandmother still had a small farm there, and I stayed until the end of the war. She died in 1946, and I sold the place and… well… let's say the rest is history."

"I see."

Lawrence knew he needed to get into the difficult things. He prepared himself, and tried to be casual in his questions.

"I need to ask you about your information concerning the reason for my little jaunt into Germany in 1944." He told Denning. "How much did you trust it?"

Denning shrugged.

"One hundred per cent. These people had proved their worth for some time, and there was no reason to suspect it was not cosher. But there are things even now that I can't go into, even with you, despite your proximity to the undertaking." He paused. "I'm sorry, but I just cannot."

Lawrence waited, hoping to imply determination. He put a hand back into the paper bag and retrieved an automatic pistol, which he kept partly concealed under one forearm.

"I'm afraid I must insist," he said. "Rutter broke his word in contacting you, so I will consider myself removed from any obligations that I gave him. You will recall that I am a convicted murderer with an erased past, so I have every expectation of shooting you and getting away with it. There are no connections between us anymore, and there is no-one around, so please make your decision as it is almost lunch time."

Lawrence thought the last part was a nice touch. Denning swallowed, unsure of how serious Lawrence was. He thought for a moment and decided that the war was a long time ago, and he was too old for cloak and dagger stuff any more. Perhaps too, he felt that he owed this man something. He sighed heavily again.

"Oh, dammit!" he began. "The long-time embedded people had never let us down. Some went back to the days when Churchill was Secretary for the Navy, and were as old as he was. They were information oriented, nothing to do with the cut and thrust during the war years. We had people in the inner circle, worming their way closer to Hitler himself, some of the officer class who hated the damn fellow and everything he stood for, and on all kinds of levels."

"And how did this information get through to British Intelligence?" Lawrence asked.

"At first, before the war, by courier. Old fashioned stuff by today's standards, but it worked all right. Then, during the war, there were more sophisticated methods, which I will not talk about," he turned to Lawrence with a determined expression upon his face, "even if you put a bullet in my brain."

"Did you have names for these people, code names, or any way of identifying them?"

"Code names, yes, but not known by me. Information was forwarded to my department from elsewhere, and we acted upon it. Our job was to use the information, not to source it. That was the employment of others."

"And the information these long-term informants produced was just trusted?"

"So long as it kept coming and was never found to be false, why challenge it?" Denning confirmed. "It was always trusted before, and until someone said different, it was taken as useful." Denning paused for a moment, perhaps challenging his own lack of doubts in those dark days. "You must bear in mind that we were grasping at straws sometimes, desperate for direction, and these information sources gave us just that."

Lawrence thought for a moment.

"And the information you had on my assignment, the dead German, Maas? It was from this kind of source."

"Of course."

"It never occurred to you that maybe one of these people could be giving false information?" asked Lawrence.

"It should have been quite obvious if they had, events would soon have identified them as false prophets." Denning's words seemed to carry some sense. "The long-term informants also had a useful by-product, they identified their own successors, the next generation of German moles. It was in their own interest to be absolutely certain of their protégés, to protect their own security."

To Lawrence, some of it made sense, and some did not, but was that not the reason for all of his doubts, and the thing which drove his mind to seek the truth of everything he had been through, twenty-two years ago? Denning broke his train of thought.

"Now, sir, unless you intend to shoot me, you remind me that it is approaching mid-day…"

Lawrence brought the automatic from under his arm and levelled it at Denning, whose face remained expressionless. A finger tightened on the trigger. Lawrence's face took on a half-smile as he raised the gun, pausing for a satisfying moment before firing.

The placid stream of water closed the gap between them and ran down Denning's raincoat. Lawrence completed the smile and put the water pistol on the bench, between the two. The older man brushed away the little beads of water, retrieved his umbrella and stood up, straightening his bowler hat. He remained there for a moment, looking around him, everywhere except down at Lawrence.

"The war was a long time ago, and I am done with it. I have served my country, and done my duty, as have others. I would remind you that events of the past are the reason that you currently take the air of the country into your body, and you should be glad of it. To all, you are a dead man, and I urge you to remain that way."

Denning took the first steps away from the bench before pausing.

"I bid you, good day, sir," he said.

Chapter Ten
The Pawn Ascendant

It began to rain again, a freshness to claim the warm August day. Lawrence retrieved the book and returned it to the paper bag, then made his way to a small, green-roofed shelter a short way off and sat on the wooden bench. He looked toward the place where the narrow path wound around the lake and disappeared behind rhododendron, where the portly form of Denning had made his way out of the park.

Lawrence had known this moment might come, when his options for truth might be exhausted and he would stare once more at a hypothetical brick wall. He began to analyse the analysis, to question his own methods of investigation and wondered if any of it really mattered after so long. He took out the book once more, and looked at the dust cover, now a little frayed at the edges, with so many thumb-through assaults. It was the catalyst that had sparked his determination to go back in time. He crossed his arms with the book against his chest, and stared out at the lake,

where the ducks were apparently enjoying the shower.

Any doubts about Denning and Rutter had dispersed. There had been plenty of time to bring down the authorities on him, had they wished, but clearly, they had not. Certainly, his history would have caused them difficulties in doing so, but he had the distinct impression that they saw him as nothing more than an irritant, reviving a past in which they had little to be ashamed of, anyway. There was something more, something that he had overlooked, something obvious, but at the same time camouflaged in plain view. Time.

Lawrence forced his mind back to the beginning. Twenty-two years was a long time, and there had been half a lifetime in between. Perhaps as things evolved, a half lifetime that he should be thankful for, but Heaven knows he had earned it, even if no-one was aware of it.

He recalled the days before Denning and Rutter had entered his life, the endless chess games that had filled the days before the noose was placed around his neck. He remembered the sensation of seconds ticking away toward the darkness of oblivion, or whatever came after. He remembered that. Then the confusion of silence, and aware that something unseen was hauling him away into the unknown. How many had been through the horrors of such disorientation and chaos of mind? Then, while his mind wandered in bewilderment, pressed into the service of blind obedience, into a situation that held little more hope than the one he had been pulled away from so inhumanely. And yet, he had survived it.

He wondered why his mind held no guilt for the killings. He knew that he should bear the guilt, at least for some, but he did not, could not. And yet, with age, no more did he feel animosity for those who had wronged him, as once he would have. But his memories were still clear, even conversations and flashes of mental vision.

He revisited his recent conversation with Denning, and then, his eyes glazed as the first of the elusive pieces fell into place. Conversation. Words. He had been over it so many times in his mind and almost forgotten. The rain stopped but it remained overcast.

Lawrence followed the first piece as it locked in his mind, and looked for the trail that led him to the next, then the next. It seemed impossible, implausible, but the more pieces he found the more it revealed another trail, another hiding place for the pieces. They were scattered and worn with time, but undeniable. He unwrapped the book again, and flipped from one page to another, satisfied that they clarified and became less fluid.

As the sun appeared through the cloud of early afternoon, Lawrence walked, finding the effort conducive to helping his memory. It was not an easy path to discovery, and reached over twenty-two years, but gradually it came through. Unaware of how long he had let the process of thought take over, he checked his watch.

He must return to his accommodation and get everything on paper. Already, he had used the second-hand typewriter that he had purchased to arrange his thoughts, but now he realised how wrong he had been, how he had used doubt instead of fact to channel his thoughts. Now, it was different, and the facts kept coming.

*

Lawrence awoke the next morning, still dressed. He had worked long into the night, and when it seemed that the clackety clack of the typewriter might cause complaint, he devolved to pencil. He took a long bath and went over it all again, still half doubting the truth of it, but coming to the same conclusions.

He had much to do. More time at places of reference, concluding the typing, and other things. Breakfast was satisfying as he had not eaten for almost a day, so heavy had the revelations dropped onto his shoulders. He had taken his typing with him, and read through again as he ate, ignoring the strange looks of diners when he talked to himself over a particular sentence.

It was tedious work and Lawrence was not a natural administrator, but after two days, he had made some order out of his reflections. He read it through several times, occasionally adding to the narrative, or changing minor incidents as he recalled them. In the afternoon, he found a stationers shop and handed over the papers in a large brown envelope.

"Ten copies, please."

The young assistant raised an eyebrow when he told her the number of sheets. She struggled with the total cost seeming more interested in the scar on his cheek.

"That will be three pounds and… err…"

"Eight shillings." Lawrence smiled. "Shall I wait? Oh, and I'd better have some envelopes."

Once he had the copies completed, Lawrence searched for a more specialist emporium. He knew that this would be difficult, and he spent some time and quite a few enquiries before he found what he was looking for. He looked around, aware that it was almost closing time, and the gentleman who followed his navigation of the shop was eager to be away.

"Have you this in in my colour?" Lawrence asked, holding up the item, and comparing it to another.

"Is it for fancy dress, sir, or some other venue, or every-day wear? asked the slightly irritated assistant.

Lawrence thought for a moment and turned to the man behind the counter.

"Er... yes."

*

Hiring a car was simple enough and he chose a Ford, expecting to need the vehicle no more than two, or three days at the most. He set off early on a Friday morning, and threw a few things in the back, including ten large brown envelopes, correctly stamped and addressed, and an old backpack that he had brought with him, containing his recent purchases. Also, on the passenger seat was the book which was the spur to his pursuits.

Stopping to fill up with petrol, Lawrence bought a standard road map book, and pulled into the first safe place to plan his journey. First, he took the best route to Gloucester, and from there he could navigate to the small village that would be his destination in the Cotswolds. Then, he would have to play by ear, and see how things panned out.

The thought crossed his mind that of course, he might be completely wrong. As he drove along, he went through it all again, tracking backwards to see if he might have made an assumption that would not fit, and if he did, he would have to start again from there. But the more he dissected it, the clearer it became.

In Gloucester, he stopped for something to eat, but it was really more time to think that he craved, and he indulged himself, his mind casting aside the uncertainties and driving him forward, literally. Taking out his references, he found the telephone number that had taken him so long to find, through so many more devious calls and cross referencing. His heart began to beat a little faster at the prospect, so near and yet so far.

Leaving the car, he opened the heavy door of the big red phone box and fished into his jacket pocket as it closed behind him, for the coins that he knew he would need. Taking a deep breath, he inserted ten shillings worth and dialled, putting a thumb on button 'A'. He waited, but there was no reply, so he thumbed button 'B' and his coins were returned.

A few minutes passed while he considered his best option, then decided to take a walk down the street, and maybe try again. The day was warm and people wandered aimlessly in their shopping adventures, and Lawrence thought to himself how different it all might have been if the conspirators of those days in 1944 had succeeded.

He purchased a newspaper and idly fanned the pages, hardly pausing to investigate what was there, his mind far beyond the local gossip and advertisements. Returning to the car, he looked over at the big red phone box, just standing there, as if beckoning him over. Once more, he pulled back the door and placed the paper on the top of the black service box, waiting until the heavy clunk gave him privacy.

The money was presented again and he waited. He looked at himself in the small mirror above the service box, listening to the burr-burr of an unanswered telephone, and was about to hang up when someone answered. His mind blanked for a moment and he spoke, forgetting to press button 'A', but then regained his composure and pushed the silver cylinder firmly home, hearing the satisfying tumble of the coins.

"Yes? Hello?" A woman's voice answered, somewhat refined, and definitely middle England.

Lawrence swallowed. He should have thought this better.

"Oh, hello. Is this Miss Miller? Elizabeth Miller?" he asked.

"Yes. Who is this?"

"Oh, hello, I'm sorry to disturb you. Er… my name is Barnes, I work for the local paper, the er…" He had forgotten the name, and so looked at the folded issue that he had put on top of the black box, and coughed to allow himself time. "Excuse me, the Gloucester Chronicle…"

"Yes?"

"Well, we were wondering if we might ask you for an interview, concerning your recent book? We do always try to support local authors."

"What was the name again?"

"Er, Barnes. Michael Barnes."

There was a brief pause.

"Mister Barnes, your paper interviewed me not two weeks ago, were you unaware of that?"

"Oh! Oh, yes. I am aware of that, but there was so much

interest that we hoped that you might consider a more in-depth review of the book. We had a few people who contacted us, who were in the services during the war, and were very interested. So, we decided to see if you might be willing to expand a little." Lawrence waited during the brief silence. "I think it can only create more interest in the book, and it certainly deserves that."

"Well, when do you want to do this?" Miller asked. "Do you want me to come to the Chronical offices? I sometimes come through to Gloucester."

That was the last thing that Lawrence wanted.

"Oh no. I wouldn't expect you to do that. I can come to you, any time that's convenient, and take up as little of your time as I can. We would be most grateful, and we have affiliations elsewhere in the publishing industry that would be interested, if you're happy with that?"

"Well, the publicity wouldn't hurt, I suppose, and I appreciate your interest." She conceded. "Look, I'm tied up tomorrow, Saturday, but if you can make it late Sunday afternoon, I'm free for the rest of the day. Do you work Sundays?"

"Of course." Lawrence confirmed, damning the day's delay.

"Until Sunday, then," she told him, do you have the address."

"Sure, I know where you are. Will around four be all right?"

"Perfect. When is this likely to go out?"

Lawrence thought for a moment.

"Oh, I should imagine within a few days or so."

"Then I'll see you Sunday, Mister Barnes, and thanks again for your interest."

*

Sleeping in the car would be far from comfortable, but he remembered far worse. However, he decided against it, and found a public house that offered accommodation, and temporary retreat, not to mention time to think with a glass in his hand. The time that he had spent referencing had so far paid dividends, even though it had not been easy, and the first thing he did Saturday morning was to plan his route to the small village to the north where the author lived. He considered driving up there right away, but decided against it, not wishing to be seen around anywhere so rural, where a fresh face would stand out like a sore thumb.

So, Saturday passed slowly and he spent the time in a strange rehearsal, refreshing his memories, finding the right way to ask a question, and often referring to the book and one of the copies in a brown paper envelope. Most of Sunday was the same. He breakfasted and wondered how the day would go, feeling that this might be the culmination of considerable concern, his doubts about himself and the journey that many would consider a witch hunt. With all of the pieces hovering above their final places, he hoped that he had got it right.

Just after mid-day, he left Gloucester and headed north, enjoying the beauty of the English countryside that he had missed for so long. Occasionally, he stopped, for no other reason than to enjoy the views and ease himself into the afternoon. Just to pass the time, he filled up the car at a small petrol station, ready for the journey back, and whatever might come after.

Time passed slowly, as it always does when tension holds back the hour. Lawrence felt his nerves isolating his doubt, but he forced them away, and felt quite optimistic and calm as he saw the first road sign to his destination. He knew that age had changed him, where once he was driven by the whip hand of something in his brain, the passing years had given him a certain probation, and yet he still craved the passions of justice, in something that only he could resolve.

*

In the holy game of chess, there is an unusual event, where against the odds, a pawn will avoid all of the assaults against it, and stand in reach of the opposite side of the board. In such an event, the player will protect the piece, for once the next move places the pawn at its destination, it may accede to something higher. It may be transposed to any piece that success dictates, but will most often be raised to a queen, that being the most valuable piece on the board, and consequently, the most useful. In an end game, the result can be a co-ordination of two queens, in the grasp of the player, but engineered by the fate of a single pawn, whose existence is immediately forgotten.

Lawrence drove the car slowly into the small, typically

English village, gardens filed with foliage and flowers, and beginning to show the first signs of a passing summer. Only one road led through, and after a terrace of rural cottages, the dwellings became more isolated and the gardens larger. He passed by the single shop, which was closed, then a red phone box, and almost at the other end of the village, a big scarlet post box, standing to attention like a Coldstream Officer with his mouth wide open, as if barking an order.

Only the occasional figure was out in the warm sunshine, as was often the case on a rural English Sunday afternoon. Lawrence checked his watch. Ten minutes to four. He parked the car across from a small, village police station, grabbed his back pack, and flung it over one shoulder, then made his way along the footpath, searching for 'Rose Cottage'. As he worked his way along, he thought he had missed the address, but just past the scarlet pillar box, he found it to be the last one, isolated by orchards and the last building before hedgerows reclaimed the road.

The cottage was a single-story dwelling, quite old but obviously refurbished and standing proud of a large garden that finished on the cusp of the footpath with a white wicket fence and gate, softened by a strip of foliage that still displayed yellow flowers. Lawrence walked to the gate and looked through the archway that framed his view of the cottages, the red tiles reminding him of jigsaws that were so common and so loved by enthusiasts.

The dark red door opened and a young girl came out, a basket in one hand and a yellow jacket thrust into the crook of her elbow. Lawrence froze. The girl was in her early twenties, fresh faced and smiling as she waked up the path toward him. She reached the gate.

"You must be the man from the paper," she said, as Lawrence found the latch and opened the gate for her.

His tried to smile back, but something stopped it.

"Miss Miller?" he asked.

"Yes," she answered. "But its Mum you want, not me. You don't think I'd be interested in that dreary old book, do you?"

It was said as a joke and Lawrence tried to take it as such, but it felt so surreal. He twisted his face into something of a response, but the words failed him. The girl past through the gate and walked away. She waved her free hand without looking back.

"She's expecting you, just give the door a kick. Bye."

Lawrence watched her go, and offered a feeble 'bye' in response, then went through the gate and walked slowly toward the dark red door, and knocked.
Inside, the woman put down the kettle at the sound of the door. She walked through from the kitchen and opened it, to reveal the person standing there. He was quite tall, with the long hair and beard of the current fashion. Over his shoulder was a rucksack that had seen better days.

"Mister Barnes?" she asked.

"Hello. Yes. Miss Miller?" He confirmed, seeming a little restrained."

Lawrence looked at the woman, in her early to mid-fifties, well dressed and still not unattractive. A pair of elegant blue spectacles enhanced the shape of her face, and her smile was warm and welcoming. She wore a pale blue dress that matched the spectacles, and her hair fell about her shoulders.

"I must say, I'm very grateful for the attention of the local papers. I had no idea that the book was becoming so popular," she admitted. "Do come in."

Lawrence walked in, realising how low the ceiling was.

"Yes," he answered. "Probably because of the death of Churchill last year, revived a lot of interest in the war stuff."

She smiled at the answer.

"I'm just making some tea. Would you like some?"

"Oh, please."

She pointed through to an open patio door.

"We can have it in the garden, do go through, and I'll bring it out."

"Your daughter is lovely." Lawrence complimented. "You must be very proud." He added as Miller reached for a teapot in a glass cabinet.

"Absolutely, she is a treasure, she'll be twenty-two in a few days."

Lawrence looked her for longer than was polite, but then took himself out into the sunshine and found a chair near a small, white table. Soon, Elizabeth Miller appeared with a tray holding the tea, complete with an assortment of cakes and biscuits.

"So, where would you like to start?" she asked, pouring from a delicately decorated pot.

Lawrence took the cup that she offered.

"I was wondering," he began, "why you decided to write the book? What your incentive to spend all of that time in research might have been?"

Miller looked pensive for a moment, a physical display of showing her intensity for the project. Lawrence found it amusing, considering what he now knew for a fact, that he had not been following the flight of a wild goose.

"I suppose," she said, "I've always been interested in this particular story of the attempt on the life of Hitler, aboard his personal train, because to date it has been so poorly documented."

"You know why that is. Of course?" asked Lawrence.

"I do now."

"Because Churchill demanded of Colonel Denning…" Lawrence offered. "That any reference to this conspiracy would not be revealed until after his death."

"Yes." Miller confirmed, a little bemused at his knowledge. "Have you spoken to Mister Denning?"

Lawrence wondered if he was bringing this into the conversation too soon. He tried to delay a little and avoided the question.

"He did write the forward to your book, did he not?"

"Yes. Yes, he did."

A cool, late summer breeze kissed the garden and Lawrence turned his head to one side, and pressed the long hair into his face, resting the elbow onto the arm of the chair, to make the action look normal. Miller shuddered slightly and made her excuses to leave the garden to find a cardigan, returning within a few minutes with a white woollen garment around her shoulders. Lawrence decided to push a little harder.

"I have heard it said that there are parts of your book that are incorrect, more that some parts are missing, misleading perhaps. Have you come across these criticisms?" He ventured.

"Certainly not." She appeared surprised. "Why would anyone say such a thing? My researches were checked and double checked. Of course, few individuals survive today, but I did have some testimonies before they died."

"I suppose your daughter helped a little," Lawrence suggested, changing the subject, "nice to have a willing assistant, although she did give me the impression that it might not be her cup of tea."

Miller looked strangely at him.

"Why are you so interested in my daughter, Mister Barnes?"

Lawrence held the moment. It made no sense to fence around. Sooner or later, he had to make his challenge, and now was as good a time as any. Slowly, he raised a hand and pulled away the long hair of the wig and slipped off the false beard.

"Because, I may have been there at the conception, Miss Miller,"

"What…" Her eyes widened as he threw the pieces onto the grass, next to his pack.

"Or should I say, Fraulein Elsa Schmidt?"

Her face froze as she looked intensely at him.

"Maas!" She exclaimed, softly. "I knew there was something. Something." She held her gaze at his face for some seconds. "After all of these years."

Lawrence shrugged.

"Oh, Maas will do, I guess, although I have many names, none of which matter, certainly in this country."

There was a long silence as both of them wondered what the next moment might bring. Elsa Schmidt reacted first.

"You still have the scar, I see." She raised a hand slightly, pointing to the mark on his cheek.

He touched it with fingers of his left hand.

"Haven't I though?" he answered. "I must say, your English is impeccable."

"As was your German." She answered, not taking her eyes from him, her face betraying the suspicion that she held. "What is it that you want, Mister Maas?"

Lawrence thought for a moment, not really knowing how to answer, or even if he should, at least not yet. He sat back in the chair and looked across the table.

"I would like to tell you a story," he began. "One that I am certain that you will find most interesting, as I assume, like yourself, I was ignorant of every chapter for such a long time."

Schmidt folded her arms. Lawrence looked into the distance, finding the place to start.

"You will forgive me if I don't have every fact, or the full narrative as you might understand it, but I think that I can now give the general outline of a sequence of events which have puzzled me for so many years, until finally, your book placed the missing pieces in my lap…"

He had gone through this so many times, but now it seemed so far away, so sterile, unless of course it was your mind trying to make sense of it all.

"After the Great War," he began. "England and Germany held a huge suspicion of each other, and I suppose rightly so. Germany experienced the Weimar Republic period, and then the Nazi ascension toward 1933, and the beginning of the Hitler years. Many in Germany had deep concerns about the future of their country, and, encouraged by Great Britain, became, especially after 1933, long-term, deep-seated informants.

Information gained from these people was, to a greater extent, extremely reliable, and no doubt, those that proved to be double agents were in time eliminated, or disregarded. But the reliability of the proven agents was exemplary, and mostly because they operated alone, only with another when recruiting their successor, and they did this with the utmost intensity, not least for their own survival."

Lawrence paused.

"Do you think I might have more tea?" he asked. "I do hope I'm not boring you, but I think you'll enjoy the narrative."

Bemused, Elsa Schmidt reached over and filled his cup. Lawrence added milk and put the cup back into the saucer once he had taken a drink.

"Now, we get to the fun part." He continued. "British Intelligence could be notoriously disjointed, and there were those in the security services that gripped their sources like a lost child, determined to maintain their status by the power that their informants gave them. This information could be passed down at their own discretion, to those that they favoured or, well, I guess to anyone they wished. And during wartime, most of British security were glad for anything they could get their hands on that the higher echelons confirmed as genuine.

But occasionally they got it wrong, and at least one of the German inductees to the spy game was not quite who they purported to be. And now I am sure of this fact."

He looked across the table while he finished the tea.

"And this is where you come in." He smilingly explained. "Someone, somewhere, within the German high command, and I'm not quite sure who, after many attempts on the life of Hitler, decided upon one last go at the big prize. But this time, it had to work. Most of those involved in recent attempts were not received too well by the general population, even though many despised Hitler and everything he stood for." He paused, looking for the words. "Patriotism knows no bounds, and their own military attacking the Fuhrer, their own leader, brought the fiercest demands for the heads of the perpetrators, and you don't need me to tell you the outcome there, even for many who were not even involved.

But there were still a few who slipped through the net, and for whatever their own reasons, were willing to have another go, providing the blame was not placed upon their heads. And so, a remarkable conspiracy was arranged, to lure the British to send someone who could be easily identified, to be the patsy when the Fuhrer went down, to be torn apart by a German public instead of the real assassins.

No doubt, there would be a ground swell of pride in those who caught this assassin, despite the fact that they had failed to stop him, but what the hell, most in Germany were ready for a change at the top anyway."

Schmidt still looked bemused. Her forehead furrowed.

"It's a little far-fetched," she voiced.

"Is it? Lawrence asked. "Much of it is documented in your book, but you obviously miss out the parts which could be a little... sensitive? Anyway, British Intelligence took it all in, hook, line, sinker, and the bicycle wheel that was revealed when the rod was jerked upward. But that came a little later, when they saw a unique possibility.

About that time, someone in British Intelligence realised that if Hitler was assassinated, then whoever took over might prosecute the war far better, and might even force the allies to a compromise which they did not want. It could also mean the cost of thousands of lives, so if he could be kept alive, it was only a matter of time before he led Germany into the final part of the game. And that was where I came in.

The potential assassins decided that the killing would take place aboard the train, Hitler's personal train, well away from Berlin. I would imagine that was because Hitler had only his personal bodyguard to protect him, and its officer was part of the conspiracy, so it kind of fell into place."

He paused the narrative.

"Oh, and there never was a sniper at the station, was there?" He asked. "That was just the bait to get the poor fish on the hook, the poor fish being myself, of course."

Schmidt shook her head, almost imperceptibly, and raised the corner of her mouth.

"And that's when it kind of went wrong." Lawrence went on. "The part that took me so long to work out." He spread his hands. "Whether I was successful or not, I was supposed to just go to the waiting room, to sit there like the lemon that I was, waiting for patriots to show me the way out, easily recognisable by the scar that the British so kindly gave me to emulate the unfortunate Maas, a little detail for which I must thank you. I presume that it was you who directed this false information toward British Intelligence so that your patsy could be easily recognised and used?"

"Why me?" she asked

Lawrence shied the question.

"We'll get to that," he answered. "Looking back, I knew they were looking for me, it was obvious. A man with a scar on his cheek. But in the heat of the moment, I had more to think about.
And then, a guard that I thought I had placed in the hereafter revived, and altered the reason for my boarding the train, not as a captured British assassin, but as a hero who had saved the

Fuhrer. Regrettably for the poor guard, his journey to the hereafter was not long in coming. I would imagine that this was a little bonus for the real conspirators, as otherwise, they would need to keep me under constraint until the last moment, and risk me bleating out a warning that might be heeded.

I have to admit, it's quite a scenario, isn't it? Here I am, the dope in the middle, placed there by both sides, the British to save their gravest enemy, and the Germans to help in bumping off their Fuhrer. You couldn't make it up."

"Anyone would imagine that you had made it up!" Schmidt said.

"The story isn't finished yet." Lawrence parried. "Because now I know you for the fourth conspirator on the train. You had to be. Who else was there during the hours when they were trying to kill Hitler? Who else could be keeping the others on the train out of the way?"

"Why me?"

"Because of something I remembered only recently." Lawrence said. "You knew me as Maas before I handed over my papers and received a clean uniform. How else could you know that, unless it was you who furnished the original information through to British Intelligence? About Maas, the dead man with the scar, the sucker who could easily be identified, and converted into the assassin, with all of the proof that you needed, including a British revolver.

What I never understood until the last few days, was why none of this was ever revealed until your book. Oh, I see now that

Denning gave his undertaking to Churchill, but why did it never surface at the time, in Germany?"

Elsa Schmidt already knew that it was pointless to protest. Maas had obviously recognised her despite the years in between, and she now certainly recognised him. What really mattered was, where was all of this leading? She decided to probe him, to fill in her own blanks of that time, and began by conceding him an answer.

"I'm sure that you can imagine the upheaval that yet another attempt upon the life of Hitler caused," she told him. "And how could he explain the fact that a Britisher had defended him against his own staff? Afterwards, everyone on that train expected to be shot, and some were. Hitler's state of mind was collapsing, as was his health and he mentally wiped the incident from his mind, and from the propaganda that could be useful to him. He swore everyone to silence."

"But you left that part out of the book, didn't you?" Lawrence defined. "And me, replacing me for a fictitious long-term female British agent who apparently revealed the plan to Hitler, and stopped the assassination, only your loyalties were not with Britain, but Germany." His expression hardened a little. "May I ask how long you were feeding British Intelligence with false information?"

Schmidt ignored the last question.

"Why would I not do for my country what you would do for yours?" she asked.

"But you abandoned it didn't you, when the cards were played out? Here you are, a respected author in the country that you fought to destroy. Luckily a perfect linguist, and able to slip into a new identity after the war and reap the rewards of anonymity, almost." Lawrence was accusative. "I imagine it was prudent to jettison the old name and pick a new one, just in case anyone might put two and two together, but Miller-Muller, you could have been a little more creative."

A dark expression crossed the face of the woman. She tightened the garment around her shoulders.

"Thanks to you, that name eluded me," she told him. "We were to be married."

Lawrence just nodded and pursed his lips.

"And Denning went along with the misinformation?" he asked. "I take it he had no idea of your true identity?"

She shook her head.

"He asked a few questions, but I think he was happy for much to be omitted, perhaps for certain loyalties, or for his own reasons. There were things he insisted upon."

Lawrence wondered if he himself might have been one of them.

"Like opposing the publishing until after the death of

Churchill?" He asked. "Because Churchill had feared exactly the same as the conspirators, that if the public became aware that he had sanctioned the operation to keep Hitler alive, when so many had suffered loss during the conflict, he would lose everything, personally and politically."

"Yes. And Denning had powerful friends. He promised to give his blessing in the forward, if I delayed until then." She leaned forward and put her elbows on the table. "And what about you, Maas? Where do you fit into all of this, after so long?"

He feigned a laugh.

"Oh, I am just the stool pigeon who fitted the description of the unfortunate Maas. Same build, same most everything, minus this scar, which they kindly corrected to improve my chances of survival, from information which I guess you had given them, so that you could pick me up easily when the time came.
My background was military, so I had a certain inclination toward the world at that time. And I had little choice in the matter, if you must know. But that's another story."

"What happened that night?" she asked, as if questioning a failed relationship. "How did it all go so wrong?"

He realised that like most of the others on the train, she had little knowledge of the activities of the other conspirators. Her role was to give them the space to succeed.

"Well," he declared, reaching back into the past, "it was a hell of a time, all right, no thanks to your man, who did his best to pull it off. I guess it was just that my best was a little better than his best."

"You killed him!" She tightened her lips. "He was a great man, and would have been good for Germany."

"But not for much else." Lawrence told her. "And it was him or me, so in the scheme of things, I think it turned out for the best, and working out the timescale, I guess he left you something to remember him by?"

"Huh?"

"Your daughter," Lawrence implied. "You seemed quite friendly on the train. With Muller, I mean. It was quite a performance."

She avoided an answer, but let her thoughts reflect in her eyes.

"I can't decide," Lawrence went on with his train of thought, almost mockingly "whether you are a German with a perfect grasp of the English language and a patriot, or a Britisher with a similar gift, and a traitor." He falsified a smile. "Either way, I suppose it doesn't matter, you certainly saw which way your bread was buttered at the end of the war, I suppose." He paused as if in thought. "Let me guess, a pregnant woman, speaking perfect English, with some cock and bull story about being stranded on the continent, and desperate to return home? Now who could make it difficult for a poor soul like that?"

"What would it matter now? So long after the war ended? Who would care?" she asked.

Lawrence raised his eyebrows and took on an expression of surprise.

"Well, actually, Fraulein Schmidt, me." he answered. "Why on Earth do you think I'm here?" You see, when the penny dropped, and all of the little pieces slipped happily into place, I did have some doubt about where all of this was going, so I did a little more digging. On the dust cover of your book, there was a brief outline of your background, your education, and so on, and so forth. But when I looked into those dark, distant, places, there was no damn sign of you."

"You never imagined I may be writing under an assumed name?"

"Well, in actual fact," Lawrence shrugged, "that's what you are doing, and it did cross my mind, which is why I had to see you in person, so that the final piece fitted perfectly."

"Very..." she looked for the right word. "... proficient of you, or should I say competent?"

Lawrence returned to a serious expression.

"I hope that you understand that I have no animosity toward you, at least not in the way that you might imagine," he told her. "As you say, the war was a long time ago. But the loose strings must be tied, if I am to find any resolve in all that happened to me at that time. Much of it, you would never comprehend." He held the thought for a second. "I paid for my indiscretions, and you must pay for yours."

She looked surprised.

"What is it that you want?"

"I want you to stop any further publication of that book, to recall it, and give the reasons why."

Elsa Schmidt looked icily at him for a few moments, then broke into an almost manic laugh.

"Are you insane?" she demanded, "You think that I would take your ultimatum seriously? After such a long time? For a no-name loser like you to try to blackmail me, a respectable English widow, an established author?"

Lawrence held up a finger.

"I think you'll find that, generally speaking, blackmail would infer a financial gain. I am asking for nothing of that kind."

"Then try it," Schmidt warned, "and see if the police feel that way."

"The police will not find me, they have no idea who I am, and even if they did, I would be long gone. You see, if I can't convince you to do the right thing, then I must persuade you in another way."

"Persuasion is a strange word," said Schmidt. "It infers a certain meeting of minds, where one party is trying to convince an equal of the validity of their argument. You, my dear Maas, lost both your argument and your equality when you disappeared into the darkness of a German dawn."

Evening was drawing the day to a close. Soon, Sunday would feel its way through the night and meet Monday on the other side. It was time. He reached down and pulled his knapsack onto his lap and pulled out one of the brown envelopes, dropping it gently onto the table. Schmidt looked at it.

"In this envelope," Lawrence explained, "is the whole story of that conspiracy, as I remember it. Everything I knew, everything that I experienced, and everything that I now understand to be the truth of it. I have included names, places, times, and what I believe to be your part in it as the engineer who put the plan together. Every remembered detail, every remembered word. Right up to our meeting today."

Schmidt laughed.

"The word of a dead man, assumed dead for years, a man with no name. A man who hardly exists."

"Yes, you are right," agreed Lawrence, casting the envelope across the table. "But it will not be me who will take these words and expand upon the truths that are in there." He slapped the rucksack. "In here are ten copies of that envelope, and they will be sent to ten British newspapers. My task is done. It is these publications who will test the facts, pursue those still alive who were involved and investigate, and assess the evidence, and that includes yourself my dear Elsa. No doubt they will come to the same conclusions that I did." He looked across at her. "And a bloody good story they'll make of it, too good to ignore, wouldn't you agree?"

Elsa Schmidt took the folder and slowly opened a few of the first pages. She paused at one of them.

"So, at least now I know your name," she uttered.

"A name long gone."

She dropped the envelope on the table and her eyes met his. Slowly, she slipped her hand into the inside of the garment around her shoulders. It returned with a familiar shape from the past, a German Luger with a small silencer over the mouth of the barrel.

"A little memento from the past," she stated. "You remember this?"

This was not something Lawrence expected. He was not sure what he had expected, being too focussed on his need to see this through to the end. Rather timidly, he held up his hands, and wondered what old Sergeant Bull might make of him. He weighed up the chances of Elsa Schmidt being willing to shoot him, and then began to realise how much her new life after the war was crumbling. It was not a scenario that he had thought much about.

"Hand over that bag!" she demanded, in a manner that clarified her intentions.

"Are you intending to shoot me?" Lawrence asked, without complying.

"It will give me the greatest of pleasure to shoot you. I have a smallholding behind the house, and equipment to put you into the ground with the greatest of ease. Then we will be close forever." She stood up. "Where did you leave your car?"

Lawrence could hardly believe that she was serious. He had wallowed for so long in the intensity of it, so why would she not? He had not considered how much she had to lose when he was scrabbling with the pieces of his obsession. Blinded by his need to right his wrong, he had failed to see the requirements of others, and in this case for Schmidt to abandon the past and go on with the life that she had constructed. Had he not in some ways done the same?

"Are you sure it works, after all these years?" Lawrence asked.

Elsa Schmidt was circling the table where Lawrence sat with his hands partly up, the woman glancing in every direction to ensure that there were no onlookers to observe them. It was getting darker, and she had the night to dispose of him.

"Stand up!" she ordered. "Put the bag on the ground, and we'll find out."

Lawrence wondered why he should comply with the order, just to be shot. His mind spun through the possibilities of what was happening. Would she do it? Was the Luger still in working order? How good a shot was she? He was older now, and if he avoided a killing shot, could he still manage to overcome the woman before another round came at him? The words of Colour Sergeant Bull nudged his memory. He waited until Schmidt's eyes searched the area one more time, then with his knees he upturned the table, sending crockery and the brown envelope crashing toward her.

Schmidt reacted and stepped backward, raising the Luger and pulling the trigger in one action.

Thup! Yes, the gun was still in working order, the sound calmed by the suppressor. Lawrence had grabbed the knapsack on his lap and hurled himself toward the nearby hedge, using the overturned table for cover. Still, her aim had been good, and the bullet tore through the soft tissue between his neck and his right shoulder, reducing the effectiveness of the muscle. He hung onto the bag and flung himself at the hedge, half pushing, half jumping through, desperate to camouflage himself from another shot.

It came soon, as the harsh foliage scratched his face but succumbed to his weight and he rolled away on the other side.

"Thup"

The bullet missed, avoiding his head by inches and throwing up loose earth that made him blink. He quickly threw an arm through the shoulder strap of the knapsack, determined not to lose it now.

He found himself in a small orchard, the branches hanging over the garden where a few moments before he had just been sitting. Somewhere behind him he heard a curse, but could not decipher the tone of German or English. Desperate to avoid becoming a clean target, Lawrence looked for the best cover, beginning to feel the pain of the bullet wound. To his left, through the lines of trees, he could see that a substantial hedge, tougher than the one that he had just broken through, stopped his passage to the village street beyond. No doubt high enough to defend the fruit of the orchard from the easy pickings of passers-by.

He could hear the woman behind him, pushing aside the foliage for another shot, but a summer dress was not conducive to pursuit in this direction, and Lawrence was glad of it. He looked to his right, where a short way through the trees was an old shed, just visible as darkness overtook the evening. At any moment, he expected another round heading in his direction and kept low and quiet. 'Hell', he thought, 'he was too old for this'.

The shed was locked, and he had already decided not to entrap himself within it, using it only for the defence it offered momentarily, as he went around to the other side. He stopped there for a few seconds, to recover his composure, and decide what to do next. If he could navigate around the house and back to the road, he had a chance to find his car and escape Elsa Schmidt's threats. After that, he had no idea.

At that moment he felt the weight of what he had brought upon himself. If he had just been willing to let the past lie, and get on with whatever years he had left, he would not now be pursued by a woman with a gun, willing to plant him in her own back garden, or wherever she decided to insert him.

He wondered how many rounds she had left in that old Luger. Lucky for him that the gun was re-calibrated by British Intelligence so long ago, and because of the extra shell, it meant that she would not have the convenience of reloading once the magazine was exhausted.

He gave himself a moment to catch his breath and examine the extent of his wound. It was already stiffening. Somewhere in the impending darkness, he could hear the rustle of soft footfalls, still some way off, but undoubtably coming closer. Lawrence looked around for a branch, or a stick, to use as a weapon of last resort, but the orchard was well cared for, and none could be found. He shuffled the knapsack to a more comfortable position on his free shoulder, the weight making him regret using so large a space between his typing, when a smaller one might have meant less pages, and less to haul.

Turning the corner of the shed, he found a space where he could slip through into a harvested cornfield, then follow the rough hedgerow, past Schmidt, he hoped, and make his way around toward the main village road. There he could make a dash for the car, or at least find a house where he might find sanctuary. He considered calling for help, but it would mean revealing his position, and at least for the moment, discounted it.

The ground was rough and crumbled beneath his feet, and he grimaced at every step. He twisted his neck to ease the stiffness, but kept moving, hoping not to be discovered.

Finally, he had put some distance behind him, and found a narrow soil path that led to his right. Looking toward the village road, he saw that a few ancient street lamps had come on, giving a gloomy light, and a certain ambiance to the place. He avoided the areas where long grass might have tripped him, and as quietly as he could, made for the street.

Once there, he hunkered down to peer around into the street, deserted for a Sunday evening, with many at the small church at the other end of the village. Looking left, he could see his car, silhouetted in what light prevailed. Keeping low, he was about to step out, but as he began to move out from the path, Schmidt's voice cautioned him to stop. With no-one visible to assist him, he turned slowly to find himself staring once more into the barrel of the Luger, twenty feet away, the mocking smile of Elsa Schmidt revealing her satisfaction of the situation.

Lawrence felt the frailty of desperation. On the side of the path, a few feet from where he stood, was the big, red post box. It would give little cover, and beyond it there was just open road. But there it stood, beckoning him, offering the hope of a few more seconds of life.

Before Schmidt could respond to his action, Lawrence leapt for the safety of the post box. The woman moved slowly forward, keeping her distance but never taking her eyes from the tall red cylinder and what was behind it.

She circled the mail box, keeping six feet from it, the gun tucked into her hip, checking that no one was around. As the figure of Lawrence came into view, she saw that his hand was raised. He had the bundle of brown envelopes pressed into the open mouth of the big red cylinder, his grip the only thing stopping them falling into it. Lawrence had the temerity to smile.

"Give them to me, or I'll shoot." she demanded.

"You told me that you'd shoot anyway," he answered. "And if you shoot me, the whole damn lot will hit the papers tomorrow, or maybe the next day."

Elsa Schmidt ground her teeth and glowered at Lawrence.

"Is it worth all of this," she asked, "for nothing more than revenge?"

Lawrence laughed.

"Revenge?" he said. "This is nothing to do with revenge."

"Then what is it?" she asked, her eyes lit up with surprise at the words. "What is it you want?"

"A reckoning," Lawrence told her, his expression hardening.

Down the street, the dim blue light of the small police station blinked on to reassure the small population of the village, still unaware of the drama outside. Lawrence looked at Elsa Schmidt and smiled the smile of his life. She swallowed hard and looked at his fingers on the corners of the envelopes, just holding them away from tomorrow's collection by a thumb and forefinger.

"Now," he said. "Shall we play this game?"